TRUE LADY

Joan Smith

FAWCETT CREST • NEW YORK

A Fawcett Crest Book
Published by Ballantine Books
Copyright © 1986 by Joan Smith

Library of Congress Catalog Card Number: 85-91238

ISBN: 0-449-20842-7

Manufactured in the United States of America

First Edition: February 1986

"Luten," she breathed, I am so glad you came. How did you know?"

He ignored the question and asked again. "Did he hurt you?"

"Not as much as I hurt him."

"You foolish, darling girl," he scolded fiercely in her ear, but even while he spoke, his lips were beginning to skim across her cheeks, to find hers. He felt her small, soft body tremble in his arms, and drew her more tightly against him, to protect this cherished hothead from the world.

The trembling from fear subsided, and a new shaking began deep within her as Luten's lips firmed on hers. It felt a little frightening, but at the same time reassuring and exciting and a host of other delicious things. When he stopped kissing her, a jumble of angrily loving words poured from his mouth, while his handkerchief brushed her tears away with infinite tenderness.

"Are you sure you're all right, darling? Why the devil did you . . . dammit, Trudie, have you no sense at all? You're quite sure he didn't hurt you?" And before she could reassure him, he kissed her again, as though he would never stop. . . .

Chapter One

"It's about time you got here!" was Lady Clappet's uncivil welcome to her brother the instant he set foot in her gloomy Blue Saloon.

"Nice to see you again too, Maggie," he answered blandly, and strode toward her. Lord Luten's thin lips curled in displeasure as his eyes roved about the overly ornate and formal room. "Do you suppose I would break a bone if I lowered myself ever so gently onto that concrete sofa by the window? Who's your upholsterer nowadays, Portland?"

"Furniture is for looking at, not lying down on," she answered comprehensively.

"Remind me to tell you sometime about a new piece they've invented. A bed, it's called." He strolled at a languid gait toward the sofa of cementlike hardness and eased himself onto it while Lady Clappet glared. Neither pleasure nor admiration made up any part of her expression. She particularly disliked whippets, and there was a quality in Luten that brought that lithe canine to mind. It wasn't the coloring; Luten had black hair, a slash of black eyebrows, and a swarthy complexion. And it wasn't the shape of his nose or face either. He had a square jaw, a good-sized Roman nose, and thin lips. It was something in the set of his sleek head, the flow of his streamlined body, the sense of wary alertness. And when she looked into his eyes, the unsettling idea strengthened. Bright, curious eyes, but not friendly, as a brother's eyes should be.

Her bosom heaved in indignation. How very like Luten to arrive two days after he was summoned, and not even bother to apologize for his tardiness, but only find fault with her decor. She wore a widow's cap on her steel-gray curls, and on her body a gown cut to conceal her spreading girth, and colored mauve to indicate her sorry condition. Regarding her, her brother thought her complexion, a mourning shade of gray, also honored her late husband.

"You ought to go about more, Maggie," he said brusquely. "Your face is beginning to resemble a garden slug."

"It is a wonder I'm not livid with aggravation!"

"You're not far from it. Why did you ask me to call?" he said, and leaned back, stretching his arms along the sofa top.

She looked with loathing at Luten, disliking his posture, the short Brutus cut of his hair, the complication of his Olbadeston cravat, the height of his collar, and even the gleam of his Hessians. His jacket, she acknowledged grudgingly, was well cut. How Luten could pass for anything but a dandy was a mystery to her. Her own dear Clappet had never been called a dandy.

"Well?" Luten demanded impatiently.

She took a deep breath and spoke in ominous accents to impress her audience. "My—son—has—left—home."

Luten lifted his dark brows and considered this pronouncement. His reply was not at all gratifying. "Oh. You drove him out with your nagging, in other words."

"*I* drove him out? It was nothing of the sort. If you had come when I first asked you to, this disaster might have been averted. Poor little Peter, adrift in the world . . . He left last night. Had Uxor pack up two bags and left without

2

so much as saying good-bye.'' A lace-edged handkerchief was lifted to her soggy eyes as her words trailed off into tears.

"He won't have drifted far. I'll drop around to the hotels and send him home. I don't see why *he* should leave. It's *his* house, and if the next step is for you to have your trunks packed up, Maggie, let me make clear while I'm here that they are not to be deposited on *my* doorstep.''

The word "heartless" was heard to emerge through her sniffles. While Lord Luten sat watching patiently, she dried her tears, straightened her shoulders heroically, and requested a glass of ratafia to restore her disordered nerves.

He poured the required restorative, looking in vain for a decanter of wine for himself. Finding none, he shrugged his elegant shoulders, gave her the glass, and with unnecessary care resumed his seat on the hard sofa.

"He is putting up with that wretched Nicolson fellow who has taken a set of rooms at Albany," she said. "Not that he bothered to tell his own mother! I learned it of Mrs. Nicolson, who had the decency to write me a note to allay my worries when she heard of it.''

"Hmmm," he said, considering his best course. Lord Luten didn't often spare pity for mankind, but in the case of his nephew Peter, he was much inclined to do so. That a young buck spending his first Season on the town should be forced to reside with a mother who perpetuated her mourning for three years was hard on the boy. Maggie was a bad-natured shrew who cloaked her humor in a veil of motherly concern. Her sort of stifling protection was more likely to goad the boy on to folly than anything else. His being forced out of his own home looked very much like the first step along the route. Yet to bring him back was a hard fate for the boy.

"Why don't you skip the Season this year, Maggie?" he

3

suggested. "You seldom go into society in any case. You'd be happier in the country at Hanch House."

"Abandon poor Peter?" she gasped. "I would not dream of it."

"I'll keep an eye on him."

She shook her gray curls sadly. "It's too late for that. He has fallen into the hands of—of one of those women, Luten," she announced, and cast an accusing eye at him.

He looked remarkably unmoved, except perhaps to interest, which should have been outrage. "Aha! The plot thickens! A *bad* woman, you mean?"

"The very worst. I think she is married as well."

"All to the good. At least she can't be angling to shackle him."

"Can she not? I wouldn't put it a pace past her to be divorced or widowed."

"The hussy!" he interjected, trying to hold his lips steady. But a second thought caused him some concern. "An *older* woman, do you mean?" Peter, not quite twenty, was a complete greenhead in his petticoat dealings.

"Oldish, so Mrs. Rolfe tells me. She has rooms in the same apartment building as Nettie Rolfe. The woman runs one of those houses. . . ."

"Gambling?" Luten asked, wondering that a perfectly respectable address such as Mrs. Rolfe's should be used for so low a purpose. The corner of Conduit and Swallow was not the heart of polite London, but it was not yet sunk to vice either, so far as he had heard.

"Worse!" she assured him, with a flashing, sapient eye.

"Oh, dear. *That* sort of house. But are you quite sure? I hadn't heard the Abbesses had invaded the West End."

"Nettie says there is a stream of young gentlemen in and out the door all hours of the day and night."

"No, it can't be. I would have heard," he said, causing her to look sharply at him. "Don't panic. I happen to own

4

some property in the neighborhood. I assure you I don't plan to let it sink into a slum. There are no brothels on Conduit Street.''

''It is not a brothel precisely. I do not mean to imply it is a regular establishment. *She* is the only one who operates out of the apartment. Or in it, I ought to say. The woman is not a streetwalker. Nettie says she entertains them right there, in the apartment, with music and dancing and drinking till all hours. She has seen Peter enter many times. In fact, she says he is the most frequent visitor. My poor baby! Nettie might have told me before he went *four times*.''

''Do you know the woman's name?''

''The card at the door says Mrs. Harrington. She has an elderly companion residing with her for appearance's sake. They pretend to be genteel. Her accent is tolerable—provincial, you know, but not low. Nettie was quite taken in by her. She smiled and said 'How do you do' the first week, till she realized what was going on, then she cut her very short. The woman had the gall to let on she was tutoring the boys in Latin—as though anyone of her sort would know Latin! We English are very wise to withhold our acquaintance a little. You never know. . . . Who would have thought, right on Conduit Street! Next I will have one of those females setting up next door, in Berkeley Square.''

''What is it you want of me, to slip Peter the clue?''

''Certainly not. You must warn the hussy away from him.''

''You have not told me *she* comes trailing after *him*. It will be better to speak to him—first, in any case. If he's agreeable to take my advice, that'll be an end to it.''

Lady Clappet considered this a moment. ''He might do so. He always speaks highly of you, Luten. I cannot imagine why. He wants you to enter his name at White's, but I think it should wait a year, till he learns how to gamble properly first. One hears shocking tales of losing fortunes at

White's. I think we have allowed him too large an allowance. Four thousand is pretty good for a minor!''

"It's more than adequate, but then Peter's fortune is large. His first Season, he'll have his wardrobe to spruce up. He'll be wanting a new town carriage, and to join a few clubs.''

"He has not done any of those decent things. I *know* he is giving his money to that woman," she moaned.

"They don't confer their favors gratis," Luten agreed blandly.

"But to be taking money from a mere boy—and the others the same. It is very *young* gentlemen she entertains.''

"Her sort ought to be whipped at the cart's tail," he agreed. "I cannot believe any lasting attachment has been formed in so short a time. Two weeks, is it, since you came to London?''

"Two weeks tomorrow, and Peter has not been home *one evening* since. Raking all over town with Nicolson and his horsey set. They will be rattling off to Newmarket for the races in May, very likely. Such a comedown for a Clappet. His father would roll over in his grave. Peter's being plucked from Cambridge too—imagine—and his father a wrangler, like you, Luten. He will never graduate now, though he lets on he has hired a tutor and will go back to university again. He only says it to appease me. He thinks of nothing but horses and racing and that dreadful woman.'' In her own mind, she couldn't decide which of Peter's vices was the worst.

"Well, Maggie, 'the dreadful woman,' at least, we can do something about," Luten told her. "As to the rest, horse-racing is a respectable way to lose money. I'll stop by Nicolson's place and speak to Peter. Shall I ask him to come home? It might be better if he put up with Nick for a spell, till your vapors have a chance to evaporate.''

"I'm desolate without him. You must send him back.''

"I'll mention it, but you must stop harping and nagging

the boy. He's nearly a man now. He wants to spread his wings a little, see the town. Give him more freedom; it's time for it. If you don't, he'll slip the leash, and you'll lose control completely.''

''We've given him four thousand a year,'' she reminded his guardian. ''How long a leash are you suggesting?''

''I'm not talking money. Don't sit up nights waiting for him, and don't make him feel a sinner if he wants to go up to Newmarket for a few days. Those are the natural diversions of a fellow in his position. He'll be married and settled down soon enough. Let him enjoy his few years of freedom.''

''I might have expected such lenient advice from a bachelor,'' she replied tartly. ''*You* enjoy your freedom so well it has become a way of life. I don't want Peter still on the town when he's your age. At thirty, it is time you should have your nursery set up. Lady Aurelia was just saying . . .''

''She said the same at the opera last week, Sis, but I pretended not to hear her,'' he answered, letting a trace of ennui creep into his voice.

It was the understanding of Luten's family that he should marry Lady Aurelia, an eligible cousin who had been on the catch for a husband the past half-dozen years. Luten had not the least intention of honoring Lady Aurelia or any other woman—not in the near future at any rate. One day he'd settle down, of course, but till he met the right woman, he was quite happy to enjoy his bachelorhood. He spent the spring Season in London, with jaunts to the race meets. The remainder of the year found him trout fishing and grouse hunting in Scotland, often spending a month in Brighton in the summer, visiting friends and receiving visitors, sitting in Parliament when the mood hit him or when some matter of particular interest to him was being debated. For the rest, he had his two country estates and his town house to see to. It was enough. And when it ceased to be enough, he bought a new racehorse or boxer or woman.

He rose and stood, arms akimbo, regarding his sister. "It's time to put off your half-mourning for Clappet. Buy yourself some new gowns and bonnets. And a pot of rouge," he added, scrutinizing her cheeks. "Have a ball, or at least a rout party. Have a life of your own, Maggie, and stop living Peter's for him."

Lady Clappet looked down at her gown, then lifted her fingers to feel her cheeks. "I had planned to go to a concert this evening, but with Peter run off on me . . ."

"Go. Go to the concert by all means. I'll have your son back tomorrow."

Luten made a curt bow, walked to the hall to regain his malacca cane, curled beaver and tan gloves, and strode out into the sunshine. It was a mystery how Maggie managed to keep the least ray of sun out of her saloon. It had three high windows facing south, but somehow no sun got through. No wonder Peter escaped as often as he could.

To escape into the arms of a cunning widow or divorcée was not acceptable, however. Luten was surprised that Peter's first real folly should involve a woman. Had he been asked for an opinion, he would have said "horses," without blinking. The woman must be something rather special to have weaned Peter from the stables. He wondered what she was like. An older woman, Maggie had said. Probably some out-of-work actress or Cyprian past her prime and sunk to preying on boys. He'd make short shrift of her.

He hopped into his curricle and headed to Albany, that exclusive double row of chambers that served as a sanctuary for London's bachelors. He felt quite righteous, playing the role of savior. Doing a good deed wasn't a normal part of his routine, but he could well spare a quarter of an hour. Not being possessed of psychic powers, he couldn't foresee he was embarking on an enterprise that would eat up considerably more than the fifteen minutes alloted and engage him in doings that made Peter's scrape sink into insignificance.

Chapter Two

"Are any of your young gentlemen coming to call this evening, Trudie?" Mrs. Harrington asked her niece as they finished their modest dinner of a chop and apple tart.

Trudie Barten leaned her head on her hand and assumed a listless air without too much dissimulation. "I am at leisure tonight. Shall we attend the duke's ball, or would you rather stay home and help me unscramble Norman's last letter? It has sat menacingly in my pocket since it was delivered this morning. I have it half-decoded."

Mrs. Harrington cast a wry smile on her charge. "Do you mind terribly that we're having such a flat time? I *did* think when Norman suggested we come here that it would be livelier for you. A young lady ought to be going out in the evenings. I know you do not truly aspire to consort with dukes at fancy balls, but a nice young gentleman . . ."

Trudie shrugged her impertinent shoulders and made a moue. Of course a young lady minded having a flat time, especially when she had come from the country to London carrying a headful of impossible dreams. For a month before leaving home, she had envisioned a round of balls and routs, beaux calling at the door and taking her for spins in the park. But she was sensible enough to know, even while she was moon-raking, that none of it was likely to happen. It was just daydreaming, except London had such an aura of glamour that it seemed within the realm of possibility that *something* interesting might occur.

"I can live without balls for a year. I never expected I would end up a tutor, though, when Norman moved us to London. Still, it passes the time and gives us some spare change. Perhaps this letter says something about money," she said hopefully, drawing a crumpled piece of paper from her pocket and straightening it out on her knee to frown at it in perplexity. "It says money—or is it mare, or possibly mirey, only he has forgotten to dot the i. Yes, that's it; the roads around Brighton are mirey. What a catastrophe! He is off to Brighton for the selling races. He'll be putting up at the Princes. No, no, he doesn't mean the Prince's Pavilion, Auntie! It's the name of an hotel there—a cheap hotel."

"There should be plenty of money at least," Mrs. Harrington said. "He got over a thousand guineas for letting Walbeck Park for the year. I daresay he has spent it all on a horse by now. There'll be stabling fees and trainer's fees and entrance fees for the races. He'll never recover a penny of it either. To be thinking he can win the Triple Crown with some bowlegged filly no one ever heard of is the height of nonsense. I can't for the life of me imagine why you encouraged your brother in this folly, Trudie."

Trudie lifted her eyes from the crumpled letter and stared out the window. Nothing was visible beyond, for darkness had fallen. Glancing at her, her aunt thought the girl was miles away. Her dark eyes were glazed, her full lips turned up at the edges. Her auburn hair, lit from behind by the lamp, glowed like fire. Just as her aunt despaired of having a reply, Trudie returned to attention.

"Oh, I don't know," she said pensively. "I think everyone deserves one folly in his life, don't you?"

"I never had one," Mrs. Harrington answered promptly. "And neither have you."

"Norman is young—too young to get married, as he would have done had he stayed at Walbeck. Since he came down from university, Georgiana Halley has regarded him with a very proprietary eye. She's hastening him into it. He's not ready. Let him take one year out of his life to live his folly. What is he losing? The rent from Walbeck will cover all the expenses, and at the year's end, he'll go back home and become a good squire. Squire Barten. And only think if he should win, Auntie! Imagine the glory of winning the Triple Crown, and then the Golden Bowl at Ascot. He means to sweep the board clean. The time to try such things is while you're young, with no heavy obligations. The Alexanders will take excellent care of Walbeck for us. I don't mind living in rooms for one year. It's rather fun," she added bravely.

Mrs. Harrington's stern eye roved the modest dining room, through the open door to the equally modest saloon, and back to her niece. "It cannot be much fun giving Latin lessons three nights a week," she pointed out.

"I don't mind. I'm not doing it for the money, you know. Norman gave us enough to live on. Indeed, I don't take any pay from Mr. Haskins, whose papa can't afford it. Peter was going to hire a tutor in any case, and he says I explain it to him better than any tutor he ever encountered, so why should I not accept a fee from him? He's loaded with blunt."

"Pooh!" her aunt said with lively disgust. "He likes to sit and moon at you across the table. I would not mind you giving Lord Clappet, Norman's particular friend, a little help, but I do not think it quite the thing for him to have brought *his* friend along. I don't just care for that Nicolson fellow. There is something uncouth about him, with all his airs and graces."

A spark of mischief danced in the dark depths of Trudie's

11

eyes. "Sir Charles Nicolson uncouth? How can you say so? Nick is top of the trees, Auntie. He told me so himself."

Mrs. Harrington snorted. Her brindled head shook angrily, and her lips pinched into a thin line. "Top of the dung pile. That's what I think of your Sir Charles. He was rolling his eyes at you, Trudie. I do believe that Rolfe woman has taken the notion Nicolson is your beau. She looked very sour when he came in yesterday evening. She spies on us. I hear her door open and close every time one of your gentlemen comes to our door. Then when young Clappet came to call for him after his lesson, she was at it again."

Trudie gave a *tsk* of annoyance. "If she has nothing better to do, let her spy. She shan't see much."

"She'll *hear* plenty! That piano was still banging away at ten o'clock last night. Nicolson was very miffed when I closed the lid on him, but to be playing a pianoforte at ten o'clock in a flat is not considerate. I never hear the Rolfes playing theirs past nine-thirty."

"It was hammering till midnight on Saturday. I'm surprised you forgot it; you mentioned it nine or ten times." Trudie felt a twinge of guilt over Nicolson, and her guilt lent a note of asperity to her answer. She knew perfectly well that he was infatuated with her, and letting him remain for a social visit after the lesson was unwise. But it was better than being perpetually alone with her aunt.

"The noise *did* go on rather late Saturday, but it stopped before the Sabbath broke. Had they played into Sunday morning, I should have felt obliged to lodge a complaint with Mr. Evans," Mrs. Harrington said.

"I won't let Sir Charles play the pianoforte again, and I shan't let Peter bring any more of his friends to be coached in Latin. Will that satisfy you, Tartar?" Trudie asked, softening the harsh word with a smile. "Papa was quite a scholar, you know, and as I've managed to master the arcane matter myself, I might as well make some use of it. It will please Lady Clappet when Peter is reinstated at university. She kicked up quite a fuss, it seems, when he was plucked, and it was only the Latin that was holding him back.''

"I have no objection to Clappet's coming," Mrs. Harrington allowed. "He has often enough been to us at Walbeck when he was in school with Norman. If only he were a few years older," she added wistfully.

"Yes, a very eligible *parti*, Auntie, but he is *not* a few years older. He is not quite twenty, and I am an old hag of three and twenty years. An ape leader, I believe they describe such antiques as I here in the city."

"Such a very odd expression."

"Shakespeare," Trudie said vaguely. "It has to do with leading apes in hell, from 'Shrew,' I believe."

Mrs. Harrington shook her head in despair. "It is amazing how a young lady who knows so much doesn't know enough to nab an eligible *parti* when it is clear as day he is in love with her."

"In love?" Trudie asked, and laughed heartily. "No, he only plays up to me to pester Nicolson. A boy not yet finished school is not eligible. And I don't know anything either, except what I've read in books. Sir Charles tells me I am a bluestocking, and a greenhead. Not a very harmonious combination, chromatically speaking, I fear."

"The devil take Sir Charles! I don't think he cares in the least for learning Latin. He comes to flirt."

"He's a brave man to attempt it with you guarding me like a Vestal Virgin," Trudie said pertly. "I only let him come to wile away the dull evenings. I'd never go out with him. Let us speak of other things, since my 'gentlemen' annoy you so," she said, lifting Norman's letter. "I'll try if I can decipher this sheet of hieroglyphics. Yes, he's bought his hope for the Triple Crown and calls her True Lady after us—since we share the name Gertrude. True Lady has gone off her feed, poor dear. They are concocting a new mélange to tempt her jaded palate. Lucky Lady, she should be called."

She studied another passage, then looked up brightly. "Oh, Peter will want to hear this! Norman has discovered a horse he thinks Peter will want to buy. It only costs two hundred guineas. Two-fifty is the top price Peter is ready to spend, you know."

As she spoke, there was a clatter of heavy boots on the stairs rising up to their rooms. "It is Lord Clappet!" Mrs. Harrington exclaimed, a smile alighting on her lips, and they both left the dining room. Lord Clappet was welcome to darken the door anytime he pleased, but he was never so welcome as on those occasions when he did not carry his Latin tomes. The aunt harbored the hope that his infatuation for her niece would mushroom into true love. When he came without Sir Charles Nicolson, he was doubly welcome. After one loud bang, Peter opened the door and pounced in.

"The greatest news, Trudie!" he exclaimed. "Norman has found me a racer!"

"I was just reading the same thing," Trudie answered, taking his hat and gloves and setting them on the hall table; there was no butler to perform this office for their infrequent callers.

Lord Clappet was tall and well-formed. His dark curls framed a face that was boyishly attractive and would one day be as handsome as even he could desire. His earnest wish was to be a sophisticated Corinthian like his uncle Luten, but his youthful enthusiasm kept getting in his way. He fancied he was already as fine a fiddler as any of the bucks. He could handle his fists without causing mirth in any corner; he had hardly missed the wafers last time he visited Manton's Shooting Gallery and was a bruising rider to hounds. All that remained was to own a string of winning racehorses. The racer of which he spoke was the first step in this direction.

In his excitement, he preceded his hostess into her small, cozy parlor, made a very short bow to her aunt, then sat down, but remembered to pop up again when Trudie entered the room behind him.

"I darted down to my bank the minute I read this," he said, the words tumbling out in his excitement. "Only two hundred guineas—imagine! I wouldn't have thought it possible. Norman is up to anything. She won a selling race at Brighton. Norman spoke to the owner, and I am to go down and take a look at her as soon as possible. I shall leave tomorrow morning with Nick. You have to make an early start in the racing season. I'll get her a good trainer, enter her in some of the lesser races for experience, and when she is fit . . ." He tossed up his hands. His audience was to understand by this gesture that the next inevitable step was that he, like Norman, would walk away with the Triple Crown.

"Norman didn't mention the sex. A promising youngster, he called it. So it's a filly, then?" Trudie asked.

"Yes, and with a streak of Arab blood in her. Her dam has won a dozen hurdle races, and her sire took the maiden plate at Newmarket three years ago. Excellent blood." He smiled happily.

"Have you told your mother?" Mrs. Harrington inquired, throwing quite a pall over the lad's enthusiasm.

"Not yet," he replied briefly. "As Norman has got me such a bargain, there is no need for her to know. I got my quarter allowance just last week and am loaded with blunt. I can handle all the expenses for the present at least. I may need a little advance if Firebird works out and is to be entered in the large races. Nick thinks I might be wiser to start out small till I learn my way around the turf; then, when I am more up to snuff, go for the big ones. But if Firebird is half so promising as Norman indicates, I mean to jump in this year."

"You'll have to tell her, if you mean to go up north for the training," Mrs. Harrington pointed out.

"Oh, as to that," he mentioned ever so casually, "I am no longer living with Mama."

"Peter, what has happened?" Trudie asked, staring. She already knew Lady Clappet for an eccentric. Such a plethora of excuses had been offered for Peter's not taking them to call that they understood her to be a virtual recluse, and a bad-natured one to boot.

"Had a little set-to. She accused me of running wild, when I have been swotting up my Latin and watching my blunt like a regular skint. Some old crone told her about a little imbroglio Nick and I were involved in," he added obliquely. Mrs. Harrington remonstrated with him, but he made little of it.

Trudie, eager to learn the nature of this affair, waited her chance. When her aunt went to fetch wine, she put the question to him, and he opened his budget.

"A couple of girls we have been seeing. Nothing wrong in it. We only took them to the masquerade at the Pantheon, and out to Richmond Park one afternoon. Fannie did hit me up for a couple of quid the second time, but when she started hinting for an apartment and a fur wrap, I dropped her like a live coal. I can't afford a mistress at the moment."

"Can you afford a hotel?" Trudie asked.

"Lord, no! I'm putting up with Nick, only for a few days till Mama cools down."

This interesting anecdote was interrupted when Mrs. Harrington returned with the wine. There followed a lengthy discussion about Firebird and related equine matters. It was close to an hour later when Lord Clappet took his leave to meet Nick at the Daffy Club. Nick was a member of the Fancy as well as a horseman. He had shares in a boxer.

"I'll drop in to say good-bye before we leave tomorrow, and see if you have any messages for Norman," Clappet said.

"Auntie has hemmed some new cravats and handkerchiefs," Trudie mentioned.

"Be happy to deliver his linens for you," he told her, placing his curled beaver on his head with great attention to its position and slant.

Miss Barten opened the door for him. At the foot of the stairs, Mrs. Rolfe's ear was to the door, and her eyes on her watch, to time the caller's visit. One hour, as regular as clockwork. It struck her as the optimum time for the business the occupants abovestairs were running. If a decent Christian were obliged to share a domicile with such females, it was more than *she* knew!

"Don't mention this to anyone, will you, Trudie?" Clappet called back over his shoulder. "Mama would ring a peal over me if she knew."

"I think you should tell her," the brazen hussy advised.

Mrs. Rolfe put a shawl over her shoulders and trotted down to speak to Mr. Evans as soon as young Clappet had entered his carriage. Either those females went, or she and the rest of the decent tenants would!

Chapter Three

An evening at the Daffy Club celebrating in advance the winning of the Triple Crown did not leave Lord Clappet and Sir Charles in the very best form for their trip to Brighton the next morning. It was ten o'clock before they were finished breakfast.

"Lord Luten to see his nephew," the butler informed them, causing some joy to the nephew, for in the normal way Luten seldom sought out his company.

"Show him right in, my good fellow," Clappet ordered.

But Luten had already found his own way to the breakfast parlor. "Peter, Nick," he said, his sharp eyes taking in the ravages of their late night—the pallor of the cheeks, the dark circles under the eyes, and the traces of red around the rims. Sir Charles Nicolson was pale and slight to begin with. He was an overly elegant young buck with a collar rising up nearly to reach the blond curls at his ears. He was afflicted with a pair of angelic dimples. These, combined with his long-lashed eyes, gave him a dainty air that he was at pains to lessen, and upon occasion to refute by an outright challenge. He modestly called himself the third-best shot in London. He could culp a wafer without even taking careful aim. It was well known in his circle that he was eager to try his luck on a live, human target.

"Have a seat, Uncle," Peter said. "Have you breakfasted yet?"

"Several hours ago," Luten answered, pulling back a chair to sit at an angle from the table. Staring hard at Clappet, he asked, "I take it you had a late night?"

"We had a couple of wets at the Daffy Club," Peter admitted.

"You hold your liquor ill, if a couple of wets have kept you in bed till this hour and turned you into a ghost besides. What other charms did the evening hold for you?" Luten looked for signs of evasiveness but saw only petulance.

Peter knew what the call was about, knew he would have to go home soon, but with a visit to Brighton and thence on to Newmarket pending, about which he wished to maintain total secrecy from his mother and uncle, he wasn't about to knuckle under yet. "I suppose Mama sent you?" he asked, avoiding the question.

"I've had a word with her, yes." Luten flicked a glance to Nicolson, who was well-bred and obliging enough to take the hint and leave them alone. "You see the inconvenience of battening yourself on friends—any privacy is impossible," he said. "When a gentleman takes into his head to leave the parental roof, he must hire quarters or be prepared to hear himself described as a barnacle." This advice was given in the hope of leading Peter back to Berkeley Square. "I should think you'd have more pride than to squeeze yourself into this cubicle on top of Nick."

"I'm not going home yet, Uncle. Mama must realize I am a man, not a boy in short coats."

"The fault is not entirely your own. Your mother is difficult to live with, but the best way for her to realize you are now a man is to behave like one."

"Dash it, I try to behave like one! None of the other fellows are clocked in and out of their home as though they were young ladies. I haven't done anything wrong. For her

19

to be cutting up stiff over . . . .'' He stopped, wondering whether he was not revealing more than he need.

"I know all about it," Luten said bluntly. "You want to be careful with women of that sort, Peter." Peter's sulking expression made him look like a very child.

"I only saw her a couple of times."

"Sure you didn't see her last night? You look burnt to the socket."

"We stayed late at the Daffy Club. You know women are not allowed there."

"There is no serious involvement with the woman, then?"

"Good God, no! She is nothing to me. She's a friend of a friend of Nick's, that's all. We only had a couple of outings."

"An older woman can accomplish a good deal on a couple of outings."

"She's not old," Peter corrected hastily. "She's very young and pretty."

"Say experienced, then. A divorcée, is she?"

"Certainly not! At least she didn't say so. I don't think it at all likely," he added, but with some doubt creeping in.

"I understood her door plate indicated it."

"I didn't notice it if it did."

"What has she cost you thus far? Is it her inroads on your purse that have reduced you to billeting yourself on Nick?"

"I've only given her a couple of guineas. Truth to tell, she was hinting pretty strong for more—wanted me to set her up permanently, but I am not such a flat as that."

"I am vastly relieved to hear it. Those women make a job of catching a well-oiled youngst— young gentleman like you and plucking him clean. You have an ample allowance to enjoy yourself, but not to establish a bird of paradise and shower her with expensive jewels. Your trust was set up carefully to see you are not rooked. When you're older, you

20

will have a better idea how to go on. For the present, then, may I assure your mother this affair is over?''

"Lord, I would not call it an affair!'' Peter objected, though he was somewhat gratified to hear it described so. Luten himself had enjoyed numerous affairs.

"But would you call it finished—over?'' Luten persisted.

"I have no intention of ever seeing her again,'' Peter said firmly.

"Good, then you'll be going home. Your mother is considerably worried.''

"Oh, as to that . . .'' Peter said vaguely.

Luten fixed him with a derogatory eye. "Yes, barnacle?''

"I ain't sponging on Nick! The fact is, Nick is going to Newmarket and I am tagging along with him.'' Peter purposely avoided mentioning Brighton, lest Luten take the idea to go with him; it was close to London.

"The races are not for several weeks yet.''

"We know a fellow has some fillies training up, and we are going to have a look around. Well, the Season ain't open yet here, in any case, and it is an excellent chance for a bit of a holiday.''

Sir Charles was known to be deeply interested in the turf. This sounded not only a reasonable destination but one that would keep Peter out of mischief and away from the petticoats.

"I expect I'll be going to Danebury myself before long, to speak to my trainer,'' Luten mentioned.

This did not throw Clappet into a conniption, as the famous Danebury training camp was not where his friend Norman had mentioned stabling and training True Lady nor where he planned to put his own Firebird. The harsh Danebury method of riding its racers into the ground was not what appealed to these young, tender-hearted amateurs of the sport.

"Perhaps I'll see you there, then," Peter answered with tolerable ease.

"We'll likely bump into each other. When are you leaving?"

"Right away—this morning."

"It would set your mother's mind at rest if you visited her before going," Luten suggested.

"You know she hates anything to do with racing, Uncle. She even rips up at *you*, and you have won the Oaks twice. I should think she'd be proud of you, instead of calling you a gambling fool."

"As long as you're going as an onlooker and not taking the plunge yourself, I doubt she'll say much against it," Luten said. He reached for the coffeepot as he spoke, and thus missed the stricken, guilty look that flashed across his nephew's face.

"I suppose it can do no harm to drop by," Peter said reluctantly. "I'll need my topboots and buckskins, and want to get more linen, but I won't let her talk me out of it."

"Stand up to her," Luten advised carelessly, thinking it was time Maggie realized she would soon have a grown man on her hands.

"I will."

Sir Charles, hovering impatiently at the doorway, was invited to join them once the lecture was over. Luten was soon being pestered so hard for his advice on tying cravats, harnessing up teams, beating the odds at the races, and other matters presumably within a Corinthian's ken that he rose and took a polite departure.

"What had Luten to say?" Nick asked eagerly as soon as he was alone with Peter.

Clappet had no intention of revealing the whole of the lecture. He answered, "Oh, Luten thinks I ought to hire myself a set of rooms instead of squeezing in here with you. That's all."

Sir Charles, fearing a prolonged squeezing, took his theme up with great vigor. "I was never so happy as when *I* got my own space."

"Yes, well there's no point going to such expense now, when we plan to spend time at Newmarket."

"Thing is, after the races are over, we'll be coming back to London, and the same old story will start up again. Your Mama will be timing you in and out. None of the fellows will feel free to drop in. And rooms are impossible to come by once the Season is started. I'll tell you who has a dandy little place he wants to sublet is Ankerson. It comes furnished and all—you might pick it up for an old song."

This plan found some favor with Peter, but he didn't want to spend his blunt on anything but Firebird, and gave some indication of this.

"You had two-fifty budgeted for Firebird. Got her for two hundred. You could take Ankerson's place for the difference."

"For the whole Season? Where the devil is it, in the country?"

"Not at all. It's on the corner of Poland Street, just south of Oxford. It'll be gone in two minutes, Peter. You'd better pick it up before we go."

"Well, I'll have a look at least," Peter agreed.

The place, though small and modest, was set up "dashed conveniently," just as Nick had described it. The glory of at last shaking free of his mother was an even stronger inducement, and with Nick's warning ringing in his ears that it would be picked up in two minutes, Lord Clappet laid down his blunt and became a paying tenant for the Season.

While this transaction was going forth, Luten drove to Berkeley Square to set his sister's mind at ease. "Could you not have talked him out of Newmarket?" Maggie asked.

"It's best to put a hundred miles between him and the female," Luten decreed.

"Yes, but if he is bitten with the racing bug while he is there, it is hardly better than the other. It is all Nicolson's fault. He is the one turning Peter's head in this directoin."

"Peter could be worse occupied. I'll soon be going up that way myself, and will keep an eye on him. At least there was no serious attachment to the woman Mrs. Rolfe spoke of. It was a passing fancy—a few days' flirtation. He had the sense to cry off when she turned grasping."

"I don't see why children must take so long to grow up," she complained, but was soon complaining of the speed with which Peter had changed from a beautiful, docile child to a headstrong young man. Her whining did much to hasten Lord Luten from her saloon and into the sunlight.

Chapter Four

It was nearing noon the next day before Mrs. Rolfe conveyed to Lady Clappet the news of her son's two recent visits to Mrs. Harrington. Her voice throbbed with sympathy and her eyes gleamed with delight as she reenacted the melodrama: Clappet's desire for secrecy and the hussy's insistence that he should tell his mother all. The morning's visit had new plot thickenings to conjure over.

Scarcely a minute after the dame had left the door of Berkeley Square, a hastily scribbled, tear-stained epistle was being trotted around to Luten's doorway in Belgrave Square. As he was not home, however, several more hours of weeping occupied the widow before her brother stood before her, elegantly attired in those black vestments considered suitable for a night on the town.

"What is it now?" he asked testily. "I wish you would find yourself a new husband and surrogate father for Peter. I am becoming demmed tired of these summonses, Maggie."

"It has happened!" she wailed, dissolving into a fresh burst of tears on the hard sofa.

Her Blue Saloon at eventide was gloomy. The walls were hung in a dark blue patterned paper that soaked up the light of three elegant lamps, without much brightening the chamber.

"I assumed some new tribulation had sought you out. I cannot for the life of me understand how every affliction finds you, so well as you hide yourself in this cave."

"It's Peter," she breathed through the folds of her moist handkerchief.

"What?"

"Peter and that woman. He *lied* to you, Luten. My own flesh and blood turned out a liar and a womanizer. I doubt I will endure this blow. When he comes back, he will find me stretched under the elms of Hanch House with his father."

"In the meanwhile, can you revive yourself sufficiently to tell me what is going on?"

"He has been back to her, after promising it was over. Last night, and again this very morning after he left me."

"He told me he was at the Daffy Club!" Luten exclaimed, harking back to the morning's visit. He remembered the pale face, the dark circles under Peter's eyes, but he couldn't remember any signs of lying.

"Oh, can human heart bear it!" Lady Clappet sighed. "Last night the hussy urged him to tell me about her. It is marriage, no less, she has in her eye, you see. Why else would she ask him to tell me? Then this very morning as Nettie Rolfe was leaving the door to bring me the dreadful news, he went again. She overheard him say, for of course she lingered in the hallway when she knew he was there, that he would write her, and that he would be back soon, and he would take care of the *linens* for her. If the greenhead is not off hiring up a cottage and furnishing it this minute, it is more than I dare to hope. It sounds dreadfully like a misalliance, does it not, Luten?"

"It sounds more like a lovenest to me," he replied. "If it were marriage he had in mind, he'd install her at Hanch House, or here."

"One hardly knows which is worse. Dear Clappet was strongly averse to irregular liaisons. Oh, I know you bloods

26

feel differently nowadays. You think me an antique, but for a grasping divorcée to have got her clutches on poor little Peter is more than I can endure.''

"It's not as bad as getting her clutches on his name and title. I didn't think Peter would lie to me,'' Luten said softly, with a frown pleating his brow. "He assured me it was over. Why would the woman not go with him, if the purpose of his trip is to find her a cottage? Mrs. Rolfe said she stayed behind?''

"Yes, he is to write her and see her soon. She has sent him off to make the place ready for her, you see, as though he were a servant.''

"You're jumping to conclusions.''

"Indeed I am not! He said he would see to the linens for her. Where does one put linens but on a bed? And where does one put a bed? In a bedroom, which is bound to be in a house. He is hiring a house. Oh, and there is more evidence than the linens.''

His raised brow invited her to continue. "Money—he has drawn *every penny* of his quarter allowance out of the bank.''

"How the devil did you learn that?''

"Quite by accident. I needed some funds and sent to the bank for them. They sent back a note for Peter, which I took a little peek at only because I thought it might be urgent, and he was not at home. The note concerned a loan,'' she announced with awful solemnity. "No amount was specified, but it said that as he had emptied his account, he would require the signature of either you or me before the loan he requested could be approved. What would he want with a thousand pounds, if not to hire her a house? And that is not to be the end of it either. She is making him take out a loan.''

Luten's brows drew together in a black scowl. "Let me see the note,'' he ordered.

27

"I've pasted the letter up again. Peter takes a fuss if I snoop. Not that I ever do!"

"Get it," he repeated.

He had no hesitation in ripping her careful work apart and reading the missive. He tapped his toe on the floor when he had finished. Watching him, his elder sister recognized the signs of rising temper. Much as she wanted Peter home safe, she did not wish him to have to endure one of Luten's towering rages. They threw even her into a fit of dismals, and she was ten years Luten's senior.

"I'll take this," he said, folding the letter up and putting it into his pocket. "I'll speak to them at the bank. As I'm Peter's guardian, they won't hesitate to let me know what's going on. Loan indeed! Lying about his doings is more infuriating than all the rest. I suppose there is no point in dashing off to Newmarket. He won't be there. That was dust in our eyes."

"He wouldn't have stripped his closet clean to go to Newmarket for a few days," Lady Clappet said; she'd forgotten that detail. "His valet, Uxor, hauled away trunks of stuff, and the foolish servants didn't tell me. I had to see for myself his dear little room, with the drawers empty of every stitch of linen, and the clothespress holding nothing but empty hangers."

"That settles it. The jackanapes has peeled off," Luten said grimly. "He told me he'd see you before he leaves—another lie."

"What will you do about the woman?" Maggie inquired, eager to detour the blame to its proper target. "You must go to her, Luten. *She* will know where he is gone. Not that she'll tell you, the brazen strumpet. She is so sly there's no standing it."

Luten's nostrils pinched dangerously, and the cold flash of his eyes would have frozen fire. "She'll tell me if she takes the idea I'm not interested."

Lady Clappet directed a withering look at this piece of obtuseness. "She will *know* you are interested. Why else would you be there—Peter's uncle."

"*She* doesn't know that."

"You may be sure the ninnyhammer has been boasting of you. He always does."

"He won't have showed her my picture. It's not Peter's uncle that will call, but Mr. Somebody or Other, who wishes to learn Latin. That is her story, according to Nettie Rolfe, is it not, that it is Latin lessons she purveys?"

"Yes, that's what she says."

"Let us see how she handles a *homo bellicosus*," he sneered, and arose from the sofa.

"You won't go to her at this hour?"

"It's only evening. Her sort open their doors after dark, Maggie. They don't close 'em, not on well-inlaid gents. I'll not be back till tomorrow."

"I shan't sleep a wink all night."

A parody of a smile pulled Luten's face into a grotesque mask. "With luck, I may not either," he said, through thin lips.

Lady Clappet sat wondering what he could possibly mean, till she happened to remember her laudanum, and sent off for it.

Luten went home to add to his toilette those expensive and gaudy ornaments that might appeal to a Cyprian. His largest diamond stud was inserted in his cravat, an emerald ring with a stone too big for its setting was slid onto his finger, and two or three gold fobs attached to his watch chain. With a shrug of his shoulders, he picked up a quizzing glass that lay on his dresser and attached it to a ribbon. He patted his pocket to ensure the presence within of a hefty wad of paper money. He had no intention of parting with any of it, but a thick wad of bills would impress an avaricious female of Mrs. Harrington's sort. His preparations complete, he had the team removed from his crested carriage and harnessed up to a plain black one that was seldom used. Mr. Mandeville, whom he was about to become, would not drive a crested carriage, but in all other respects, he would be the pink of the ton. A financier perhaps, having the sound of big money attached to it, would impress the female.

Inside the upper apartment on the corner of Conduit and Swallow streets, Mrs. Harrington got up off her chair, stretched her arms, yawned, and said she was for bed.

"It's only nine-thirty," Trudie pointed out.

"The light is too poor to knit on these dark woolens, and I have read the newspapers. I could write a few letters," Mrs. Harrington said listlessly.

The ladies had spent the entire day without company, except for Peter's flying visit that morning. It had been a long, extremely tiresome day, and the immediate future promised more of the same. It was frustrating for Trudie to know that bustling, teaming, social London was out there, just at her fingertips, but held aloft from her by the lack of connections, and the inelegance of the apartment. In fact, they didn't even have a carriage to accept an invitation in dignity, should one be offered. But she refused to admit to Aunt Gertrude that she was suffering. She had encouraged Norman in this plan, and for a year she could stick it.

There was no warning sound of footfall on the steps, for Luten had crept up softly and held his ear to the door a moment before knocking. The first knowledge of a caller was a sharp rapping at the door. "Who could that be?" Mrs. Harrington asked in alarm.

"I've no idea," Trudie said, but she walked with hopeful anticipation to the door, expecting nothing more than a call from one of the neighbors. She was greeted by a tall, elegant gentleman with dark hair and eyes. His wide shoulders nearly filled the doorway, and on the shoulders sat a jacket that bore little resemblance to the provincial tailoring she

30

was accustomed to seeing on gentlemen. It looked as if it had been poured on him, so smoothly did it sit. No sooner had she ascertained he was a stranger than she noticed the large diamond stud he wore. It was impossible to miss it, twinkling and shooting off sparks from the hall light. She was sure it was some mistake—the man wanted Nettie Rolfe probably—but it was the most pleasant mistake encountered thus far in London, and it brought a smile to her lips.

"Mrs. Harrington?" the man inquired in a polite, well-modulated voice as he smiled in apparent pleasure at the lady who stood before him.

"My aunt is home. May I tell her who is calling?" she asked, and opened the door to admit him. Her mind was alive with conjecture. Who could he be? Was it possible Gertrude had a rich young cousin about whom she'd remained silent all these years?

The ladies had brought with them one female servant for the cooking and cleaning, and her husband, Bogman, to act as general factotum for the heavier work, and protector from the evils of the city. Bogman also donned his best jacket and answered the door upon occasion, but this evening he was polishing their shoes in the kitchen with a towel around his waist. His presence on the premises, however, made it possible to admit an unknown man.

"Mr. Mandeville, a friend of Sir Charles Nicolson," he told her.

Trudie's first reaction was disappointment, and her second was curiosity as to why Sir Charles should have sent a friend to Gertrude, who cordially disliked Nick. It must have something to do with Norman.

Luten, running a practiced eye over the girl, was relieved to learn she wasn't the infamous Mrs. Harrington. It would be enough to kill a man's faith in humanity if this bright-eyed young chit should be a member of the muslin company. Her general appearance was of a young girl fresh off

31

the farm. Her gown was modest but fashionable; her coif-
fure pretty but not at all in the current mode. Her clear
complexion, her full cheeks—everything about her was
healthy- and honest-appearing, and it was a pity she must reside with the aunt, he thought.

Trudie led him to the parlor, where Mrs. Harrington had
resumed her seat upon hearing a guest being shown in.
"This is Mr. Mandeville, a friend of Sir Charles, Auntie,"
she said, and behind Luten's back she lifted her brows in
confusion.

Long practice allowed Luten to perform a creditable bow
while his mind scurried to figure out that the aging dame
scowling at him beneath her gray brows was obviously not
the one who had trapped his nephew. The niece was the
vixen, then, despite her innocent trappings. All her country
charm was interpreted differently, seen as a cunning disguise.

He turned a questioning gaze back to the younger female.
"I am Miss Barten," she told him. "Pray have a seat, Mr.
Mandeville. We are curious to hear Sir Charles's message."

He listened closely and could hear the breath of the country in her accent, but it was genteel country. "Message?" he
asked. "I didn't bring a message."

"Why did you come, then?" she asked with appalling
frankness, while her large bright eyes returned to his diamond stud, then flittered to his emerald ring, which was
being employed to attract her attention and test her interest.

He slipped one quick glance to the aunt, then said to Trudie, "Sir Charles recommended you as an excellent teacher
of Latin, ma'am. I have come to see whether you will be
agreeable to take me on as a student."

"A student! But you're so old!" she exclaimed, her
frankness descending to outright insult. It was clear she preferred young birds for plucking. "And you asked for Mrs.
Harrington. Nick knows very well Auntie doesn't know any

Latin," she pointed out. Her eyes were bright with suspicion, but despite the oddity of the call, she wasn't eager to shoe Mr. Mandeville to the door and resume the tedium of watching Auntie write her letters.

"I misunderstood him. I thought your aunt's name was Barten," he explained, and of course said not a word about Nettie Rolfe's part in the misunderstanding.

Mrs. Harrington had taken the dandy's measure and decided she didn't care for him. "Miss Barten does not give lessons," she said firmly. "She has tutored a few close friends, but she does not advertise and does not take strangers."

"Nicolson will be happy to give me a character, if that is the impediment," he said warily, but he was surprised that the diamond hadn't been character enough for them.

"No, the impediment is that she does not give lessons," the lady insisted, bestowing her haughtiest contempt on the caller.

While the elder spoke, the younger continued to examine Luten from the side of her eye. He was extremely handsome, well outfitted, and well-spoken. He was also a friend of Sir Charles, which made him not *quite* a stranger. Eligible gentlemen were rare enough that she felt some desire to know him better, especially now that the other gentlemen had left town.

"I am tutoring a few friends, but really I have no notion of setting out a shingle," she explained, using a kinder tone than her aunt. "Why have you decided to study Latin at such a late date in your life, Mr. Mandeville?" She sat down as she spoke and nodded her permission for him to do likewise.

"I hardly consider myself to be doddering into the sunset yet!" he answered, conferring his most ravishing smile on her. It softened the harsh lines of his nose and mouth and did actually appear to remove five or so years from him. "It's

33

not really a full course I'm interested in. The fact is, I've been elected to Parliament and wish to insert a few quotations in my maiden speech. My friends tell me it is all the go. I never had the advantage of a classical education and have often felt the lack of it. I was put into a bank when I was twelve, for I had some knack for handling figures."

Trudie's eyes were drawn again to the flickering diamond, and she said, "You appear to have prospered without benefit of the classics."

"Beyond my highest expectations, insofar as my career and earnings are concerned. Now that I have accumulated a good fortune, I am aiming for a political career. Vansittart, the Chancellor of the Exchange, was instrumental in my winning a seat. He feels I could be of help to him in his ministry; I seem to have the knack of handling money."

Mrs. Harrison was impressed by the man's patron and joined the conversation. "I hope you don't plan to raise the taxes."

Trudie also looked at their guest with greater interest. "Is it just a few famous quotations for the speech you are interested in?" she asked. This could be accomplished in half an hour, and who knew what else might be accomplished as well? Already the words of Cicero and Vergil and Horace were tumbling through her head.

Luten cast an impatient look at the aunt but answered civilly. "For the beginning, at least, to see how we go on together." His wish was to imply he was good for more than one call, if they rubbed along well.

"Could some of your colleagues not help you?" Mrs. Harrington asked.

"No doubt they could if I asked, but I am a little proud, and don't mean to advertise my lack of formal education," he answered.

Trudie was of the popular but unstated opinion among Englishmen that pride was no vice; quite the reverse. "I think we might help Mr. Mandeville, Auntie. We should all do our bit to make Parliament a polite and learned place.''

Luten's smile escalated from approval to intimacy so quickly that she was set to wondering. Being as innocent as a nun, she concluded he liked her, and she wasn't slow to return the smile.

"Could we—ah—take care of it now?" he asked, darting a glance at Mrs. Harrington, who sat like an owl, watching and listening.

"It is rather late," Trudie pointed out. "My aunt was about to retire. I will want to make some preparations for the meeting. Could you come back tomorrow?"

He lowered his tone to avert Mrs. Harrington's detection and said, "If you think we would disturb your aunt, we could do it elsewhere—go to my place."

Trudie stared with blinking eyes. "Oh, no! Are you in that great a hurry?"

"My speech is coming up very soon, and of course I will want to practice a little."

"Miss Barten is certainly not leaving her house at this hour of the night with a strange gentleman," Mrs. Harrison said. "She has been seeing too many students lately and is fagged. Besides, it is quite improper for you to suggest it, Mr. Mandeville."

"I'm sorry," he said promptly, and began backtracking to undo the mischief. "When may I return?"

"Tomorrow morning?" Trudie suggested.

"Morning?" he asked, blinking in surprise. "I thought evenings would be more . . . appropriate."

"Daytime would be better," Mrs. Harrington said.

"Mr. Mandeville works, Auntie," Trudie pointed out. "He is a Member of Parliament. He is busy during the day."

As he was eager for a private talk with the young woman, Luten discovered a free space in his timetable at eleven the next morning. This hour was agreed upon as suitable to both parties. Next he went on to try for news of Peter.

"Sir Charles was going to come with me to make me known to you," he invented, "but he went out of town this morning with a friend—Lord Clappet, I think he said. Perhaps you know Clappet. He is a great bosom beau of Sir Charles."

A warm smile lit Trudie's face and she answered, "Oh, yes, it is really Peter, Lord Clappet, who is our friend. It is he who brought Sir Charles to us. They went to . . ." She remembered in time that the trip to Brighton was a secret from Peter's family, and for all she knew, Mr. Mandeville might be a friend. Luten regarded her, his black brows lifted in a question. "To Newmarket," she said, but in a flustered way.

"They went a bit early. The races aren't till May," he said.

"Yes, they did."

"Nicolson didn't mention just why he was going," Luten continued in a careless way, as though he were just making conversation, but it would be natural for her to explain now if she knew, and if she was innocent. Luten looked at her from beneath his lashes. He found himself hoping she would give some unforeseen reason for the trip, some motive that excluded herself. What he saw was a faint blush color her cheeks, a quick warning glance to the aunt, and what he heard was a longish silence.

When Trudie spoke, she changed the subject. "What is the topic of your speech in Parliament, sir? It will help me to cull suitable quotations if I know what you will be speaking about."

"Money," he answered. "Large sums of money."

"Is it spending, raising, or wasting money you will be discussing?" she inquired.

"I am not in the Opposition, ma'am. It is Tierney who

rails against the awful waste. My subject will be the careful husbanding of the nation's funds.''

She nodded. ''Anything to do with thrift will be useful, then.''

''Quite. With the *nation's* funds one must be cautious, whatever one's own habits,'' he said, taking the opportunity to hint at personal largesse.

She couldn't quite refrain from smiling at his diamond, which was really unattractively large, ostentatiously so. Seeing her glance, he lifted the hand that sported the emerald ring, and patted the folds of his cravat. Then he drew out his watch, allowing the heavy golden fobs to rattle to her attention.

''What a handsome ring, Mr. Mandeville,'' Trudie commented, for she had some idea these adornments were being purposely drawn to her attention.

''I rewarded myself for a particularly brilliant coup on the market last year,'' he explained.

''I tremble to ask what coup the diamond represents. Is it possible you were alive in the last century and were the one who reaped the rewards of the South Sea Bubble?''

''That was well before my time. It was Harley, the Earl of Oxford, who is usually credited—or shall we say discredited—with the scheme. We Tories deal quite differently with the national debt, but I'm not pushing Consols as a good investment by any means.''

Trudie nodded, only minimally interested in his financial advice. ''What does your diamond represent?''

He bestowed another of his intimate smiles on her, but this time it was tinged with flirtation. ''Why, to tell the truth, I bought if for a lady, but she spurned my advances, so I had it mounted into a stud to wear myself, till I find a lady willing to accept it.''

Mrs. Harrington pokered up and looked rather pointedly

at the clock. Trudie smiled and glanced at the decanter of wine that rested on the table. Luten observed them both and concluded he would have better luck tomorrow when he got the young female off by herself. He rose, thanked them most civilly for accepting his offer, bowed his adieux, and left.

In his carriage, he removed the excess of jewelry, put it into a side pocket, and went on to a rout party. Peter's scrape, however annoying, was by no means monopolizing Luten's time and thoughts.

"Cheeky fellow," Mrs. Harrington griped. "We have hit a new low, catering to Cits."

Trudie emitted a long sigh and replied, "I thought he was rather handsome."

"A man who decks himself up like a jewelry display window to impress his betters is no gentleman, my dear. Give him the quotations he wants to use in Parliament and have done with him."

"How odiously snobbish of you to disparage Mr. Mandeville only because he is a self-made man. I think with a little coaching he could be . . ."

"He is too old, and too common for you," her aunt said swiftly. "How very like Nicolson to burden us with his second-rate friends. It is the outside of enough for him to send total strangers to our door. I wish you had turned the man off."

"It can do no harm to see him once more," Trudie answered mildly.

He was the most interesting man, in fact the *only* real man, they'd met since coming to London. There was a whiff of the city about him to be sure, but that could be brushed off with tactful hints. And Mr. Mandeville would be susceptible to such hints. He must be very clever to have advanced so far in the world, and he wanted to make a good appearance.

The tedium of London had brightened, and though Trudie was obliged to listen to several other animadversions on Mr. Mandeville's manner, she paid no heed to any of them. She thought she had found an access into polite society, and meant to cultivate Mr. Mandeville's company.

Chapter Five

"Did you see her?" Lady Clappet demanded the next morning, before her brother had handed his hat and gloves to the butler.

He made no reply till they were in the lugubrious Blue Saloon. "I saw her."

"What had she to say?"

"She admitted she knows Peter, but of course gave no idea why he went to Newmarket. She says that is where he is gone—not that it's necessarily true."

"Did you get the thing settled? I hoped we might be rid of her by now."

"What did you expect me to do, murder her? She's got Peter under her thumb. Why should she hand him back to us, only because we want it? She's not a fool. I begin to think the best thing is to buy her off."

"Pay her money?" Maggie asked reluctantly.

"It's done all the time. The Beauforts offered Harriet Wilson twenty thousand pounds to rescue Worcester from her."

Lady Clappet turned a nasty shade of mauve from the sudden infusion of blood into her pale cheeks. "Twenty thousand pounds!" she gasped.

"Yes, but Miss Barten isn't so high a flyer as Harry."

"Miss Barten? The woman's name is Mrs. Harrington."

Luten shook his head. "Harrington is the aunt, or called so, at any rate. The female Peter's involved with is a Miss Barten. She has an eye for gaudy jewelry."

"Did she ask for money, for jewels, to free Peter?"

"Oh, no, we were much more civilized than that. I am to take Latin lessons from her, starting this morning. Last night I only made contact, presented myself as a rich Cit, ripe for plucking."

"This is wasting valuable time, Luten," Lady Clappet objected.

"We can afford it. Peter's out of town. She won't bother going after him if she thinks she has a plumper bird in hand."

"How long will it take?"

A cocky smile settled on his lips. "About two minutes, once I get her away from the chaperone. Getting rid of the old hag will be the major problem. She sticks like a burr and is loath to see her girl take on any more clients, but the chit rules the roost. I can't believe Peter means to marry her—the aunt spoke openly of other clients. Unless she has an offer of marriage from Peter, she'll be easily bought off."

"And if she *has* an offer?" she asked fearfully.

"Then she won't get a Birmingham farthing. A penniless female plying her trade to earn a living is one thing; an adventuress trying to pull a greenhead of a boy into marriage is something else."

"Dear me, yes. She is much more dangerous."

"I really think she has no more in mind than being set up in a cottage near Newmarket for the racing season. That's bad enough to be sure, but Peter is reaching the age, you know. And so far as women of that sort go, she's not at all bad. She has a ladylike way about her, a lively little thing, well spoken and so on. There were even a few papers and books in the room."

41

"Of course there were! She claims to be a tutor," Lady Clappet said sharply. She disliked that shadow of a smile that was hovering at the corner of Luten's lips, and his oblique praise of the woman.

"So she does. She is ingenious, you must admit."

The woman was a witch. First Peter, now Luten. "I want you to buy her off, Luten," she said, taking her decision quickly. "Once Peter gets a taste of that low life his dear papa so abhorred, there is no saying where it will end. Offer her a couple of hundred pounds."

Luten gave a snort of laughter. "She stands to get a thousand every quarter from Peter. She won't be likely to settle for less."

"A thousand pounds! It is too much!"

"She'll never settle for a couple of hundred."

"She shan't get a penny more," Lady Clappet said firmly. All signs of mourning were abandoned; a very martial light gleamed in her eyes.

"We'll see. We may scrape through without giving her anything at all. I mean to try my charms on her. If I can gull her along, get her to give up Peter . . ."

"Yes, Luten, but then *you* are stuck with her."

"My foolish sister, do you take me for a knave? Naturally I would not actually steal the boy's mistress." A soft moan sounded in his sister's throat. "I'll only lead her to believe she may have me for the taking. I shall insist on monopoly rights; she will turn Peter off, and *voilà*!" He threw up his hands. "I bolt on her. It will show her a useful lesson. She hasn't dealt with a *man* before, I think. She's only preyed on boys."

"Do you think it will fadge?" she asked doubtfully.

"I have no idea. I think she considers me ready for a Bath chair, but we'll soon know. I am to be there in half an hour. I'll come right back to you. Had Nettie any luck in getting them evicted, by the way? You mentioned it earlier. They weren't in the throes of packing last night.''

''Evans, the maintenance man, took the tale to the owner, but nothing has come of it so far. Nigel Patterson is the landlord, it seems.''

''In the worst case, I can speak to him, but to do it before she turns Peter off would only send her pelting after him to their cottage lovenest.''

He pulled out his watch, read it, and rose to take his leave.

''Why are you using three fobs?'' she asked. ''And that great ugly emerald ring of Papa's—you do not usually wear it.''

''It is to impress the female. Last night my tie was weighed down with the Luten diamond. I'm driving my curricle today to show her that I have two carriages. I can't be seen in my crested one, since I'm posing as a Mr. Mandeville.''

''Such a lot of bother as she is causing. It does not seem right for her to be able to put us all to so much trouble.''

''We shall get our own back when *she* is put to the bother of finding herself a new protector,'' he consoled her, then he strode from the saloon. His face showed no irritation at the inconvenience to which he was being put. On the contrary, his lips, usually a thin line, were curved into a little smile.

The smile stretched into a full-blown grin when he noticed the twitching of Mrs. Rolfe's curtains half an hour later as he approached the door of Miss Barten's residence. There would be another dash to report this visit to Evans, he supposed.

Mrs. Harrington wore no smile of welcome, but a severe countenance when he was shown into the parlor. To his amazement, Miss Barten actually had half a dozen Latin books laid out on a table, along with paper, pen, inkpot, and other signs of her alleged profession. She looked so dauntingly demure in her dark gown and lace fichu that he was struck for one awful minute with the idea that it was all a mistake. No Cyprian he ever knew, and he knew several of them, dressed so plainly.

"Good morning, Mr. Mandeville," Trudie said, dropping a curtsey. There was some air not far removed from the coquette in the smile she bestowed on him. It was enough to assure him of her calling and to conclude that this innocent facade was a clever and quite effective contrivance. Upon closer inspection, he remarked that her toilette had been spruced up from the preceding evening.

Her titian curls were more becomingly arranged, the cheeks quite possibly touched with rouge. He did not know she also wore her best morning gown and had washed and pressed the lace collar especially in his honor, tucking a silk rosebud into it for added enticement. Trudie saw no harm in making a discreet play for this extremely eligible gentleman who had fallen into her path, provided he proved to be a bachelor, an item to be confirmed that morning.

A few remarks were passed on the glory of the spring day. "I drove my curricle, to enjoy the breezes," he mentioned, and took note of the interest the words elicited. "I plan to get out to my country estate this weekend. One dislikes to be cooped up in such fine weather. Even a thirty-room mansion is too confining in the spring. I long for the freedom of stretching acres, the brooks babbling. I hope to get in a spot of fishing at my lake," he added, tossing in every evidence of wealth he could lay tongue to.

Trudie smiled at the obviousness of his stunt but took due note to his possessions all the same. "Very true. My aunt and I as well have been complaining of the same thing, with more cause too. We, you will not have failed to notice, are confined to something less than a thirty-room mansion. We are accustomed to a good deal more space. We have let our country home, Walbeck, for a Season."

He posed no embarrassing questions as to why this un-usual course had been taken, nor did he pursue the location of this hypothetical estate.

"Shall we get down to work now?" she suggested, look-ing at the table, where two chairs had been placed an incon-venient but very proper three feet apart.

"Yes, certainly," he agreed. He looked to the chaperone in the corner, who had thus far said nothing but good day, though she had heard with disgust the vulgar enumeration of his worldly goods.

"I have been perusing these books for possible quota-tions," Trudie said, and drew forward a neatly written sheet on which rested Latin quotations and their English transla-tions. "I thought Horace's *Epistles* might yield some-thing," she mentioned. "He is much quoted by literary gentlemen nowadays. He would have been at home with Sheridan—such a wit! Vergil, I think, is a trifle bucolic for us, though there might be something in his *Georgics*."

Intrigued, Luten took up the sheet and glanced at it. He frowned, wondering how she had accumulated such relevant passages in such a short time. Trudie noticed his expression and misunderstood it. "This one deals with husbandry, but could be used to refer to husbanding money as well," she pointed out. She added a few other quotations orally, caus-ing him to frown harder than ever. She actually knew Latin!

"You must not be discouraged, Mr. Mandeville," she encouraged. "You won't have to memorize all these. Only select the few that are suitable, and we shall go over them a few times for the pronunciation."

"This is extremely obliging of you," he said. "I'm afraid I have put you to a great deal of trouble."

"Not at all. Actually, the work was half done for me. My father studied classics at Oxford—an interest he continued till his death—and had made an extract of his favorite speeches. I only referred to it, but unfortunately he has done

45

it by author rather than subject. It would be an excellent notion for someone to publish a book of quotations by subject matter, to save writers all the bother of ferreting through dozens of books for the proper words.''

''An excellent notion. I would be the first to buy such a book.''

''Now, how shall we set about this? Why don't you look over the list, and mark those you think useful. Then we'll practice the pronunciation for your speech.''

''Fine.''

''Would you like some coffee while we work?''

''That would be very nice.''

He hoped to see the aunt fetch the drink, but she just pulled a bell cord and summoned a decent-looking servant. It was a male servant at that, which was more stylish than a female. Luten began to perceive that Miss Barten was going to be more difficult to deal with than he had thought. His aim was to remove her from the apartment, which was achieved by a hasty selection of quotations, the only criterion being that he already had them by heart, to speed up the ''memorization and learning of pronunciation.''

''You are a very fast learner, Mr. Mandeville!'' she congratulated, more than once. ''I have never seen anyone learn so quickly.''

''I put my mind to things,'' he explained briefly.

Before half an hour, the lesson was completed, and the embarrassing matter of payment arose. ''Shall we discuss your fee outside?'' he asked. ''It's such a fine day, and you were complaining of being cooped up. I had allowed an hour for this lesson, and we've finished early. Would your aunt mind if we took a spin?''

Mrs. Harrington's stiff face showed that she minded very much, but as Trudie was already darting for her pelisse and bonnet, Luten confirmed who was the boss in the business.

The dashing yellow curricle and team of high-stepping

bays harnessed up to it showed that whatever of Mr. Mandeville's personal toilette, in the matter of transportation, his taste was excellent.

She ran her eyes over the teams' points. "Sixteen miles an hour, I expect?"

"Only fifteen in the city," he answered modestly.

"A pity we haven't time for a jaunt into the country. Such a laggardly gait, fifteen miles an hour," she said, but her real interest was to discover his marital status. With more speed than finesse she added, "Does Mrs. Mandeville enjoy such a lively drive, sir?"

"Not at all. Mama uses a landaulet," he assured her. The knowledge in his eyes at her artless angling for information caused her to blush. "Or did you refer to my wife?" he asked.

"Yes, I meant your wife," she admitted, her chin jutting forth. Having been caught out, there was no point denying it.

"I don't have a wife." The jutting chin of his partner receded in satisfaction. He whipped up the team, and they were off at a good clip, but not so fast as fifteen miles an hour.

"It would be your only having an hour at a time for your social life that accounts for it," she said.

"My social life occurs in the evening. It happens I am at liberty tonight. Am I fortunate enough to find you also free, Miss Barten? I hoped we might go somewhere for dinner, perhaps a play afterward. . . ."

There had been no mention of including her aunt, which caused her to hesitate. A chaperoned evening such as he suggested was very tempting. "I don't know what my aunt may have in mind," she parried, to test the waters.

"What Mrs. Harrington has in mind need not concern us. Are *you* free?" he asked bluntly.

She stared at his suggestion and the blunt way he pro-

47

posed it. "I couldn't go out alone with a stranger, Mr. Mandeville! It wouldn't be at all the thing."

He turned and looked at her with a conning smile. Birds of paradise who set up as innocent females were beneath contempt. "I'm not such a dangerous fellow as all that. I will undertake not to beat, rob, or otherwise molest you."

Her shoulders sagged in disappointment. Aunt Gertrude was right. Mr. Mandeville was extremely common; he didn't even know the behavior expected in polite company. But he was handsome and amusing and might yet be hinted into propriety. "It would be considered fast for me to go out without a chaperone, since we are so slightly acquainted" was all she said. She waited with held breath to see if the invitation was broadened to include her aunt.

"Do you care so much for the opinion of people you don't even know?" was his reply.

"Of course I do. A lady's reputation is very important. If folks took the idea she was fast, she would have no hope of making a good match," she explained, putting the thing in its simplest form so that even a Cit must accept it.

Luten nodded. "I see. You have some good match in your eye, have you?"

"I am speaking in generalities only."

"Let us be more specific. Do you have a gentleman already, Miss Barten?" he asked, with awful bluntness.

She replied, "No," with equal candor.

"Why will you not come out with me, then?"

"I didn't say I wouldn't, Mr. Mandeville, but I would have to insist my aunt accompany us. It is the way things are done in polite society."

"Your aunt dislikes me. We would have no opportunity to become better acquainted if she came along."

"I can only say she would dislike you more if she knew what you have in mind," she said crossly. But soon relented and added, "Let us get to know each other now, since it seems we will not have another opportunity."

"It suits me. How long have you been teaching Latin?"

"For two weeks—only since we came up to London." She went on to explain about Norman's having let his estate for a year in order to buy a racehorse and try his luck on the turf.

Luten listened, giving some encouragement when he felt it was called for and maintaining always the pose of believing her unlikely tale. "You met Nicolson through your brother's interest in racing, did you?" was his question when she had finished.

"No, through another friend, Lord Clappet," she told him, not reluctant to drop such a respectable name.

There was no tensing of her companion's shoulders to betray his interest. He had been waiting for the name to arise. "Clappet is a good friend of yours, is he?" he asked blandly.

"He is the best, really the *only*, friend I have in town."

"Have you known him long? How did you meet him?"

"Through Norman. We've known him a few years."

"Now I see why you wouldn't go out with me this evening," he teased, and looked for signs of guilt.

She was completely unfazed. "Oh, no, it's nothing like that. You already knew Clappet is out of town this evening," she reminded him.

"Will he be back soon?"

She was alerted to attention at the sound of his voice, some keener interest than should have been there. Was it possible Lady Clappet had sent him to spy, to learn what he could about Peter? She knew Peter's mother for an eccentric, and answered airily, "Good gracious, we are not so close as that. I don't know his itinerary. Why do you ask?"

"I'm trying to discover how much time I have to batter down your defenses," he answered, smiling lazily at her, but still he didn't extend the evening's invitation to include her aunt. He wasn't that eager to see her. She decided Mr. Mandeville was a lost cause, and fell silent.

"We haven't settled on your fee for tutoring me," he said a moment later. "Will five guineas be sufficient?" He chose a ludicrously high fee, to reengage her interest.

"A crown is my usual fee, Mr. Mandeville," she answered coolly.

"When a gentlemen hires a lady, he usually pays more than that," he answered. His tone had become strangely insinuating.

"That must depend on what he hires her for, I presume. Tutors are paid at the rate I mentioned. I occasionally tutor youngsters in Latin for the going fee. I see no reason to change it because the student is older and richer."

"I shouldn't think you make much of a living at a crown per student, with only a few students a week."

"I do not make my living at it! I have told you my circumstances," she said, becoming angry at the tenor of his remarks.

His own patience broke, and his anger rose to meet the occasion. "I have told you a few untruths as well, miss. Let us cut line. You have come to the city to try for a rich patron. You won't find a richer one than I."

Trudie stared, unable to assimilate the change in her partner's manner. "I beg your pardon!" she huffed, her voice rising to a squeal of indignation.

"There's no need to apologize. I'm not against a woman's earning her keep if she must."

Lord Luten was a notable whip. All his expertise was required to control his team when Miss Barten reached out without a word and grabbed the reins from his fingers to pull the horses to a dead halt. She turned a wrathful, fiery eye on him, while two bright red spots gathered on her cheeks.

"Next time you set out to hire a mistress, Mr. Mandeville, may I suggest you try Covent Garden, rather than insult a decent lady. I am surprised such an experienced gentleman as you should require the hint, but then breeding is obviously not your long suit.''

His thin lips drew into a sneer. ''I'm always willing to listen to advice from a professional,'' he assured her.

She threw the reins in his lap, jumped down from the seat, and walked angrily through the streets, with really very little notion where she was going. They had driven east, for Luten wasn't eager to be seen with an undistinguished member of the muslin company in his open carriage.

He frowned to see the direction she took. Trudie turned at the first corner she came to, which removed her from the residential district. She was now in an alien territory never before seen or imagined, though the name Long Acre would have been recognized as a place to avoid even by her. She passed a few carriage makers' shops, where young bucks were loitering, happy to have the amusement of a young lady to whistle and shout at. She gathered up her skirts and walked faster, turned another corner, and came to Endell Street, where a large building was advertised as a closed bath.

Not daring to look over her shoulder, Trudie didn't know she was being followed by a pair of the bucks from the carriage works. As there was no crowd around the baths so early in the Season, she stopped to take her bearings and decide how she was to get home. She opened her reticule to check her money, not that there was a hackney cab in sight. She had exactly a shilling and tuppence.

She turned to glance back to the corner for a cab and saw the two young bucks advancing at a swift pace, their faces full of mischief. Her heart began a fierce pounding, and she continued her walk, which was quickly accelerating to a run. The bucks speeded up. They were suddenly by her side, each taking one of her arms to hold her captive. There wasn't another soul on the street to come to her rescue.

"Let go! Let me go this instant!" she cried.

"What's the hurry, my little fancy?" one of them asked. "A pretty thing like yourself shouldn't be alone on the streets of Long Acre. No saying what might happen, eh, Charlie?" he asked his friend.

"Let me go, I say!" she insisted, pulling and squirming to disengage herself from their clutches.

"Let you go? Why, we are offering to go with you, love, back to your place." The second man laughed.

She was hardly aware of their looks. She saw they were young and extremely foppish, but despite their silly appearance, their arms were strong and their expressions extremely menacing. They tightened their hold on her arms and began pulling her along, vastly enjoying the sport of harassing a lone female.

Though she was frightened, Trudie didn't think the bucks could do more than annoy her on a public street in broad daylight. She dug in her heels to impede their progress while looking around for a likely doorway to dart to for help. "If you don't let me go this instant . . ." she blustered.

"Yes, my pretty? What will you do? Shout for help? Bow Street is a few blocks away. You'll have to sing loud." The bucks laughed heartily at this sally.

There was the welcome sound of an approaching carriage behind them. She lifted her foot and struck the one she supposed to be the leader as hard as she could with her toe while exerting the force of her body to wrench free of the other's arm. Her kick caused no pain to anyone but herself, for the dandy was well protected with Hessians, but the surprise of it made him release her arm. She raised her reticule to take one swing at the side of his head, then ran shouting into the road to stop the carriage. It was hardly necessary. Luten had already drawn to a halt and sat grinning at her predicament.

"Out of the frying pan, into the fire, eh, Miss Barten?" he called, just before he turned a black gaze on the bucks.

"Luten!" one of them said to the other. Had Trudie been less agitated, she would have recognized the name, for Clappet often spoke of his uncle. Luten didn't call the bucks to account as he might otherwise have done. He wasn't eager to have his identity revealed.

"Beat it," he growled, and with admirable obedience, they complied with his suggestion.

"Hop up," he said to Miss Barten, and offered her his hand. She was not quite so swift to act as the bucks, but with a survey of the neighborhood, she didn't tarry long either. He whipped up his team and they were off.

"Thank you," she said stiffly, then averted her head and said nothing more for the length of the block, while she recovered her breath.

Luten was equally terse. He said, "You're welcome."

Eventually Trudie had wind to give vent to her feelings. "It's really shocking. . . ." But she was still too overcome to continue, so Luten spoke.

"It certainly is," he agreed, but his voice wasn't as serious as she felt it ought to have been. "If a woman isn't looking for that sort of attention, however, she really ought not to go for a stroll in Long Acre alone."

"You know why I was there!"

"I don't, really. I thought, when you so precipitately parted company with me, that you would head back to civilization. Why did you come this way?"

"Because I was lost, naturally."

"Ah, as you were more or less en route to Covent Garden, I thought perhaps . . . It *was* Covent Garden you suggested to me, was it not, as the best spot to make an assignation?"

"Mr. Mandeville, I have thanked you for rescuing me.

Pray do not make it necessary for me to bolt again. Take me home, at once.''

"It will be better if you calm down first. Your aunt will think it is I who have caused your distress if you go home with your face all ablush, and your toilette, if you will pardon my saying so, very disordered."

She looked down and saw her robe had got twisted around during her fracas with the bucks. Her ribbons were all askew, and her purse was hanging open from being used as a weapon. She smoothed her skirts and ribbons, clasped her reticule shut, and folded her hands in her lap, determined to let her spirits settle, as he suggested.

"That is much better," he complimented her. "Half an hour's drive through a well-traveled park and you'll be your usual demure yourself."

"I wish to go home at once."

"It's a long walk" was his answer to that.

"I thought you only had half an hour to spare."

"A damsel in distress is reason enough to delay my business."

"I should think so indeed, when it was *you* who put her in distress."

"If that is true, I'm sorry, but it wasn't necessary for you to behave quite so rashly. Even women ought to blend some common sense with melodramatics, don't you think?"

"I certainly behaved rashly to drive out with a stranger. My aunt was correct; I'll pay her more heed another time."

"I'm delighted to hear there is to be another time. I feared your mishap this morning might put you off."

She gave him her most withering glare. "Not at all. I don't conclude that *all* men are villains, only because three this morning have behaved with such unconscionable lack of manners."

"Three? There were only two," he reminded her, but

54

soon read her meaning. "I still maintain only two behaved unconscionably. The third had some provocation."

"What provocation? Didn't I help you with your Latin, as you wanted?" she demanded.

He gave a sardonic laugh and drew on the reins, pulling his team to a halt. "It wasn't the lure of a dead language that took me to your apartment, Miss Barten."

"Then what in the name of God was it? Whatever made you think . . ."

"You know what I want. This," he said, and swept her into his arms for a kiss, after first taking a peek around to confirm that no one who mattered was around.

His arms were like human coils wrapped around her, holding her arms immobile. There was an instant's shock while she realized what he was doing. Mr. Mandeville was giving her a very fierce kiss, in broad daylight. Her head was pressed back against the squabs, held immobile by the pressure of his lips against hers. His lips felt hard, savage, totally unloverlike. It wasn't a kiss at all; it was a punishment.

She twisted aside, breathing hard, and stared into his eyes, which glared back at her, glittering with hatred. Luten stopped, and while he stared, his expression changed.

She was afraid! Scared out of her wits. Oh, she was angry too, but fright was foremost. He noticed when she gulped and swallowed the lump in her throat. An edge of white teeth came out and grasped her lower lip, while she waited, obviously wondering how to escape him. He released her and pulled back, feeling a perfect fool.

She edged away carefully and looked toward the street. A respectable-looking man and woman were just rounding the corner. She took heart at the sight of them. The color slowly returned to her blanched cheeks, and the vinegar was back in her tongue as well.

"That is Great Windmill Street ahead, is it not?" she asked, straightening her crushed bonnet.

He looked to the sign. "That's what it says. Why do you ask?"

"I know my way home from here. This district is safe." She put her hand on the door to open it.

"When I take a woman for a drive, I like to deliver her home safely."

"I suggest you expand that policy to include *ladies*, Mr. Mandeville," she said coolly. "If you ever succeed again in conning a lady to drive out with you, that is. But really it would be better if you stick to your *women*."

The muscle in his jaw quivered, and he picked up the reins. "If you don't want this team jobbed again, I suggest you let me down," she said. For a moment their eyes met in a battle of wills. When Trudie reached for the reins, he let them drop.

"Thank you," she said, and hopped down. She walked briskly without looking over her shoulder, but she listened for the sound of the carriage following. When she'd gone a half block, she knew Mandeville had given up, and was relieved. What an ordeal! Her heart was still hammering from the fright of it. Whoever would have thought Mr. Mandeville would be so coarse, so vulgar, and rude as that? She trembled inside to remember the way he'd attacked her. If they had been alone . . . But she'd never be alone with him again. And she wouldn't let on to Aunt Gertrude what had happened either. It wasn't till she reached her own door that she remembered she hadn't got the crown for the Latin lesson.

Luten sat, watching her slender form as it hastened to the corner and disappeared around it. The girl was an enigma. A Cyprian who was afraid of men. But not of boys, apparently. Despite his lavish boasting of money, she hadn't accepted his invitation. And what was his next move? He was reluctant to consider it. His instinct was to go after her and apologize, and his duty was to report to his sister. He sat frowning for a long while, then drove to the park, to think some more.

Chapter Six

Some days, a person is further ahead to stay in bed. This proved to be one of those days for Trudie Barten. As though being accosted by two fops, molested by a libertine, and having to walk home alone were not enough, worse was in store. When she reached Conduit Street, she saw her aunt standing alone and bewildered on the curb with their trunks around her. Trudie hastened forward, speechless with shock.

Mrs. Harrington had had time to recover her speech. "We have been evicted," she announced in a hollow voice. Beneath the offense and astonishment, Trudie heard a tinge of fear. Really it was enough to frighten two lone women, loose in London for the first time in their lives. "Our belongings put into the street."

London was proving a dreadful disappointment. Failing to crack society was bad enough, but to find the city full of so much vice and ill will was almost beyond their comprehension. "Evicted? How is it possible? We paid our rent."

"It is the doings of that old quiz Mrs. Rolfe," Aunt Harrington confided behind her fingers. "She's been smirking at me through the curtains the past five minutes. Evans came the instant you left and asked that we leave. Naturally I refused—I was never so embarrassed in my life. He showed me a petition signed by all the other tenants in the building—even that nice Miss Blythe, and the civil servant on the third floor too. They all want us out, Trudie. I made sure it was Nicolson's banging on the pianoforte that accounted for it, and promised Evans it wouldn't happen again. I even told him he could take the piano away, for it is wretchedly out of tune in any case, but he said . . ." She came to an indignant pause, her thin bosom swelling. "He said females of *our sort* were not welcome."

Trudie was as bewildered as her aunt. "What's that supposed to mean?"

A word was whispered in her ear. Her first response was to laugh, but before long, she was remembering her morning's experiences. Mr. Mandeville had thought the same thing. Who was responsible for this heinous rumor?

"It's your having young gentlemen in for tutoring that accounts for it," Aunt Gertrude said. "I knew some harm would come of it. Your innocent diversion has been misread as nights of unbridled lust."

Trudie started to hear such unfamiliar phrases fall from her aunt's lips. "This is nonsense," she scoffed. "I have my key. I'm going back into our apartment, and we shall see whether we are evicted. It is illegal, as well as a slander against our characters. In fact, I have half a mind to hire a solicitor and sue Mr. Evans." Her brave words gave her courage, but Mrs. Harrington soon returned her to gloom.

"It was not Evans's decision. The building is owned by a Mr. Patterson, you recall. He is a great man in the city. There's no point thinking we could win a case against him. Neither would it be at all comfortable to go on living here, when everyone—even Miss Blythe and that nice civil servant—thinks we are . . . like that," she said decorously but with a very significant nod of her head.

"That's true," her niece agreed reluctantly. "We cannot

stand on the curb to discuss it. Let us go into our apartment to make plans at least.''

''We cannot. That is, we could go in, perhaps, but the door has been taken off its hinges. Mr. Evans calls it a Kent Street Ejection, which must be the most degrading kind, by the sly way he said it. He says it is practiced in Kent Street in Southwark, when tenants fall into arrears on their rent. Anyone passing by would be free to look in at us and laugh or to come in off the street and pester us for that matter.''

''This is infamous,'' Trudie railed impotently. ''We paid our rent.''

''He reimbursed me for the unused portion of it. I will not stay where we are so patently unwanted. Pray do not ask it, Trudie. Having to leave Walbeck Park and come up to London was bad enough, without having to be despised by our neighbors.'' A tear gathered in Mrs. Harrington's age-dimmed eyes as she spoke. She blinked it away, but it had been seen, and a terrible angry frustration began to build up in her niece.

''All right. All right, Auntie,'' she said, to calm her, but she would have revenge on whoever had done this to them. And who could it have been? Mr. Mandeville had heard the rumor as well. Mr. Mandeville—she would like to put the blame in his dish, but there hadn't been time, unless he had begun the rumor last night. Was it possible?

She stood for a moment considering what was best to be done. She was proud enough to share her aunt's distaste for remaining in this apartment. Obviously they must take rooms elsewhere, find some other apartment to let, but it would be difficult to do with their two large trunks in tow. The trunks must be picked up by a carter, but till the carter arrived, they must be guarded. She had very little taste for standing on the curbstone to guard them herself.

''Where are the Bogmans?'' she asked.

''In the kitchen, packing up what can be easily carried.

There is no need to leave fifty pounds of flour behind, and a good leg of lamb, already dressed.'' She continued with a longish list of items, which, while expensive to replace, could obviously not be hauled across London to another set of rooms, though the linen and silver and dishes certainly must be.

"I'll speak to the Bogmans," Trudie decided.

Mrs. Bogman said very firmly, "You ought to go to your brother. He'll decide whether to hire a lawyer and go to court. I think it is that nasty Mrs. Rolfe as ought to be sued for a slanderous detraction."

"Someone ought to be, except that it would give us so much unwanted publicity. I really ought to consult with Norman, though. Bogman, could you look after our trunks and things while I take a quick trip over to Brighton? Have the things stored at a cheap hotel or inn near the edge of town, till I have discussed this with my brother."

"Why, you've more sense than him and his shatter-brained friends all put together, missie," Bogman told her. "What would you want to talk to him for?"

She drew a weary, uncertain sigh. "This may be a matter of honor, I fear, and Norman knows more about that than I do."

" 'Tis a sharp pity you hadn't known sooner, and you could have got a drive with Lord Clappet, but it's a short distance. You could be back by tomorrow. The wife and I will look after things here, missie. We'll need a little blunt for the hire of the cart and room at the inn. Where can we leave word for you to know where we've gone to?"

"Let me see." She considered her options and soon realized that she had no friends in London. Her few acquaintances were out of town. "You could leave word at Clappet's house, perhaps, though his mama is a Tartar. Oh, the very thing! Leave word with his servants at the new set of rooms he hired before leaving London. They're on the corner of Poland Street, just south of Oxford. In fact, I'll go myself at once and see if we can leave our trunks there to save hauling them off to the edge of town and back. They'll be no bother to Clappet; he's gone for a few days."

"That would save time and money," Bogman agreed.

Trudie took Bogman with her to the curb to explain this course to Mrs. Harrington. Even in this fairly polite corner of the city, passersby had stopped to stare and smirk at the sight of two ladies on the street. Fingers pointed, and leering laughs floated toward them, every one inciting a furor in Miss Barten and fear in her aunt. Bogman guarded the possessions while Trudie, trying for an air of nonchalance, found a cab and went with her aunt to Peter's apartment. It was a wonderful relief to get away from prying eyes in the safety of the carriage.

Uxor, Clappet's valet, was there arranging his master's new lodgings. He was not at all happy to be turfed out of a mansion and a soft job as Lord Clappet's valet and put in charge of a cramped set of rooms where he was, apparently, expected to be servant and cook as well as valet. His thin, ferretlike face tightened in disapproval as he listened to Miss Barten's story.

He doubted her claims of friendship with his master, but as she was familiar with his trip to Brighton and the reason for it, he knew she was at least an acquaintance of his undiscriminating lordship. He reluctantly allowed the belongings to come and be stored but did not offer the hospitality of a roof for the servants, as she hoped. They returned to Conduit Street to arrange the matter with their servants. At least the small mob had disbanded. Bogman's efforts with the poker had been instrumental, but he didn't tell the ladies so.

"And now we must be jostled over the roads to Brighton, to rub shoulders with horsemen and race track touts," Mrs. Harrington exclaimed.

"Also with the Prince Regent and the aristocracy, Auntie," Trudie pointed out.

Any complaint brought forth a reminder of the princely associations of Brighton, till at last Mrs. Harrington went to the coaching house without an actual grimace on her face. The grimace didn't arrive till they had reached Brighton and a hackney cab was rattling them over to the west side of town, to what she assumed must surely be the very worst part of it. She eyed askance a cluster of brick and timber cottages and a narrow, inelegant road cluttered with ragged humanity. They didn't stop right there but were taken to the Princes Hotel, where Norman had rooms and where they hoped to find him.

He wasn't in, but the Princes was the sort of establishment where the only wonder a young woman's asking to be let into a man's room caused was that she should be accompanied by a chaperone. Despite Miss Barten's genteel appearance, and despite the chaperone, the honor of entering a client's chamber during his absence was denied her.

"You can wait for him in the lobby," the clerk said.

"Perhaps a cup of coffee while we wait?" Mrs. Harrington suggested, with a hopeful glance into the dining room.

"The very thing," Trudie agreed at once, for one of the clients was ogling her from the corner of his shifty eyes.

The ladies knew as soon as their slippers encountered a sandy floor that the dining room would be no better than the lobby, but at least they weren't leered at. After two cups of coffee and close to an hour's wait, it was clear they would not be returning to London that night, so they booked a room at the Princes and left word at the desk for Norman to call them when he arrived.

Mrs. Harrington cast a dispirited eye around the dismal chamber. Its unclean condition was not so visible in the fading shadows of eventide as it would be the next morning. She saw enough of the linens to tell her charge they would

63

lie down on top of the counterpane with their pelisses over them, and with their towels for pillow cases. Within half an hour it was necessary to light the lamps. An hour after that, Norman had still not come, but hunger pangs had set in. They sent below for a meal, which was every bit as bad as Mrs. Harrington forecast it would be.

As she ate and Mrs. Harrington nibbled, Trudie thought about their predicament. Mostly she wondered how such an awful thing had happened to them. It had to be Mr. Mandeville; yet where had he got the idea she was a lightskirt? The idea had come from his own low mind. He had no notion of propriety, just money and arrogance. She longed to retaliate for his various offenses, particularly that nasty, punishing kiss.

Her anger and frustration had ample time to grow. Seven o'clock crept to eight, to nine, and still Norman didn't come.

It was nine-thirty when he came bounding up the stairs, three at a time, his dusty face a perfect mask of astonishment. "Good God, Trudie, what brings you and Auntie to this wretched hole? You are lucky you haven't been set upon by thieves and worse. Come to my room at once, where you will be safe."

This speech did nothing to calm their exacerbated nerves. Neither did the appearance of Norman's room, which had once been a replica of their own but was now so covered with dirty linens, newspapers, dusty boots, empty glasses, cigar butts and other signs of a gentleman's occupancy that it wasn't immediately recognizable. Aunt Gertrude took one look, and one gasp of the stale air, and said they would retire to her room instead.

"Have you eaten yet?" Trudie asked. She examined the youth before her with the keenest interest and hardly recognized him as her younger brother. His fine, dark hair had grown an inch; his usually decent provincial toilette had been replaced by a spotted Belcher kerchief at his neck, buckskin trousers, topboots that were very likely leather but appeared to be constructed of caked layers of mud. The jacket and trousers on his tall frame hung more loosely than before. His face, really rather a handsome face, had become tanned from constant exposure and lean from starvation. And beneath all the decrepitude and grime he looked incredibly happy. His brown eyes sparkled.

"Not since noon," he answered. "But what on earth brings you here to Brighton?"

"We require your assistance, Norman," Mrs. Harrington said. "The most wretched thing has happened."

Trudie saw the flash of apprehension on her brother's face, the fear that he would have to leave this raffish paradise he had discovered. She was very loath to burden him with their problem, and cast an admonishing glance at her aunt.

"A little difficulty, Norman. It is nothing of great account. The fact is, we had to leave our rooms on Conduit Street and want your advice on where we should go."

"Leave? Why the deuce did you leave? You paid the rent, didn't you?"

"Yes, it was the neighbors. We—we did not care for them in the least. They were very noisy and troublesome."

Mrs. Harrington had lived with the Bartens long enough to understand the new situation without explanation. She gave Trudie one accusing look but said nothing.

"I don't see why you took into your noggins to come pelting all the way down to Brighton," Norman exclaimed. "Why didn't you see a real estate agent and hire another set of rooms?"

"That would have been much more sensible," Trudie agreed quickly. "But you know Auntie always wanted to see Brighton and the Prince's pavilion, so we decided to come here for a few days first."

65

"That makes sense," Norman said. His hunger soon gave such peremptory signals that he had to tend to it. Another plate of the dry mutton and wet potatoes was brought up, and he attacked it with relish.

"You must leave this place, Norman," Mrs. Harrington told him. "It is unhealthy."

"A regular den, but it's cheap, you know, and I'm hardly here except to sleep. Where are the Bogmans?"

"We left them in London," Trudie said vaguely. "Did Peter and Nicolson arrive yet?"

"Yes, I have been with them since late this afternoon, checking out Firebird. They took the idiotic idea Firebird was a filly, when I called him a youngster, plain as day, in my letter. Anyway, I'm glad to be home," he sighed.

That Norman spoke of this slum as "home," when he was accustomed to an elegant country mansion, spoke as plainly as was necessary of his delight in this sabbatical. Trudie decided she would not trouble him with their London problem. They would go back, find another set of rooms, and await the year's end, when they could return to Walbeck Park.

As he ate he told them of True Lady's progress, her various and ever-improving times on the track, her assorted leg troubles.

Though his eyelids were drooping, he seemed ready to talk till morning about True Lady and every other "bit of blood" in the neighborhood. At midnight, his aunt decreed, "You're ready for bed, and so are we. We shall meet at eight in the morning parlor for breakfast; then you can take Trudie and me to the coaching office."

"But what about the Royal Pavilion? Don't you want to see it?" Norman asked. "I thought that was why you came."

"Yes, so it it," Trudie said quickly. "We'll leave our handboxes at the coaching house and go to see the pavilion.

The coaches leave frequently—perhaps we can catch the early-afternoon one.''

"You ought to stay a few days, now you're here. I'll get you a room at the Ship's Inn. I got my linens, by the way. Very useful.''

He yawned as he spoke, shaking his head in an effort to stay awake. He cast a very tired, very happy, very young smile on them.

"I'm having the greatest time," he said. "I hope you're enjoying yourselves as much as I am. You *are* enjoying this holiday, aren't you?" A doubting frown puckered his brow when the response wasn't as quick as he expected. "If it's money that is the problem, I can get rid of the groom and train True Lady myself. Everything costs more than I had thought.''

Trudie crossed her fingers in the folds of her skirt and lied for Gertrude and herself. "We're having a lovely time, Norman. Money's no problem. You wouldn't have a fair crack at the Triple Crown if you didn't have a proper groom.''

The pucker disappeared like magic. "It's nice to have you both here. Have you heard any word from home? I thought some of the neighbors might have written; I gave her your address. My own wasn't settled.''

"I haven't heard from Georgiana," Trudie said, since it was "her" Norman obviously meant. She hadn't written to Georgiana either. Half her reason for encouraging Norman in this folly was to get him away from the girl.

He listened, and nodded his head silently. After he had left them, Mrs. Harrington gave vent to all those feelings she had been holding back with such difficulty.

"Let him have his year," Trudie said. "Norman is sensible; he won't go overboard. We shall go back to London and wait for him there. I shan't say a word about Mr. Mandeville or Mrs. Rolfe. He would only feel obliged to make a great ruckus about it.''

"Mr. Mandeville?" her aunt asked. "Why, don't tell me he misbehaved himself, Trudie! You never mentioned a word about your drive with him, now I stop to think of it. The ejection from our apartment put it of my mind, but you were *walking* home, weren't you? What did the brute do?"

Trudie had had enough for one day. She admitted to the least of Mr. Mandeville's offenses, to explain her comment. "He asked me to go out to the theater with him—unchaperoned."

"The commoner! But do you really think it was wise to hop down from the carriage and walk home? Why, you might have fallen into who knows what fracas!"

Trudie hid the tell-tale staining of her cheeks by rifling in her bandbox for a nightgown. "Nothing happened. We were nearly home," she said.

Trudie lay awake for a long time, listening to the comings and goings in the hall and the echoes of revelry from the taproom below. The mattress felt as if it had been stuffed with turnips. Lumps and knobs pressed into her back, adding to her misery. Everything had turned out so wretchedly. London was lonesome and boring and expensive. She missed her old friends from home, but most of all she regretted that London was so horrid.

She knew it could be very different. Before Norman left with the carriage, he had driven them to Hyde Park, where the ton met at the barrier at four o'clock. Ladies in furs and beautiful bonnets gossiped while their gentlemen ogled all the ladies, even her. They had walked along Bond Street to see the shops to. It had all seemed just the way she dreamed it would be. That day, she had thought she'd meet those people eventually. They couldn't all be as bad as Mr. Mandeville.

Mr. Mandeville. Was he the one who had started the rumor about them on Conduit Street? Guilty or not, he was the only suspect she could think of, and her animosity against the man made Christian forgiveness impossible. It wasn't fair; it wasn't right that he should treat them so badly and get off scot-free. If she ever met him again . . . But she wouldn't, of course. And that made her sad too.

Chapter Seven

Lord Clappet and Sir Charles Nicolson attended on Norman at eight o'clock the next morning. They were outfitted in the highest kick of fashion, with gleaming new spotted Belchers arranged with careful disarray at their necks. Each carried in his fingers a jockey's riding crop, not useful for driving at all, but giving the uninitiated a hint they were dealing with gentlemen of the turf.

The choice of a filly for Peter was still to be made. He preferred descendancy from one of the three founding fathers of thoroughbred-dom: the Godolphin Barb, the Byerley Turk, or the Darley Arabian. An astonishing number of the racers up for sale laid claim to this bloodline.

"In fact, they ain't *real* thoroughbreds without it," Sir Charles decreed, hitting the edge of the table with his crop to emphasize the point and to show off the crop.

"You didn't tell me Firebird was a colt, Norman," Peter said. " 'Promising youngster,' you called him. I made sure it was a filly. I like fillies. They're a tad smaller, but you can't match 'em for pluck."

"If it was a filly you wanted, you should have said so," Norman grouched. "And for God's sake put down that crop before you knock over my coffee."

"Don't want him," Nicolson said firmly. "We'll go

around to the auctions and pick you up a filly, Peter my lad. Where would you suggest, Norman?''

''If it's better bloods you're after, Newmarket is the place. I'll be going there myself immediately, to begin intensive training with True Lady.''

A burning anxiety gnawed at Peter's innards. Here was Norman getting a jump on him. He too wanted to go to Newmarket immediately and begin intensive training of his winner. He listened, jealous as a green cow, while Norman continued.

''For twenty-five pounds you can train there for the year. Sand gallops and turf gallops go on forever. Best training ground in England. Jockey Club there—all the knowing 'uns. If you had more than two hundred guineas to spend, Peter, you might get a filly out of Cheveley Park. Excellent stud farm. Cost you a monkey, though.''

Their talk was interrupted by the descent of the ladies. After admiring their Belchers and crops, Trudie found a private moment to tell Peter she had left her trunks with his servant, which threw him into confusion.

''Why did you leave Conduit Street?'' he asked.

She explained discreetly, hoping to make little of it, but he wouldn't be put off. ''I don't care for old Nettie Rolfe myself, but she ain't noisy, and she ain't bad ton. A friend of my mama, in fact. Tell the truth now, Trudie. What happened to send you scrambling down here?''

''We'll discuss it later. I don't want to trouble Norman,'' she explained quietly.

''You're welcome to use my rooms in London for the present at least. I shan't be home for the devil knows how long. I'll send a note back with you for Uxor, to keep the old bleater in line. Stamp on him if he cuts up stiff.''

Mrs. Harrington was occupied hearing Norman's plans to remove to Newmarket. ''Thank God, you are leaving this place,'' she sighed.

When it was time to go to view the pavilion, Trudie took a seat in Clappet's carriage, letting her aunt and brother go with Nicolson. She outlined very discreetly the advent into her life of Mandeville, saying nothing of his more farouche behavior in the carriage, and asked Peter whether he was acquainted with the man.

"Never heard of him. Sounds like a demmed Cit to me. He don't sound like anyone Nick would know, and if he *did* know him, he would never in the world send him 'round to see you alone. The scoundrel learned somehow you were there without a man to protect you and was trying to take advantage of you. Upon my word I think he was, Trudie. I believe you ought to tell your brother. Mandeville ought to be called to account."

"That is precisely what I do not want—for Norman to become involved in a duel."

"Duel? Nothing of the sort. Norman ought to draw his cork, darken his daylights, give him a sound thrashing."

The image lingering in her mind of Mr. Mandeville's broad shoulders did not incline her to think it was Mandeville's daylights that would be darkened if it came to a fistfight. "I've decided to say nothing about it. My aunt and I have left Conduit Street, and he won't know where to find us. It's better this way."

Had there not been a trip to Newmarket in the offing, Clappet would have insisted on calling the man to account, but his head was full of more vital matters, so he agreed to remain silent. "Oh, that is the famous pavilion up ahead, by the way," he pointed out as they entered Marine Parade.

She looked at the oriental splendor of spires, domes, and minarets rising white and gold above treetops, and was suitably impressed. It really was a fairyland of enchantment, but it failed to enchant Trudie that day. She was worried not only about Mandeville, and finding a new flat, but about Norman too.

"I hope he takes better care of himself at Newmarket than he does here," she sighed.

"What he needs is a housekeeper," Peter said idly.

"Yes," she agreed mechanically, but soon she saw the plausibility of filling this role herself. At heart she was sorry to miss out on the excitement and fun of training True Lady and of watching her run. Why should she and Aunt Gertrude not go to Newmarket, hire a cottage, and have Norman stay with them, where he would be decently cared for, and at less expense than hiring two places?

Trudie discovered to her great delight that the same idea had occurred to her aunt. Mrs. Harrington had not only thought of it but outlined to Norman the advantages. By the time they all met back at the Princes, the thing had been arranged.

"I shall nip up to Newmarket and scout out a tidy little cottage for us while you go back to London to collect the Bogmans and your stuff. I'll write you there, and you can all join me at Newmarket," Norman said. "Where will you be staying in London?"

"They're staying in my rooms," Peter said. "In fact, I'll drive the ladies to London myself. I have decided to go to the bank and arrange a loan and buy my filly from Cheveley Park. I'll have to make some excuse to Mama as well for being away from London so long. I'll tell her—oh, dash it, I don't know what I shall tell her, but I *will* go to Newmarket."

"Let us leave early this afternoon, Trudie," Mrs. Harrington said, fearing another night at the Princes.

Sir Charles was frowning while this was discussed. "Thing is," he pointed out, "can't stay at Peter's flat if he is there himself."

"I'm staying at your place," Clappet informed him, and put his hand out for the keys. Sir Charles put the key ring on the end of his crop and handed it over with only a little scowl at his friend's presumption. Not the thing to quibble in front of the ladies, but Peter was taking a bit for granted, it seemed to him.

"Will you go to Newmarket today, Norman?" Mrs. Harrington asked.

"There's a race over the sticks this afternoon that Nick and I plan to attend."

"Over the sticks, eh? I should like to see that, by Jove. What time is the match?" Peter asked.

"Two," Sir Charles answered.

It was finally communicated agreeably enough to Trudie at least that the ladies would take luncheon with the gentlemen at the Old Ship, after which the former would have the use of Sir Charles's carriage for a tour of the city while Peter joined the men at the match. When this trip took under two hours, they had time not only to see the shops but to dawdle impatiently about the circulating library for half an hour before meeting the gentlemen back at the Old Ship for tea, then a dash to see True Lady.

It was five o'clock when they set out for London with Clappet, which ensured their arriving well after dark. He assured them five hours was the longest it could possibly take, but in fact it was not far from midnight when they rattled up to the apartment on Poland Street. They were all tired and hungry, and at such an advanced hour the best place to eat was where they were. Mrs. Harrington herself went to the kitchen to prepare them gammon and eggs while Clappet pointed out to Trudie the convenience of his rooms.

Uxor stood glaring like a wet hen. "My friends will be using the rooms for a few days, Uxor," Peter explained. "I'll be shutting the place up for a while after they go, so you can go back to Berkeley Square and await word from me."

"And where shall I tell her ladyship you are gone to, milord," Uxor asked haughtily, "that you won't be requiring the services of your valet?'' His eyes cast mute aspersion on the Belcher kerchief, the travel-dusted outfit, the riding crop, still between Peter's fingers. "You have become a jockey, have you?''

"Don't tell her anything, or I'll boil your Friday face in oil,'' Peter barked.

"Will the ladies be bringing their own servants?'' the valet asked.

"Of course they will, numbskull. You take off as soon as they arrive. They won't want your ghoulish phiz getting in their way. Till the Bogmans come, however, you will offer the ladies any assistance they require.''

"Yes, milord,'' Uxor said in a voice that suggested vengeance for this misdeed.

It was one o'clock in the morning before Clappet took himself off to Mr. Nicolson's rooms at Albany. "I shall do myself the honor of saying good-bye now, ladies. No point coming back tomorrow before I leave for Newmarket. I already have to go to the cursed bank, and had better look in on Mama or she'll ring a peal over me when next we meet.''

Trudie had no difficulty sleeping that night. It wasn't just fatigue from the unusually exciting day that accounted for it. It was the rosy aspect of her changed future she anticipated. They would be leaving London, going to Newmarket to enter a brand-new style of life. Through Norman, she would meet the other gentlemen of the turf. And with a man as part of the family, there would be no misunderstandings of the sort that had arisen here in London with Mr. Mandeville. There was just one little wrinkle in her happiness, and that was that Mandeville should get off scot-free after his treatment of her.

Chapter Eight

Lady Clappet was not at home the next morning when her son called, for the reason that she had darted over to Belgrave Square to complain of him to her brother. Lord Clappet was certainly told where his mother was and that she would be happy for him to join her there. In fact, a footman was sent off to alert the mother of Clappet's arrival, but Peter left before the servant got to the corner of the street.

"I am in the devil of a hurry," he explained briefly. "Tell her I stopped by and that I am fine." He remained at home for two minutes by the clock before nipping down to the bank to sequester himself in the banker's office for some highly confusing conversation. He spoke of "short-term obligations" and "a bit of dire necessity, if you want the truth," but said not a word about racehorses, Newmarket, or any related subject.

"What, precisely, appears to be the difficulty, milord?" the banker asked, for Luten had coached him well.

"Who said anything about a difficulty? It's a personal matter, and that's all there is to it. I have to have the money."

"But *we*, milord, must have a reason."

"There is no question of my being good for it. Deuce take

it, I own an abbey, don't I?'' he thundered, but finally fell into a sulk when even this didn't move the banker to pity.

"Certainly, milord, and if you would just ask your uncle Lord Luten to countersign the note, a loan could be arranged on the spot.''

"This has nothing to do with Luten. It's my money, ain't it?''

"Indeed it is, in trust till your twenty-first birthday, at which time a quarter of it comes into your hands outright, the remainder . . .''

"I know all that! I'll remember your unwillingness to help me when the time comes,'' he added coolly.

Not wanting to alienate such a good customer, the banker found himself able to advance five hundred without Luten's signature.

"Could have got the thousand if I'd had the sense to ask for two,'' Clappet muttered as he pocketed the cash and went out the door. All the same, there must be something at Cheveley Park he could afford and still have enough over to handle the expenses of training and racing.

Meanwhile at Belgrave Square, Luten spoke vaguely to Lady Clappet of having "settled the matter'' of Peter's lightskirt, though he feared he had done nothing of the sort. He must go back to Conduit Street and try again, but was singularly reluctant to do so. He had felt a monster when Miss Barten bolted from his carriage and walked home. He even wondered whether Maggie wasn't mistaken about the girl. She had been horrified when he kissed her, if that attack could properly be called a kiss. He wondered how Peter kissed her and felt the clutch of anger at the very idea.

She was genteel-seeming. She really *did* know some Latin—how had she picked it up? And Peter was supposed to be swotting up his Latin. After considerable thought, he decided to present himself to her under his true guise, with his real aim out in the open. He had a mental picture of the two of them laughing over the misunderstanding. He supposed, on scanty evidence to be sure, that she had a fine sense of humor. She had a winning smile at least; also a hot temper, which charmed him in ladies. She would call him "an odious man," in that sweet, slightly rustic, and very blunt way she had.

"I don't see that there is anything to grin about," Lady Clappet snorted as she pulled her furs about her broad shoulders. "But at least Peter is safe. When he returns from Newmarket, I shall apologize and ask him to come back home."

"I was not grinning," Luten pointed out, still grinning, in his sister's opinion.

She returned to Berkeley Square immediately, missing Peter by no more than fifteen minutes. While she was still remonstrating with her servants for failing to detain him, Uxor appeared at the end of the hallway. He said nothing, but his face was capable of much mute intelligence.

"Uxor! You're back. What have you to tell me?" she asked eagerly.

"Oh, nothing at all. The master has put an embargo of secrecy on his doings," he said importantly, but she could see he was bursting to tell, and had soon got the secrets out of him.

"Petticoat dealings," he teased, and waited for more urgings from her ladyship.

"Good God, what has happened? If you tell me he's married, Uxor, I shall . . ." She could say no more, but her blanched cheeks and staring eyes, the white hand clutching her heart, implied that even death wasn't beyond her.

"No, not married. Not *yet*," he added mischievously. "He's moved them into an apartment. 'Look after them, Uxor. They are my special friends,' he said. Bag and baggage they've moved in. A young strumpet and an older one, with two servants I never saw before in my life."

"Where? When?" she managed to breathe.

"Last night at midnight. The rooms are on Poland Street. He made me take his own things there the day before."

"You should have told me!"

"I had an embargo on me," Uxor reminded her.

"Send for Luten," she moaned, and reeled to the sofa, propped up by Uxor and a footman. Her servants, wise in the ways of hysterical ladies, didn't have to be told to run for hartshorn and feathers to be burned.

Luten was sent for and came like a good brother. Uxor took center stage with very little reluctance and repeated his tale. Having broken his embargo of silence, he now embroidered the story to the top of his bent. "I overheard the servants," he said, making his audience fish for the details.

"What did they say?" Luten asked.

"Kent Street Ejection! That's what happened to them. The lot of them were turfed out of Conduit Street and set up shop on the street corner. They came running straight to his lordship's new place to tell him. I've no doubt the young one is still lying on his lordship's pillow as she was when I left, though it was past time any decent Christian be up and about, as they no doubt would be if they hadn't kept the master up till morning plying him with wine."

Luten's nostrils pinched into slits, and an icy gleam shone in his eyes. "Lord Clappet spent the night at this new apartment as well?"

"No," Uxor admitted reluctantly, but pulled his chestnuts from the fire by adding ingeniously, "She wouldn't let him stay, after it was *he* that was put to the expense of hiring the place. She turned him out of his own door."

"Where did he go?"

"To Newmarket, he *said*." Uxor's tone implied that not even a swaddling babe would believe it.

Lady Clappet moaned, beyond words. Her white hands went out to her brother in a silent plea, which was ignored. Luten was already on his feet, swiftly striding to the door.

He had come in his crested carriage. He didn't bother to change it for the dash to Poland Street. He ordered his groom to "spring 'em" and sat with his arms folded in the comfort of his well-sprung chaise, plotting a revenge of some heinous but rather obscure nature.

When he approached the apartment, a cold, purposeful expression had taken possession of his face. His posture was not that of a wary whippet today but of a bulldog. There was a determined set to his shoulders and a pugnacious angle to his jaw. He lifted the brass knocker for one loud crash before turning the knob and entering the rooms. Mrs. Harrington was in the kitchen with Mrs. Bogman, determining whether the dressed leg of lamb, surviving its trip, was edible. Bogman was in the pantry, rooting on high shelves for candles and other usable items possibly hidden away and forgotten by the former tenant. It was Trudie who got halfway down the hall to the door before it opened and Luten stormed in.

She took one unbelieving look at him and felt terribly like swooning. He was even more formidable than she had remembered. Fright drove the blood from her face. She said, "You!" in a faint squeal, and fell back a step.

"At your service, ma'am," he answered, his voice laden with sarcasm. His bow was a low, sweeping, dramatic parody of obsequiousness, but all too soon his blighting eyes were scrutinizing her haphazard toilette. It angered him more than anything that she should look so demmed innocent, with her curls tied up in blue ribbons and a smudge of dust on the side of her nose.

The pause gave her time to realize which of them was the interloper. She gathered her shreds of courage and said, "Get out. Leave this place at once!" in quite a firm voice.

He paced forward. "I was about to offer you the same advice, miss. If you're wise, you'll take it."

"How dare you! I have a right to be here."

80

"No doubt *you* think so. There is, unfortunately, no law forbidding females of your sort from preying on credulous youngsters. In Lord Clappet's case, however, there is a family to protect him. You chose your quarry ill, Miss Barten."

"What have you to do with Peter?" she demanded.

"I am Lord Clappet's uncle, and guardian."

"Luten?" She stared hard, with a frown on her brow.

"You were aware he was under my guardianship, I see. No doubt that's why you removed him to Newmarket, for easier plucking."

"But you said—you *lied* to me! You only came to Conduit Street to spy."

"Precisely. I assure you my taste in females runs to quite another complexion than yours."

"I know it very well," she shot back. "Peter has often told me you choose the gaudiest birds of paradise to be had in London."

Luten ignored the jibe. "Is he here?"

"No."

"When will he be back?"

"He won't, not today."

"Very well, let's get the gloves off and settle it between ourselves. I want you out of his life," he said. The menacing glitter in his eyes and the hard set of his jaw still caused a tremble, but with Bogman in the pantry, Trudie wasn't actually afraid for her physical safety. She was, however, very much aware of the insult implicit in his attack. The knowledge of it brought an angry flush to her cheeks.

"What is it you're afraid of, that I'm angling to marry him? Is that it, or do you take me for no more than a light-skirt?" she demanded.

"They're not mutually exclusive. Either is unacceptable to his family."

"I see. Without bothering to inquire who I might be, you have decided I'm not fit to marry Peter!"

"Any female who sets herself up in hired rooms to purvey what she chooses to call Latin, to any hedgebird off the streets, is not fit to be Lady Clappet," he informed her. And he also took note that it was marriage, no less, the chit had in mind.

"I *was* purveying Latin, nothing else! And *you* were the only hedgebird I made the ill decision to tutor. I'm sorry I ever let you inside the door."

"A lady wouldn't be put out of her apartment for teaching Latin," he pointed out.

"So you were involved in that, were you? I thought as much." Her anger reached new heights as she remembered the ignominy she and her aunt had been subjected to.

"That was entirely your own doing. I used a little subterfuge to gain admission, and I don't apologize for it. Now let's get this unpleasant business settled. It's no more to my taste than your own. Any visions you entertain of rising to a countess are futile. If you're reasonable, you'll take what you can get and leave. Go and try your luck elsewhere. We both know the likeliest location, don't we, Miss Barten?" he tossed in, with a sneer.

Her first flush of anger had burned itself out. The reeling indignity that had occupied her mind, robbing her of rational thought, was replaced by a cooler emotion, not untinged with scornful amusement. Being innocent of the charge, she was able to see the humor of it. "You are offering nothing other than advice and insults then, Lord Luten?" she asked pertly.

"If the truth is offensive, you mustn't hold me accountable for it. We know you had Peter withdraw all his allowance, know he is trying for a loan at the bank. It will not be granted. All you stand to gain from him within the next three months is what he's not already squandered on you. Between Conduit Street and this flat, the purse must be growing thin."

"Not at all. I paid for Conduit Street myself. He has plenty left for me to get my greedy clutches on," she cautioned. The charade was beginning to amuse her. It was the only revenge she'd ever have on Lord Luten, and she meant to milk it dry.

"We—Lady Clappet and I—are willing to give you one thousand clear, on the understanding that you not see him again. Take it or leave it."

This offer was greeted with a scoffing laugh. "Only one thousand? Why, you must take me for a greenhead. Peter's allowance is four thousand a year. And in a few years, when he's twenty-one, he comes into a quarter of his money, if I am not mistaken."

"You've done your homework well. It must be taken into consideration, however, that you can sell your lessons elsewhere after you've given up Clappet. A whole semester's salary without 'teaching,' in fact." He managed to imbue the word "teaching" with every manner of lechery.

Trudie looked at him, casting one bright, brief flash from her narrowed eyes. Luten had insulted and annoyed her once too often. Though he didn't know it, he was about to be repaid. "Ah, but Peter is such a talented young boy, you know. One does not often encounter his ability and willingness to learn." She saw his lips pull into an angry line, saw his hands jerk uncontrollably forward, as though he wanted to strike her. "He will not be easy to replace," she said, and fluttered her lids at Luten in a meaningful way.

He swallowed his spleen and assumed a pose of interest in her invitation. "You were offered an equally precocious student not many days ago."

"Precocious?" she asked, smiling doubtfully. "No, surely the word implies youth! You are too long in the tooth to be precocious, Lord Luten, though I make no doubt you're well accomplished." She thought his teeth would soon be ground down to a more youthful length, to judge by the way he was grating them together now. "You will not take offense, I know, when I tell you I prefer *young* gentlemen like your nephew."

"It stands to reason an unlicked cub would be better for your purpose, but then your ultimate aim must be to feather your nest, and I am in a better position to do that than a boy who has not yet control of his fortune."

"Do you know, I find it hard to believe you want to feather my nest?" she asked, holding back a laugh. "Destroy it, is more like it. Rip it right down from the branches and stamp on it."

"On the contrary. I'm not averse to some liveliness and spirit in my women. My offer still stands," he said. Luten was trying for an air of flirtation, but it was all he could do to keep his fingers from the girl's neck, and she could see the strain he was under.

For one long moment they stood silent, each taking the other's measure. He meant to buy her off, and she meant to turn it to her advantage in showing him a lesson. Luten was in dire need of a lesson.

"I don't recall the terms of your offer. It was vague, if I am not mistaken. A dinner and a night at some play . . ."

"We didn't get down to specifics."

"How very remiss of us! Shall we do it now?"

All the while they stood in the front hall. Trudie feared to let him into the drawing room lest her aunt come and discover him. Listening for sounds from the apartment, she heard none but still kept Luten in the hall; it would be easy to shove him out the door from there, if anyone came.

"Name your price," Luten said grandly.

"I see Lord Luten is ready to be as generous as Mr. Mandeville. Did you also make a killing on the market?"

"Have you got something against inherited money?" he demanded.

"Only that it breeds such self-satisfaction in the inheritors.'' Luten swallowed this infamous remark without retort, and Trudie continued goading him. ''I am very tired with having to leave my hired rooms every time a charge is laid against me. It would be so peaceful to have a little cottage of my own. A hired cottage,'' she added hastily as she saw the look of denial settle on his countenance at such a large outlay.

''That could be arranged,'' he agreed.

''Furnished, of course, for I have only my own plate and linens. I have two servants who must be paid, and will want some money for living. Four thousand a year should about do it,'' she suggested, a smile peeping out at the familiar figure of Lord Clappet's annual allowance.

''I made sure you would want to *better* your circumstances,'' he retaliated.

''Oh, I am not grasping, Lord Luten. A lady has to live, and you said yourself you had no objection to a girl plying her trade if she must. All I ask is a decent living,'' she said modestly, lifting her fingers to pat her hair as she looked at him from the corner of her eye.

''A cottage in the country,'' Luten said pensively, while his mind raced to consider a likely spot. He wanted it close enough so he could go and chide her from time to time, without being so close as to make it likely she would pester him and, worse, Peter. She must vanish without a trace. He didn't want Peter to get the idea he'd stolen his mistress from him.

Her own wish was to put Luten to the absolute maximum of inconvenience, preferably roaming over the countryside for days. ''Cornwall would be nice,'' she said tentatively.

''Cornwall! That wouldn't do me much good!''

''Thoughtless of me. It is rather a long drive—why, I'd never get to see you,'' she added with a fond smile. ''Tunbridge Wells, then?''

His lip curled in derision at her choice of this hotbed of

romantic intrigue, where all the déclassée females went to find a rich patron. "I thought Tunbridge Wells might be to your taste," he said.

"Yes, indeed. I have spent a few Seasons there. The chalybeate springs are so invigorating. The historical associations are very much to my taste—the visit of Queen Henrietta Maria, the park retained in her honor, right in the center of town. And the company too is so lively and amusing," she added provocatively.

"A small cottage at Tunbridge Wells, then," he agreed.

"Not too small! I have my aunt, you remember, and the servants. So is it a thousand per quarter, plus the cottage?" she asked, assuming a businesslike manner.

"Agreed. Is there anything else?"

"A carriage and team would be nice," she ventured, looking to see if he accepted this addition. His face, while considering, was not downright negative. "Just a small open carriage, but stylish. I suppose cream ponies would be too expensive?" she added on a wistful sigh.

"Much too expensive. I'll get you a gig and one horse to draw it."

"All the better class of—of mistresses have two horses." She pouted, but her cheeks grew pink to mention herself in this low class of female. "Of course, I'll need a clothing allowance, but you need not fear I'll be pestering you for jewelry. I am not at all interested in jewelry," she added as a sop.

"A woman is wiser to ask for cash. About the clothing allowance, I prefer to select and pay for the gowns myself. Your accessories you can provide from your allowance."

There was a sound from the kitchen, not really close at hand but suggesting that the others were finishing their chores. "Very well. Go now," she said, ushering him toward the door.

"I'll find you here, after I've made the arrangements?" Luten asked.

"Yes, I'll be here," she said, and felt a dreadful premonition that she would indeed be here, and not safe beyond his wrath when he got back.

"It will take a few days," he pointed out.

Miss Barten breathed much easier at this good news. "There is no hurry," she assured him.

"Where is Peter? Will he be back in the meanwhile?"

"No, he is gone to Newmarket."

"You must turn Peter off. Tell him—that is, don't tell him who your new protector is. Just tell him you have decided you two do not suit. Write him a letter. I don't want you seeing him again."

There was another sound from the kitchen, and Trudie nudged him faster toward the door. "Why, after getting to know you better, Lord Luten, I think Peter and I do not suit. He is a trifle boyish for me."

Luten made a bow, finally ready to leave. "I take that as a compliment to myself, ma'am."

"It was meant as one," she said sweetly, and finally got the door closed behind him.

Luten left, surprised that he had gotten out without succumbing to the urge to either strike her bold face or berate her loudly. Conniving, cunning, grasping, unfaithful wretch! His heart was pounding in anger, but at least he'd got her off Peter's back. She would release Clappet, go off to the cottage at Tunbridge Wells, which would be hired on a month's lease, no longer. He'd go once or twice to see her, just enough to let her hope he was seriously interested. Demme and he'd have to purchase a horse and gig. He wouldn't let her at any of his own bloods with those cow hands. His frown faded, and a malicious smile took its place. Yes, he'd buy her a horse and gig all right, and they'd be the most ignoble outfit for sale in the whole of London.

Mrs. Harrington came into the hall. "Was someone at the door, Trudie?"

"It was a mistake. The man was looking for someone else," Trudie prevaricated, and went to her room to unpack a gown. She was on nettles lest Luten come back before they had all left for Newmarket, but at least he would certainly not be back today, which gave her time to think and plan and remember all Luten's sins, not omitting that he was willing to steal what he believed to be his nephew's mistress. He mustn't think her so bad either, she thought, since he wanted her for himself.

Chapter Nine

Lord Luten received a note from Peter's bank and went there to learn all the details. The banker was frightened at the livid hue his customer's face assumed, and very much surprised that no abuse was heaped on himself.

"I understand," Luten said. "Naturally you could not offend such a good customer as Lord Clappet will be in the near future. Five hundred pounds, eh?"

"He wanted a thousand—for a personal matter, he said. I couldn't get anything else out of him."

"That's quite all right. I happen to know what matter my nephew referred to. I'll take care of it."

He took care of Miss Barten's stunt of gouging an extra five hundred out of Peter by searching out in the stables of London a mangy, sway-backed hack, which he bought for five guineas at Newmans', the largest livery stable. The groom couldn't imagine what an out-and-outer like Luten wanted with the old jade, but supposed it must be a prank. He found a gig that did justice to the nag. It was a faded, dilapidated rig, the wood bereft of paint, the irons rusty, and the wheels wobbling unsteadily on bowed shafts. Miss Barten would be lucky if she got halfway to Tunbridge Wells without a breakdown. Such was Luten's faith in his desirability that he still thought she would go on to the cottage and wait for him.

A day was spent on the trip to Tunbridge Wells to hire a cottage. He could not find as bad a shack as he wished, but on further consideration, he thought if he went too far, she would go running back to Peter and reveal the whole plan. It might even push him into marriage. Miss Barten was a cunning woman, and despite her deplorable character, she was not only pretty but genteel in her manners when she wasn't pressed by greed.

At Tunbridge Wells, Luten found a rather quaint Queen Anne–style cottage just at the edge of Queen Henrietta Maria's Park. The parlor was low and dark, the bedchambers, while numerous enough to accommodate her household, were small and dingy. The terms were one hundred per annum, or thirty guineas per quarter. He hired it for three months, reckoning he had got out of the dilemma cheaply, at under fifty guineas. He'd have to pay the woman some part of her first quarter's allowance as well, but he'd pay it on a monthly basis. With luck, Miss Barten would soon pick up a new patron at this second-rate watering spot.

Lady Clappet, figuring some monetary outlay had been necessary to turn the girl off, didn't press too hard to learn the sum, in case Luten should take the notion it should come out of her pocket. Her brother didn't ask her for the money, nor did he intend to dun Peter's account for it. He derived so much amusement from the deal that he considered it payment enough. As a further snub to the chit, he didn't call in person to make her aware of the arrangements but sent around a very curt note, with a request that she reply to let him know she had not changed her mind. He would send the carriage and gig to her on Thursday morning and expect to see her at the cottage on Friday.

Trudie could hardly believe her luck that Luten did not come in person, for of course she hadn't told her aunt of the arrangement. She wrote back very civilly that the cottage sounded extremely attractive, and she looked forward to seeing him on Friday. With a malicious smile, she added a postscript in Latin from Horace's *Satires*, claiming that all she wanted from life was a small cottage near a wood, free from worldly cares, with nights and suppers of the gods.

Thursday she received a note from Norman that he had found them a cottage at Newmarket, and they could come at any time. Heaving a vast sigh of relief, she sent Bogman off to the coaching house to book them passage on the next vehicle leaving in that direction. Before they got away from the apartment, the gig and the old nag arrived at the door, delivered from Newmans' stable. She was curious enough to go out and have a look at it; she saw the ancient animal, his head drooped with fatigue before starting the trip, and his eyes bleary with age. The gig sagged even when empty.

Mrs. Harrington went out with her and was thrown into confusion. "What can it mean, Lord Luten sending this to Peter? Who is it for?" she asked the groom.

"For the young female what lives here," the groom answered, as confused as the others.

Trudie rushed in to explain the confusion. "It is obviously for Peter's servant—it must be a cart for delivering green groceries and things. I'll handle it, Auntie."

"You'd better send it back to Luten," Mrs. Harrington said doubtfully. "Clappet has no stable here." On this speech, she went back into the house.

"Where is Luten to be found? Would he be at his home?" Trudie asked the groom.

"No, ma'am, when he dropped round at the stables a while ago, he said he was on his way to his club. That'd be White's, in St. James's Street."

"I suggest you take it to him there," Miss Barten decided.

"Ah, 'tis some kind of a joke," the groom said, nodding his head.

"Yes, I want the carriage returned to him at his club. And tell him—tell him the female on Poland Street is not at all amused. In fact," she decided, worried that he might come before she left, "tell him his friend went on ahead to Tunbridge Wells with another friend. Perhaps Lord Luten would be kind enough to drive the carriage down to us. I fear I could not handle such a lively stepper as Dobbin."

Trudie regretted that she must miss the commotion at White's when his lordship went out to see his carriage, but she was too busy hurrying the others out of the house half an hour earlier than necessary to give it much thought.

Luten sat ensconced in a parlor with a few cronies at his club, playing a desultory hand of cards while talking and drinking coffee. He noticed a larger than usual group gathering at the front window that looked out on the passing show of St. James's Street, where only the fops and dandies paraded. A respectable female was denied the privilege of traversing this particular street, at peril of losing her reputation. A noisy clamor of laughing and joking was going forth at the window.

"What can it be? What's going on?" one of the men asked, and rose up to join the others.

"Is it possible the Prince Regent is trying to walk the length of the street?" one of the wits inquired.

"Trying to ride, perhaps," another quipped, and shoved back his chair.

Luten got up and went with them to view whatever spectacle the morning was offering. He recognized the gig and nag at a glance and knew he was about to be the butt of much merry roasting. His greater worry was that Miss Barten had come in person to chastise him in front of his friends. This at least was spared him. It was a page of the club who came in and announced, through unsteady lips and in a loud, fluting voice, the message. "Your lady friend, milord, says she don't care for your taste in horses and has accepted a drive to the house you got for her at Tunbridge Wells with another bloke, and she'll meet you there, as agreed. And would your lordship be so kind as to drive this here animal down there for her yourself."

Knowing he was pulling off a rare stunt, the saucy fellow bowed ceremoniously while a roar of guffaws and taunting shouts rose up to the ceiling. "Will I have the chariot wait outside, milord, or will you have it drawn 'round to the stables and brought back when you're ready to leave?"

"Taken a grandmother under your wing, have you, Luten?" one fellow shouted, to a loud round of approval.

"By Jove, Luten, I thought you had a better eye. Where'd you get this one, at the glue factory?"

"No, I swear I saw Dobbin pulling a dun cart on the Chelsea Road yesterday," another taunted.

Each friend had his say while Luten stood mute and furious, trying to conceal his condition beneath a mask of spurious good humor. "Finished with your compliments, gentlemen?" he asked during a pause. "I'll take the rig to Tunbridge Wells at once, fellow," he told the page. "There's no need to pull it 'round to the stable. Anyone going my way?" he asked, making a jest of it.

"That creature won't get you as far as the corner, let alone to Tunbridge Wells," he was told.

"What's up, Luten? Is it a bet?" one knowing one asked.

"No, a dare," he replied, swallowing his ire, and he went out the door with his head high and his shoulder straight, to hop into the seat, which immediately cracked beneath his weight. He went falling ignominiously to the floor, in front of all his friends. He muttered a curse under his breath as he scrambled up and got a perilous perch on the seat's edge, but, with a mind to his audience, raised his hand and waved as he jiggled the reins. He held his smile till he had jogged beyond view.

Before Luten got to the corner of Piccadilly, he realized he had no wish to drive all the way to Poland Street in the dawdling cart, with his friends looking, pointing, and laughing at the spectacle, but as he had stepped boldly out of White's without summoning his groom, he had little choice but to continue. He stopped a servant met just at Green Park and had him take the outfit back to Newmans' with a curt message that it had served its purpose, as the stable had done. He did not wish for reimbursement, nor for any future doings with an establishment that could not follow simple orders. His ire partly mitigated by this piece of ill humor, he paced rapidly to the apartment. He was greeted by drawn blinds, a locked door, and similar signs of a vacant set of rooms. She actually had gone on to Tunbridge Wells, then, he surmised.

Without wasting a minute, he hailed a hackney cab, returned to his club for his own carriage (and another round of roasting), thence straight on to the little cottage by the park at Tunbridge Wells. It too was locked and barred. He strolled around the park, returning to the cottage at frequent intervals throughout the next few hours, at which time the awful realization was accepted that Miss Barten had played off another trick on him. She wasn't coming, and it was that five hundred Peter had borrowed at the bank that was financing her independence. Why else had he borrowed it, but for her?

His account with Miss Barten was once again out of balance, but the time would come when she paid for this day. He went thundering back to London in a towering rage. She had never had any intention of accepting his patronage. She'd made a May game of him.

He reached Belgrave Square late at night, tired, hungry, dusty, and too irritated to eat or rest. He sat drumming his fingers on a mahogany table with marble insets in the shape of a short-pointed star. "Very well, Miss Barten," he said in a menacing voice. "You want to cross swords with me, we shall see who cries craven first."

His information that Peter was at Newmarket was unreliable, since it had come from Peter and that female. He made a fresh toilette and spent the remainder of the night running around the city, questioning friends and parrying questions on the stunt at White's. He learned Peter had been at Brighton with a woman who sounded exactly like Miss Barten. They had been seen not only in Peter's carriage but in a public inn together. The informant mentioned that there had been a largish group. She was drawing poor, innocent Peter into her rackety set, filling his head with God knew what pernicious ideas.

If he didn't put a bullet through that vixen before this was over, he'd be surprised. But no, shooting was too good for her. She deserved a slow, tortured death, contrived in the most public and degrading manner possible. Luten derived some small satisfaction from mentally arranging her demise, but as he lay in bed imagining ingenious tortures, he decided he was more softhearted than he had ever realized. In the last scene, he always seemed to be rescuing her from her perils and being thanked for his heroics by a much humbled and affectionate Miss Barten.

Chapter Ten

Mrs. Harrington took a look around the dull, flat country-side and said, "I doubt we shall like it here at Newmarket, Trudie."

Her spirits revived somewhat when Norman was on hand to meet them at the coaching stop with the family carriage. She would have preferred that he wore a clean shirt and decent cravat, but at least he was there.

He bounded forward to help her descend. "I have found us a dandy little cottage, one of the brick lodges right beside the heath," he said, even before saying hello. "We shall all be as snug as bugs in a rug."

What she felt the need of at that moment was space and air. "Has it got a good-sized drawing room?" she inquired.

"Oh, there is a drawing room, certainly. The greatest luck, Trudie," he rattled on, turning to include his sister in the news, "the stables are enormous."

"How nice," Trudie said faintly, and smiled a wan smile.

"Is it clean, Norman, in good condition?" his aunt asked.

"We haven't had time to clean it, but now that the Bog-mans are coming, it will be put into shape in jig time. Where are the Bogmans?"

"They will be on the next coach," Trudie told him. "They are bringing our belongings—the linen and plate."

"Excellent," Norman said. "There aren't any linens at the house. I have been sleeping on a curtain I ripped from a window. But there is a set of old cracked dishes—two of the cups even have handles. About the stables, Trudie—a dozen loose boxes and as many stalls! The roof is in perfect repair, and there is a cozy room for John Groom, with an excellent feather tick on the floor."

"Sleeping on a curtain! No handles on the cups!" Mrs. Harrington asked, bewildered.

"It is no matter," he assured her. "I've been taking all my meals except breakfast at the inn. Oh, and the location of the cottage couldn't be better. Within a stone's throw of the practice runs. They are in excellent condition. The club is very strict about which course can be used on any given day, to keep them in shape."

"Is the cottage handy to town?" Mrs. Harrington inquired as Norman helped her into the carriage.

"Downtown? Why, what would you be wanting to go there for? There is nothing worth seeing in town."

"Is there a conservatory?" she asked hopefully.

"Eh? No, who would want a conservatory? A place with such frills would have cost me a monkey. Even Northfield— that's what my lodge is called—was very expensive, but I have struck a deal with Peter and Nick. They are putting up at an inn, since I have to billet you ladies, but they are stabling their nags with me."

"Wouldn't it be more convenient for them to stable their nags at the inn? They must do a deal of walking," Mrs. Harrington said.

"I don't mean their hacks or carriage horses," he explained. "Naturally *they* are stabled at the inn, but when they drive out to the tracks, they leave them with me during the day, then at day's end, they bring their racers back to

Northfield and ride their hacks to the inn. A very tidy arrangement, really. Ideal. They help pay the rent of Northfield for me, and it saves them on stabling fees elsewhere.''

"Clappet and Nick have already made their purchases, have they?'' Trudie asked.

"Peter bought a colt, after all his ranting about wanting a filly. The nag he got is a cribber, but Lightning is a sweet goer, I must say—that's Nick's bit of blood.''

Mrs. Harrington was very little interested in these equine matters. She asked, "How many bedrooms has Northfield got?''

"Five or six, I think. I have set the best one aside for you, Auntie. Trudie and I shan't mind going without clothespresses and mirrors in our rooms.''

"My room *does* have a bed, I hope?'' Trudie asked curtly, and was assured that it had.

After a quantity of such oblique remarks, the ladies were not surprised to see Northfield was less than elegant. From the outside, and at a distance of several yards, it looked an impressive enough place. The brickwork was not perishing in the least, and the building was not yet tilting in any direction, but as they drew closer, the peeling paint around the windows, the opaque condition of the glass, and the general decay of the surrounding vegetation came into prominence.

"Isn't it pretty, Auntie? Such a lovely fan window above the doors,'' Trudie pointed out, selecting the best feature of an indifferent facade.

"This is nothing. Wait till you see the stables!'' was Norman's ill-advised comment.

Within, the place was every bit as bad as Norman had inadvertently implied it would be. Having been hired by three gentlemen the Season before, it was badly abused. Nothing but drunken orgies, Mrs. Harrington was convinced, could account for a fine marble mantelpiece having six bullet gouges in it. How else but in a drunken stupor could a sofa have suffered a disfiguring burn? Why were three pillows resting on a table, and why did one chair have no legs but sit with its seat on the floor? The remains of a varnished leg protruding from the uncleaned grate suggested their fate.

Trudie exchanged a resigned look with her aunt and said, "We have got our work cut out for us."

"A bit of elbow grease will have us as fine as ninepence in no time," Norman assured them.

"I expect houses are in short supply so close to the racing season," Trudie mentioned, trying to smile.

"And so close to the practice runs," Norman added. "You can hear the noise very well from here, so you always know when there's something to watch."

"How convenient!" Mrs. Harrington said, but Norman was impervious to irony. "You have certainly taken great concern for our comfort, Norman. I daresay there is a terrific amount of dust and dirt kicked up.

"We shall take dinner at an inn tonight. Tomorrow, when the Bogmans come, we shall oversee the cleanup."

"An excellent idea." Norman looked around the drawing room and actually saw it for the first time. "It needs a little brightening," he admitted sheepishly, "but really, the stables are something out of the ordinary, I promise you."

"That, of course, is a great consolation to us," his aunt said, in such a tone that even Norman recognized sarcasm, and blushed.

To atone, he took them to the best inn, where he hired the best private parlor available. He wanted to make up for the solecism of the house by being particularly considerate, but his enthusiasm overcame him, and in the end he spoke of nothing but horses.

The shadows of evening had grown long by the time they got back to Northfield. Aunt Gertrude took up a brace of tallow candles to tour the chambers abovestairs while Trudie went to the stables with her brother to inspect his racer and see the cribber Peter had been fool enough to pay four hundred guineas for.

True Lady had been admired at Brighton. She was a fine filly with a good deep chest, long, strong legs, and an intelligent eye. The animal had been placed under the supervision of a certain Bingo Rourke, who was giving Norman invaluable tips on winning races. Bingo was also to be the jockey, when the great races arrived. Next she was taken to see Nick's filly, Lightning. As she was being ruthlessly overtrained by someone other than Bingo Rourke, her chances of ever giving her owner anything but grief and expense were not high. While she was admiring Lightning, there was a sound of splitting wood from the next stall.

"That cribber of Peter's is at it again!" Norman declared, and darted around to hit the colt's rump, while Trudie followed fast at his heels.

The top bar of the stall was between his teeth, and the floor was littered with pieces of wood that still bore the imprint of his teeth. While he gnawed at the wood, Fandango inhaled, drawing in noisy breaths. He was not at all happy to be interrupted at his meal, and threw his head back and whinnied, while his eyes rolled dangerously.

"Demmed cribber! I'll be charged for the repair of this stall if Peter don't do something to stop him," Norman said angrily.

"Red pepper!" was her reply. "That's what Papa used when our gig cob took to biting her stall. He put red pepper on it."

"And salt too, I suppose, to make it nice and tasty. A muzzle is what he shall have. I ain't standing buff for putting in new stalls. Furthermore, Peter puts him in a different box every night. This is the third he's chewed up."

The criminal owner appeared at the stable door at that moment. He and Sir Charles had arrived by hack from town. While Nicolson bowed and did the pretty with Miss Barten,

Peter had his ears chewed off quite as thoroughly as Fandango was chewing at the stall.

"I want a muzzle on this cribber, or out he goes," Norman decreed.

"I ain't muzzling my thoroughbred," Peter maintained stoutly.

"Thoroughbred? Thoroughbred cob is what you've got here. You was duped, Clappet, and if you had any sense, you'd sell this old screw for dogmeat."

Peter investigated the chewed-up lumber, making little of the damage, then pulled Fandango's jaws open to check for slivers within.

While Norman and Nick examined the stall, Peter asked Trudie how things had gone in London. "As a matter of fact, a little difficulty arose," she said reluctantly. "Could we step outside and talk about it? The smell here is rather strong."

He stared that anyone could find the acid reek of manure and horseflesh less than ambrosial, but humored her whim and strolled outside.

"You may, perhaps, be hearing from your uncle Lord Luten, Peter," she began reluctantly. "The fact is, he called on me before we left your apartment."

"Did he, by Jove? How did you come to meet him? I hope you didn't tell him I'd bought Fandango."

"I didn't know it at the time. The thing is, Peter, he disliked it that I was using your apartment."

"It's none of his dashed business. It's just like him to be butting into my affairs. I hope you sent him off with a flea in his ear."

"Well, yes, I did, actually," she said, which set Clappet to stare in wonder that anyone should stand up to Luten.

"*Really?* What did he say?"

Since Luten was now involved, there was no way to keep the story from Peter, and she explained the situation from the beginning, adjuring him not to say anything to Norman. "So what do you think I should do?" she finished, and put herself in his hands.

"You won't have to do a thing. Luten will kill you," Peter said. He stood blowing silent puffs of air through his lips, trying to calm his nerves at this dreadful tale.

"I think he would like to, but it is really the outside of enough for him to be accusing me of being . . ."

As Peter considered the story more fully, he realized that Luten was actually in the wrong, for once. It gave him much pleasure, and a little courage. "Yes, by the living jingo. He ought to be called to account."

"But you mustn't tell Norman!"

"Got to tell him," Peter advised sadly. "Luten will kill him too. Best shot in—second-best shot in—well, one of the best shots in the country in any case, whereas Norman couldn't hit an elephant at ten paces. Nick is a capital shot, but Norman never had the eye for it. Nick is up to all the rigs."

"I hoped the matter could be settled in some other way than killing people," Trudie exclaimed.

"Keep mum about it, you mean?"

"Yes, I won't be in London, and Luten won't be here, so perhaps it will all just blow over. I just wanted you to be aware of the matter, in case your uncle said anything, you know."

Peter silently shook his head. "He *will* be here. Luten always comes to Newmarket in the spring. Member of the Jockey Club. Got half a dozen nags running. He won the Oaks twice. He may not be here for a week or so, but long before you and Norman have gone, you must certainly expect to see him."

Trudie's heart felt as if it were shrinking inside her. "Could you explain to him that it was all a mistake?" she asked.

102

"Be very happy to. Not that he'll believe me. He ain't a cloth head, after all. Sent all the way to Tunbridge Wells searching for mares' nests—and the stunt at White's—they were no mistakes. The thing is, Luten is proud as a Spanish grandee. You don't happen to have any relatives in Cornwall or Wales?" he asked doubtfully.

While they were still discussing it, Sir Charles decided it was time to relieve Miss Barten of Clappet's insufferable company and went after her. "Norman is going to have a porker on his hands if he don't stop overfeeding True Lady," he mentioned. "I do believe the filly toes in as well."

"Nick is up to all the rigs," Peter said, eyeing his friend in an assessing way that Sir Charles found very suspicious.

"What of it?" Sir Charles bristled.

"Can I tell him?" Clappet asked, and Trudie nodded.

"But don't tell Norman," she said to Nick.

"Tell him what? What the deuce are you two up to?" he asked angrily.

"Luten called me a lightskirt, and I had him rent me a cottage at Tunbridge Wells, only I didn't go to live in it, of course," Trudie said, the words tumbling out all in a heap. She felt terribly like crying and was thoroughly ashamed of herself for bothering these two young boys with her problem, except that there was no one else to turn to, and even if they were young, they were city boys at least, whereas Norman was a complete flat. And really she didn't want to ruin Norman's one year of pleasure.

Sir Charles put a consoling arm around her shoulder and patted her wrist. "There, there, m'dear. Pull yourself together and try if you can make sense this time. It sounded as if you said Luten rented his lightskirt a cottage at Tunbridge Wells, which he never would do. Not for a minute. He always puts his ladybirds up in the first style of fashion, right in London."

"You heard her right," Peter said, and removed Sir Charles's hand from Trudie's wrist. He kept hold of her fingers, but Sir Charles felt he had the better of it. He still had his arm around her shoulders.

Trudie shook off both her protectors and took a deep breath, then explained exactly what had happened. Sir Charles counted himself very much a man of the world. He had the rules of Almack's and the Code Duelo by heart. He belonged to the best clubs, was accepted in the best saloons, and was the object of the only word of praise ever heard to issue from the lips of Mr. Weston, London's premier tailor. It was once said that Sir Charles did Mr. Weston's jackets justice. Even Beau Brummell had called him "a pretty fellow." Obviously he would must know what was to be done in this case.

He cocked his well-coiffed head, grimaced to hide his dimples, and took his decision. "You must find yourself a real beau, Miss Barten. It stands to reason, if Luten sees you are attached to someone else, he won't fear you are dangling after Peter. That's what has got his dander up, you know. He thinks you're making a play for his nephew's title and blunt. He'll have to apologize; you accept. It will all blow over without going to the Court of Twelve Paces."

"But I don't have a beau," she pointed out.

"Newmarket is full of bucks. You won't have a spot of trouble," Peter assured her.

Sir Charles cleared his throat a couple of times in a meaningful way, but Trudie didn't jump to the obvious point he was making. Even that clunch of a Peter didn't twig to it.

"Auntie is particular about my friends," Trudie objected.

"Then Norman will have to demand an apology from Luten, and be prepared to do the right thing," Peter said flatly.

Again Sir Charles cleared his throat and again was ignored, so he gave a verbal clue. "Really no problem, Miss Barten. I shall be happy to act your beau, if Luten comes hounding down here after you, as he's bound to do. Demme, I wish I'd been at White's though! No point thinking he'll take Tunbridge Wells sitting down either,'' he added aside to Peter. ''If he knows you are here, he'll be down on your head before you can say one, two, three. You haven't time to find a beau. You'll have to use me.''

''That's a shabby trick to serve a friend,'' she said. Her demurral was said so prettily, and her little face in the moonlight looked so kissable that Sir Charles found himself infatuated into folly.

''Not at all. It would be an honor, Miss Barten. 'Pon my word, it would. You'll have to let me call you Trudie. Been meaning to ask you if I might. My friends call me Nick, by the by. Might as well get used to it, so it will come out natural after Luten gets here.''

That word ''Luten'' struck her heart like cold steel, after hearing the two young men discuss him in such uncompromising terms. ''Do you think it would work? Will it satisfy him if he thinks you and I are . . .''

''He won't raise any ruckus when *I* am involved,'' Nick said confidently. ''He is my aunt Marion's first cousin. He wouldn't want to shoot a connection, especially a *young* connection. Not the thing. Luten is too proud to involve the family in such a low sort of a scrape. He'll knuckle under— hasn't any choice actually.''

''We'll do it, then,'' she decided.

The solution cheered her, especially since it gave Luten a well-deserved comeuppance. If he were a real gentleman, he would apologize. She found herself looking forward to his apology with eager anticipation.

''Tell you what, Trudie,'' Nicolson said. ''I'll take you to the assembly if he comes. Let him see us standing up together. We'll all go, Peter and your aunt and Norman and us. Luten will look nohow.''

Trudie returned to the house with a lighter heart. She

hadn't really so much feared Norman would be forced into a duel as that he would do something harebrained like apologize to Luten. Norman wasn't a hot-blooded young man, but apparently Luten was of quite a different kidney. Only pride would stay his hand from murdering a boy. It would be interesting to see his pride crumble when he realized he'd been made to look a fool and had no recourse but to smile and apologize for it. In the midst of all her thinking, she didn't forget that Luten was a womanizer. And he put his ladies up in the first style in London, whereas he had bought *her* a broken-down jig and hired a cheap cottage at Tunbridge Wells!

Chapter Eleven

Norman was up and out before the ladies arose the next morning. The Bogmans arrived, and the arduous task of bringing order to the chaos of Northfield was begun. Norman had told them it was the sand gallop being used that day, not the one nearest them. It wasn't till the next day that they had the pleasure of listening to the thud of hooves and enjoying the constant shower of dirt that filled the air. In the afternoon, Trudie walked out to the edge of the heath and watched the horses training on the nearer turf gallop. There were more men than women present, but several respectable ladies were there, so that Aunt Gertrude could not call it ramshackle, as she was wishing to do. She did insist that Trudie be accompanied by a groom, and since Norman's was not busy, he went with her.

It was a novel experience to stand and watch the racers pelting down the heath, with various trainers, jockeys, and owners standing about talking, drawing out watches to time their bloods, and jotting notes in little books. The groom explained to Trudie what was going on.

Later, her brother and his two friends joined her.

"Lightning is going beautifully," she complimented Nick.

Peter took instant umbrage and informed her that Lightning was even then being withdrawn from practice due to a case of bucked shins. "Furthermore, Fandango outdistanced her by five seconds in the last trial."

Nicolson didn't remain long. He had to go back and look after Lightning's shins. Norman and Peter soon followed after him. "I shall go home now," Trudie told the groom.

As she turned to leave, she was diverted by the sight of an animal that put in the shade every other horse she had admired that morning. The filly was being led by a buck who outdistanced all other gentlemen to a similar degree. He smiled to see her admiring his filly and soon used it as an excuse to speak.

"Good day," he said politely, and lifted his hat. Manners were easier on the turf than in London. She had exchanged a few words with other strangers and didn't take exception to this greeting.

"Good morning. What a beautiful filly you have there," she complimented him.

"Why, thank you. Thank the pretty lady, Sheba," he commanded the animal, and drew to a halt, stroking his filly's neck. Sheba rolled a mischievous eye at him and tossed her mane. "You are a newcomer to the turf, I think?" he asked. He spoke with an echo of Irish brogue, just enough to make his speech interesting, without rendering it comical.

"This is my first trip to Newmarket," she replied as she took the man's measure. She beheld a startlingly handsome young fellow. His jet black hair glinted in the sun, but even more striking were his eyes. They were of a clear and very bright dancing blue, fringed with lashes a mile long. The severe geometry of his face and its weatherbeaten complexion prevented any air of fragility, however. It was all angles, from the square jaw to the straight line of his nose. His physique was without flaw, unless his shoulders could be called almost too wide. His toilette was in the highest kick of fashion, though it was the fashion of the turf: buckskins, topboots, and a Belcher kerchief at his throat.

"You must have a string of racers training, since you are here so early," the man said.

"Oh, no! My brother and his friends are each training one entry for the races. I do not own any racehorses."

"I meant your family, of course," he answered, smiling. Sheba took into her head to rear up and paw the air with her front legs. The man busied himself quieting her down, giving Trudie a chance to continue examining him, and his calmly masterful way of dealing with this lively one. "You must excuse Sheba's manners," he said, laughing. "She's always jealous when she sees me speaking to a young lady. She is half human, I swear."

"Have you raced her yet? Is she a winner?" she asked. She didn't want to break off the conversation just yet. Really the man was incredibly handsome and seemed every inch the gentleman.

"She's won several small races. I shall be entering her in the Oaks this year."

"My brother and his friends also plan to enter the Oaks," she told him.

"Oh, really? I probably know them. I'm an old hand at racing. Would it be presumptuous of me to inquire your brother's name?"

"Norman Barten," she answered with a little blush, for his manner indicated it was her own name he was angling for.

"Mr. Barten," he said consideringly. "I don't seem to recognize the name. I know mostly everyone who comes regularly."

"My brother just arrived a few days ago. We have hired that lodge, just there," she told him, and pointed over her shoulder to Northfield.

"Johnson's place has excellent stabling. A good location too, so close to the heath," he praised.

A few more comments were exchanged, and soon the gentleman told her his name was Ralph O'Kelly, more usually called Okay by his friends.

"I thought I detected a hint of Irish," she exclaimed, pleased at having caught it.

"I was born on the ould sod, but nowadays I'm an habitué of Newmarket, Ascot, Doncaster—all the leading meets."

Mr. O'Kelly sounded the very sort of gentleman to appeal to her brother, and possibly to help him, since Norman was a very tyro at the turf. In a few moments, Trudie said she had to leave. He warmed her heart by saying he hoped they would meet again soon, and meanwhile he would be looking out for her brother. She mentioned that evening that she had met Mr. O'Kelly, and asked Norman if knew anything about him.

"A tall, good-looking fellow?" he asked.

"Yes, he has a filly, Sheba, and probably a whole string of racers," she replied.

"I've seen him around. He knows everyone—at least everyone seems to know Okay O'Kelly, if that's who you mean."

"His friends call him Okay," she admitted.

To make up for taking the afternoon off, Trudie helped her aunt in the drawing room that evening.

"It will never be elegant," Mrs. Harrington pointed out, quite unnecessarily, "but at least let it not be said the Bartens have sunk to living in squalor."

The next day Miss Barten was on thorns to get back to the heath to look for Mr. O'Kelly. The awful image of Lord Luten was slipping to the back of her mind. She was by no means an accomplished rider, but Norman's hack was in the stable and required exercise. It was not so high a stepper that a lady couldn't handle it.

The air was cool as she cantered along, viewing in the distance a mist rising up from the uneven heath, but in the trees overhead, the birds sang of spring. She took up a position along the edge of the track, where a few gathered groups waited patiently for some action. Soon a pair of fillies came galloping along, the divots from their heels thrown up behind them. Other groups and single colts and fillies went past, each causing a ripple of excitement. At last Trudie spotted her quarry. Mr. O'Kelly came riding by, mounted on a bay hacker, not his Sheba. He recognized Miss Barten at once and drew up to speak. "Good afternoon, Miss Barten. All alone?"

She felt ill at ease and wondered if perhaps it wasn't quite the thing to be in this raffish place, without the excuse of its being at her very doorstep. "My brother and friends will be along shortly. I just rode out to exercise my brother's mount."

"May I join you?" he asked, already dismounting.

"I would be very happy for your company."

"It might be best if I stay with you till they come" was all he said, but she surmised she had strayed into error to have come alone.

"It's very exciting, watching the runs," she said, to account for the happy smile she could feel lighting her face.

"In my opinion, we are standing on the most interesting piece of land in the country. How does your brother's training program come along?"

"Well, I believe. He has a filly, True Lady."

Their interest was diverted to the track as a few racers pounded past. Mr. O'Kelly named each one and gave an opinion of its chances. "The Duke of Welsham's Barb," he said a moment later, when one lone horse and rider darted past. He was apparently familiar with every bit of blood on the turf.

"Do you know all the horses?" she asked.

He turned and smiled down at her. The sun struck his handsome face, casting a magical glow over it. "No, I haven't met True Lady yet, but I look forward to making her acquaintance. I have learned your brother hired Bingo Rourke to ride her. Though he is a countryman, I can't give Bingo my complete approbation. Too soft—the national failing of his race—but at least he won't break the lady's spirit. Your brother is out in his hopes if he thinks to win the Oaks with her."

"Why do you say so, Mr. O'Kelly? It's early days yet. There is time to train her up."

"Oh, that was not my meaning!" he exclaimed, surprised. He pointed to a mound of earth, where an ancient tree was enclosed by a rude fence. "There will be wildflowers blooming on the Boy's Grave by April. I have been out to check for sprouts. I've spotted the green spikes of lilies of the valley, and something else that looks like buttercups."

She blinked and frowned. "I beg your pardon?"

"You're not familiar with the legend? My dear lady, your training in superstition has been badly neglected!" he teased her with a delightful smile.

"I never heard of any legend. Who is buried there? What boy?"

"That is reputed to be the grave of a shepherd who was killed for losing one of his master's sheep. His friends buried his body there, under that mound, and planted wildflowers. When they bloom in April, a Newmarket filly will win the Oaks at Epsom. It's held true since 1780, when the first race was won by Diomed. True Lady cannot be a Newmarket filly, or I'd have known about her. I'm not superstitious myself," he added with a smile, "but a friendly Leprechaun told me never to enter anything but a Newmarket filly in the Oaks, and if you don't follow a Leprechaun's advice, you end up in the hot place."

"Have you ever won?"

"I did once, actually, but was disqualified after the fact. It was claimed my entry was four years old—the race is for three-year-olds. An astonishing accusation, and never proven either, but Alvanley's filly was named the winner. The Jockey Club boys stick together. Luten and his friends arranged it amongst themselves."

"Lord Luten?" she asked, her pulse quickening.

"Yes, do you know him? I hope I've not trod on the toes of a good friend of yours." Mr. O'Kelly looked abashed at his faux pas.

Trudie was quick to clear up the matter. "I am slightly acquainted with the man. He is by no means a friend. Quite the contrary!" she said stiffly. "But could you not prove them wrong?"

"You might as well try to argue with God. My papers were claimed not to be in order. It is the Jockey Club that handles all that sort of thing. This was before they started the Stud Book in 1808. They could never get away with it today. I make sure to buy only well-documented bloods. Most breeding stock is owned by members, and they decide quite arbitrarily amongst themselves what is to be called a thoroughbred. I believe the chief qualification is that the animal come from their own stud farms. They're saying now the male line must trace back to the Godolphin or Byerley or the Darley, although it was not initially a requirement at all."

She listened to this tale of inequity, but it was mainly the word Luten that registered in her mind. "Why do you not join the Jockey Club yourself, since you are such an avid member of the turf, Mr. O'Kelly?"

"It's a closed club, in fact if not in theory," he said vaguely. "There is a saying that all men are equal on the turf and under it—in death, you know—but the fact is, if your blood is not bright blue, and especially if it has a hint of green like mine, they don't want you in the Jockey Club."

"But that's horrid!" she exclaimed. She went on to commiserate, believing every word he spoke, for he spoke them with such charming looks.

He shrugged and dismissed this gross inequity. "At least Sheba is fully documented. I got her from Cheveley Park, the best stud farm around, and right here, in Newmarket."

"My friend Lord Clappet got his colt there."

Mr. O'Kelly's eyes glinted with interest, and his smile suddenly grew brighter, but he carefully refrained from dwelling upon the name Lord Clappet. "You will want to see where old King Canute bred his horses," he said, and went on to explain that this was another legend she must profess to believe if she was to become a member of turfing society.

There was a thunder of hooves down the track, and they both looked to see what was coming. "Here comes my Sheba!" he exclaimed, and went closer to the track. Trudie went with him to see the filly bolt past at a breakneck speed. Her knotted muscles flexed in the sunlight, and her coat was as smooth as molten gold. It seemed to Trudie that she went at least twice as fast as any of the other racers. Mr. O'Kelly smiled after Sheba's retreating form. "A winner," he said confidently.

Just after Sheba thundered past, Trudie spotted her brother and his friends advancing toward her across the field. They had stopped to watch Sheba. Trudie waved her hand and beckoned them to her, to introduce them to Mr. O'Kelly. "Mr. O'Kelly owns that beautiful filly you were just looking at," she told them.

"Sheba?" Peter asked. His eyes grew wide in admiration. "What a bang-up bit of blood. I have been admiring her anytime this week. I notice you always run her alone. I expect your aim is to keep her time a secret, eh?" he asked knowingly. "What is her speed?"

"As you so cleverly figured out, Lord Clappet, it is a secret,'' Mr. O'Kelly replied, but with none of that toploftly air that would offend. He wore a charming smile.

"Part Arabian, is she?'' Sir Charles inquired.

"So her papers say. The Easterns are all double cousins. I cannot tell a half Turk from a half Arab, and neither can anyone else, unless he has it on a piece of paper. Her nose is hooked, and most of the Barbs have a little hook at the end of their noses.''

"Where did you get her?'' Sir Charles asked.

"Cheveley Park.''

"I got my Fandango at Cheveley too,'' Peter said, wishing to drop the name himself.

"He was gulled,'' Nicolson announced happily.

"Ah, but one is gulled in style at Cheveley Park,'' O'Kelly consoled. "They weren't asking much for him at any rate. Why did you bother buying him, milord?''

"Well, he was cheap,'' Peter pointed out.

"I cannot think money would present a problem to you!''

"A trifle short at the moment,'' Peter admitted.

"Aren't we all,'' O'Kelly said. "This is a rich man's game. The prices being asked this year are ridiculous. I paid—well, it is no matter, but I had to scramble to buy my Sheba. I nearly succumbed to Fandango as well, when I saw how little they were asking for him. Our tastes are similar, Lord Clappet.''

They discussed pasterns and knees and hocks for a considerable length of time. Before they parted, a wizened man in a leather waistcoat ambled by, with a basket in which rested an assortment of racing memorabilia slung around his neck. "Buy a charm?'' he asked. "Racing plates worn by Eclipse, a hank of her hair braided into a watch fob and mounted in glass, the riding crop used on her when she won the Ascot in 1770.''

"That's a dandy crop,'' Peter said, lifting it to heft between his fingers.

Mr. O'Kelly shook his head in disbelief. "Eclipse must have been a walking hairstack. There are a dozen vendors hawking this spurious stuff. Why, I do believe that is the same crop was stolen from the stables yesterday morning."

"I've had it for two weeks! I bought it right in town," the man said, grabbing back his treasure to trot off at a fast pace.

"Blackleg," O'Kelly scoffed. "You have to beware of all the touts and Greeks that hang around a place like this. Don't put a bid to buy Newmarket Heath either, if you're offered it for an old song," he suggested.

There was a bout of merry laughter to show this joke was fully appreciated. "Took us for a bunch of Johnnie Raws," Peter said in a knowing way.

"Those crooks ought to be run out of town. I cannot imagine why the law permits them to operate," O'Kelly said. "I daresay they pay a percentage of their ill-got gains to the Jockey Club for permits to operate."

"The Jockey Club is above reproach," Sir Charles felt obliged to tell him. "I have applied for membership myself."

"Perhaps you will be accepted. It is *Sir* Charles, if I remember correctly?"

"That's right. What of it?"

"Nothing. The Jockey Club has a fondness for sirs and lords."

There was a little more general talk, then Mr. O'Kelly took his leave.

"A knowing cove," Clappet said. "Demmed fine mount he has there too."

"His Sheba is a goer," Sir Charles allowed, "but the fellow is out if he thinks there is anything havey cavey with the Jockey Club. Top of the trees."

"I wish I had met O'Kelly before I bought Fandango," Clappet said. "Maybe I could trade him for a filly. I shall speak to O'Kelly about it next time we meet. Where does he put up, Trudie?"

"He didn't say."

"Someone at the inn will know," Sir Charles said.

That evening, Clappet and Sir Charles did not drive out to Northfield to visit. As soon as he twigged to the reason they had not, Norman tacked up his mount and went into town to search them out. They had succeeded in discovering the lair of O'Kelly. Even better, O'Kelly had that same evening decided to remove to the Golden Lion, their own inn. Their conversation over the next days was heavily peppered with the wisdom of Okay O'Kelly. Trudie expected every evening when Norman returned to Northfield that he'd say O'Kelly was dropping around, but he never did. It was always Norman who went to the Golden Lion, so Trudie got her news of him second-hand. Of Luten she got no news at all, and had become quite easy in her mind that that affair was over and done with.

Chapter Twelve

What revenge could be bad enough for an impertinent, grasping, lying female who had not only ensnared Lord Clappet but had made a flaming jackass of his uncle as well? That was the question that bedeviled Luten as he made his preparations for Newmarket. Public exposure, preferably at a cart's tail, occurred to him, only to be rejected as ridiculously lenient. Dunking in a pond for the witch that she was beguiled him for five minutes. The two criteria eventually settled on were humiliation and publicity. The humiliation, complete and utter, must occur in a public place, to serve as a warning to others of her sort (and to retaliate for Luten's public disgrace at his club).

After Miss Barten's stunt in sending him off to Tunbridge Wells, Luten was convinced Peter could not be at Newmarket, as she said. He would not dash around the countryside again, being made a fool of. Certainly not! He'd send his groom to do it for him. By the time his groom returned to London with word that Clappet was indeed at Newmarket, Luten was at his wits' end with impatience. He set out at four o'clock in the afternoon, thus ensuring himself of an uncomfortable night at a public inn.

He arrived at Newmarket the next day before the sun had set, and had time to lay his plans. He didn't happen to own a house near Newmarket, but hired one of the finer lodges each spring at a price that would have made purchase wiser. He drove directly to Sable Lodge, where all conveniences awaited his pleasure. His staff preceded him, going each year in March, to have the house standing ready for any chance days he might wish to spend there. After an excellent dinner, he donned evening apparel and drove into town to begin his search.

He discovered in town what inn Peter was putting up at but soon heard there that Lord Clappet was out for the evening. With the girl, then, but where? No amount of quizzing of the inn staff gave him the least notion where to look. It was Luten's groom who learned at the stable that Clappet had left the inn in evening attire a few hours earlier, planning, he believed, to attend the local assembly. The last words were uttered with all the contempt of the city groom for provincial doings.

"At the assembly rooms at the White Hart, milord," he finished, lips curling into a sneer.

Luten's reply was uttered in a similar way. "That sounds a spot likely to appeal to his friend."

Luten hastened to the White Hart, unaware that his heart was beating faster with excitement. Just so did it hammer when the fox was sighted during the chase. Revenge was at hand—and still he had no idea what form it would take.

He could have wished for a rowdier party. The patrons were displeasingly respectable. The participants were the locals, with a sprinkling of turfing society, those aficionados who came long before the races began. Several of his own friends were there, to make him welcome. He was obliged to waste several minutes in polite chitchat, even after he had spotted his nephew and the female.

While he chatted, he noticed that Miss Barten was still in her disguise as a provincial lady. She didn't wear the white gown of a deb, but a pretty royal blue, set off with white lace and pearls. It was a modest outfit, but then modesty was a part of her act. Her curls caught the reflection of overhead lights, giving her a copper crown that was easy to keep track of as she moved about the room.

Luten was spotted by his quarry two minutes after he discovered her. She had time to seek out Nicolson and warn him the time had come to be her protector. Soon she was aware of Luten's dark, menacing eye following her movements from across the room. She felt an apprehension of doom. He could hardly murder her in front of a few hundred witnesses, but that black scowl told her he would like to.

"Remember, Nick, you are my particular friend. We are not betrothed or anything of the sort. Just good friends," she reminded him. As she spoke she looked around the hall for Mrs. Harrington and Norman. She wanted to keep any unpleasantness from their sight.

It proved very difficult indeed. Aunt Gertrude had spotted Luten and came darting up. "Trudie, the worst luck! That wretched Mandeville man is here, the one who didn't pay you for the Latin lesson in London, and wanted you to go out to a play with him unchaperoned."

Trudie willed down her fear and answered as calmly as she could, "Yes, I've seen him."

"Have nothing to do with him. I mean to cut him dead if he speaks to me."

Nicolson intercepted a worried look from his partner and jumped into the breach. "There is a rollicking country dance starting up. Shall we have a jig, Trudie?"

The dance floor seemed a safe spot. She accepted and went with trembling knees to the center of the floor, still watching Luten. He went straight to Peter. They were talking about her—there was no misreading the signs; the angry, short looks in her direction, the gesturing hands, Peter's weak denials, indicated by his shaking head.

"Well, Master Jackanapes! Enjoying yourself, are you?" Luten asked.

Peter felt that those eyes were burrowing right into his skull, but he tried to answer bravely. "Very much, Uncle. I don't know why you are in one of your rages. You knew I was coming to Newmarket."

"I had the notion you were coming with Nicolson, not Miss Barten."

"I did. Nick and I are putting up at the . . ."

Luten cut him short. "What sort of establishment have you set up for the woman?"

"I?" Peter asked, his voice rising to a squeak of protest. "Really, Uncle, I don't know where you got the cork-brained idea Miss Barten is anything to me. Nick is sweet on her, to be sure. As to where she is putting up, why, she stays with her aunt and brother at Northfield."

"She palmed the 'aunt' off on you as well, did she? Do explain, cawker, for I cannot believe even *you* are gullible enough to have let her talk you into billeting a man as well, who is the alleged brother."

"Alleged? Demme, I have known Norman Barten any-time these eight years—an excellent old Warwick family. We were at Harrow and Cambridge together. I nearly died of shame when Miss Barten told me what had happened in London. I gave her and her aunt the use of my apartment for a few days while they waited for Norman to hire a lodge for them. That's all. Norman is training up a filly for the races, and the ladies are keeping house for him."

Luten listened, hoping for discrepancies in this story. Finding none, he attacked on another front and was again repulsed. "Since when have you taken into your head to hire yourself an apartment in London?"

"Why, you told me yourself it wasn't the thing, squeez-ing in with Nick. I only sublet a few square inches. To tell the truth, I'm sorry I hired it. But it was going at a great bargain. Why, the place would have been gone in two minutes if I hadn't moved fast. And I'll use it after the races.''

"What about those nightly visits to Conduit Street?"

"What about them? And they weren't *nightly* either. Naturally I visited Norman's family when they were in town and had no other acquaintances. I've stayed at Walbeck Park any number of times. Trudie was kind enough to help me out a little with my Latin, for you know Mama is in a pucker at my being plucked last term.''

The story had the ring of probability to it, and Luten sought for any possible flaw. "I'm not quite a fool, Peter. Ladies of quality do not purvey Latin lessons.''

"There was no purveying about it. Her papa was a famous scholar, you must know, and he taught his daughter Latin; she seemed to have a head for it. I took Nick around to call a few times, and . . .''

"It's news to me if Sir Charles Nicolson has any interest in Latin. He'd do better to learn English, and you too.''

"To tell the truth, Nick wasn't much interested in the Latin, but he developed a tendre for Miss Barten, and since she's perfectly eligible, there was no harm in giving him a hand.''

"Perfectly eligible ladies are not given a Kent Street Ejection," Luten said. He was playing his last trump card, and he knew it.

"It's infamous carrying on, if you want my opinion. If the ladies wasn't a pair of greenheads fresh off the farm, they'd have hired a solicitor and taken old Nettie Rolfe to court. She's the one set tongues wagging. I can't imagine who'd be fool enough to listen to her ranting.''

But Luten knew and was writhing under it. "I thought there was a brother who should have done something about it.''

"Norman wasn't there, and Trudie is such a thoughtful girl she didn't want to trouble him with the story. She really is very sweet and generous when you get to know her, Uncle.''

"Sweet and generous girls" did not make laughing stocks of their acquaintances. The whole thing was hard to swallow, as it put Luten in such an unattractive light. Miss Barten was angling after Nicolson instead of Peter. That was his only error. Nicolson, while not a close relative, was a connection. A wide spreading of his paternal wings might include Nick. "So it's Nick she has in her eye, is it?"

"She only tolerates him, if you want the truth. For one thing, she's three or four years older than Nick."

"That old?" Luten asked, surprised.

"She's twenty-three, but she has no town bronze, and seems younger. The Bartens are more than respectable. She has a dowry of five thousand—a respectable heiress is as good as Nick can hope to do. The Nicolsons would likely jump at the chance of attaching her."

"They wouldn't be eager to see young Nick marry an ape leader. Twenty-three is a bit over the hill for Nick."

"He'd be better off settled down. I've heard you say so yourself. Between his portion and her own, they could buy up a tidy little estate somewhere—set up as landowners, have a few kids."

This dismal future was put forth in a perfectly perfunctory way. Luten listened, hearing echoes of a few family conversations. The truth was that a Miss Barten with five thousand pounds was as good as Nicolson could be expected to do. In other words, he had been made a fool of again. Worse, he had made a fool of himself. Miss Barten, if Peter was telling the truth, was more victim than fiend, but this did not totally acquit her of having led him a merry chase. The score was by no means settled. Merely it would have to be handled in a different manner. The black anger was shading to gray, a sort of antic quality creeping over him. Some playful retaliation must be given for the affair at White's and the futile trip

123

to Tunbridge Wells, but he had caused quite enough real and unnecessary trouble to Miss Barten.

Looking at her in this new light, he noticed that her appearance had undergone another metamorphosis. Her face was no longer conniving and grasping, but intelligent. The light in her eyes was caused by a memory of some esoteric Latin extract she'd been dipping into. It would be a pleasant change to converse with a lady who took an interest in something other than gossip and fashion.

"In that case, I believe I owe the lady an apology," he said.

"You certainly do. And for God's sake don't tell Norman what you thought, or he'd be obliged to blow your brains out. That is to say, he can't shoot worth a tinker's curse, which is why Trudie don't want him to know the things you did, for he'd be obliged to try."

"I suppose you have all given this a good deal of discussion?" Luten asked, brow rising in ire.

"Naturally we had to sort things out—Nick and Trudie and I. The aunt don't know the half of it either. Trudie was nearly in tears when she told me the story. The poor thing felt it was her fault, in some way, that the whole town was treating her like an old shoe. She didn't know which way to turn."

Peter felt he had handled the matter with perfect discretion. He knew his uncle well enough to realize that his frowning pause was caused not by anger but by embarrassment—and something else. Some emotion that looked very much like regret but soon looked more like resolution. The two stayed talking till the country dance was over. Nicolson began hastening Miss Barten back to her aunt at its end, but the fleeing couple were soon overtaken by Luten's long, purposeful strides.

"Miss Barten!" he called from a few yards away.

She stopped in her tracks, turned slowly, and stared at

him. Her first reaction was fear, pure and simple. As she noticed the doubtful face of her pursuer, she took courage. "Lord Luten? Or is it Mr. Mandeville this evening?" she inquired. Her tone hovered between politeness and irony.

"Take your pick. In either case, I wish to apologize."

"I should think so!" Nicolson exclaimed. There was no doubt about *his* tone. It was all relief. He added in a low aside to Miss Barten, "Peter has talked him around. I shall nip off now."

Luten offered her his arm. She accepted it reluctantly and they walked off together. "Champagne?" he offered. "The country dances are tiring, are they not?"

"I'm tuckered out, and so very het up," she admitted. Luten bit his lip at these signs of rusticity. "But there's no champagne. You're not in London now."

"Nor even in Tunbridge Wells. The gods don't sip on orgeat, I bet," he laughed. She was quite shocked that he should refer openly to his disgrace, and do it with such good humor too.

"Don't pretend to be shocked, Miss Barten! The quotation is your own. Also the location. Now that I know the truth, I'm surprised it wasn't Coventry you chose for our lovenest. I'm sure that's where you were wishing me."

"That's much too close to home, milord. I hail from Warwick myself, you must know."

"You wouldn't wish to burden the county with such an unregenerate idiot as Lord Luten. I have to concur with you there."

They proceeded to the end of the dance room, where the refreshments were being served. Luten took a glass of fruit punch, and Trudie asked for orgeat. After one sip, she was ready to condemn it. "This is more barley water than anything else. We serve it to our field hands in hot weather, only not in such pretty thimbles, of course."

He found her frank country manners charming and decided to confer a treat on Miss Barten. "I shall make a promise here and now to serve you champagne when you attend my ball, later in the Season." He smiled.

She only looked startled, and not at all gratified. "Did you enjoy Tunbridge Wells, milord?" she asked archly.

"No so much as you did, I suspect."

"You really did go, then? I was by no means sure that elegant rattler and prad you sent 'round would accomplish the trip."

"They didn't attempt it. I drove my own rig down."

"That was wise of you."

"And are you not going to apologize for *your* part in the infamous affair, Miss Barten? I think I got the worse end of the bargain."

"I'd bear that in mind in future, if I were you, Lord Luten. I'm sorry the misunderstanding occurred. I can't truthfully say I regret having repaid you for your behavior."

Luten blinked at her intransigence, and after he had gone out of his way to charm her too. Was she not aware that he stood very near the summit of social London, while she inhabited the outskirts of Newmarket and Warwick? "The virtue of truth can be overdone. One usually *pretends* at least to regret misdeeds," he pointed out.

"Yes, I suppose so," she answered vaguely. She sipped the orgeat as she scanned the dance floor beyond, looking for Mr. O'Kelly.

Luten felt the onset of impatience and asked, "So it is Nicolson who is your particular friend now, is it?"

It was no longer necessary to maintain this lie. "Both Nicolson and Clappet are my friends. You don't object to my being an acquaintance of your nephew, I hope? He spent enough weekends with us at Walbeck Park," she added, quite unnecessarily.

"Not in the least. My only objection is that Peter didn't

make you acquainted with his family. It's odd he did not do so."

"It's Lady Clappet," she explained. "She is quite a queer old nabs. But you must know that—she's some relation to you as well, I expect?"

His lips thinned noticeably. "My sister," he informed her.

"That would explain it."

Luten was ready to mount his high horse, till he observed the glint of laughter in her eyes. A strange, undefinable color—those eyes. Were they blue, green, hazel? After a pause long enough to determine the eyes were hazel, he answered, "Despite the family tendency to oddity, I am not quite so eccentric as Lady Clappet. Peter might have introduced you to me. In any case we have met now, and I hope we may see each other again. Peter tells me you have hired Johnson's lodge. May I do myself the honor of calling on you there one day?"

"No! You mustn't think of it!" she exclaimed sharply. "What will my aunt think? She believes you are Mr. Mandeville."

"So I am. Luten is my title. I also have a name, which I use occasionally when dealing with . . ." He stopped short. There was something about this outspoken lady that called forth a similar manner of speech from him.

"No, really it would be better if you stay away."

The statement angered Luten to the core. He wasn't accustomed to hearing himself turned off so abruptly by young ladies of meager fortune. His chin went up, his shoulders stiffened, and he stood trying vainly to think of some cutting riposte. But all he could think of to say was "Why?"

"I told her about the drive—that is, something about it. Not the whole, or she'd have had Bow Street down on your head. And besides, you never paid me for the Latin lesson."

Luten's cheeks were suffused with a blush at this re-

127

minder of past indelicacies, and perhaps the fleeting memory of dreams in which he had anticipated future ones as well. "The payment is easily remedied at least."

Miss Barten did not brush this token speech aside but considered it practically. "You can give it to Peter. He'll see that I get it. I can't be seen taking money from you here."

"A crown, wasn't it?" he asked.

"Yes, I shan't charge interest." Her darting eyes discovered Mr. O'Kelly entering at the doorway, and she excused herself, in her usual blunt fashion. "I have to go now."

"I hoped we might have the next dance."

"No, thank you. I'll be busy. Good evening."

With the barest sketch of a curtsy, she hurried away, leaving Luten alone feeling foolish. He joined a party of friends from London, without again glancing at Miss Barten, or at least taking some pains not to be seen staring at her.

The affair, in both their minds, was terminated, but unsatisfactorily so. There remained some rankling sensation of not having exacted sufficient revenge on her part, and of new offense on Luten's. He had offered a generously decked olive branch, and she had spurned it. She had refused to stand up with him, had denied him the privilege of calling on her, and hadn't shown the least interest at that hint that he would be pleased to see her at his ball. Those invitations were not freely sprinkled about by any means. Many a noble deb dangled after one in vain.

Mr. O'Kelly attracted a good deal of attention when he appeared in the doorway, resplendent in his black evening clothes, his wide shoulders nearly filling the frame. Many female hearts were set aflutter, but it was Miss Barten's that rose like a thrush when Okay smiled and advanced toward her.

Others than ladies were observing Mr. O'Kelly. "Isn't that Okay O'Kelly just come in?" Lord Enfield remarked to Luten.

"Yes, it is. I wonder what lamb he has in mind to fleece this year," Luten said. His eyes narrowed in suspicion when he saw Peter and Nicolson darting toward the doorway.

"I couldn't say for sure, but it is your nephew's set he hangs around with," Enfield cautioned. "I have often seen them together. He is on great terms with the young lady you were with earlier. Barten, I think she is called."

Luten drew a weary sigh. "Somehow, that doesn't surprise me. Thank you for the tip, Enfield."

He disappeared into one of the dark corners of the hall and observed the scene silently for a few dances, long enough to see that Miss Barten had fallen into the hands of a creature who was likely to do her more harm than he had done. She would definitely require rescuing, and so would Peter. Oddly, there was no sign of disapproval at the daunting chore before him. He wore a lazy, but really quite happy, smile.

Chapter Thirteen

When Lord Luten left the assembly room at the White Hart, his nephew breathed a deep sigh of relief. An impromptu meeting among the three gentlemen and Trudie was held over the punch bowl, to decide how they should handle Luten's presence at Newmarket.

"He's bound to hear I have bought Fandango," Peter said worriedly. "He'll write straightway to Mama. I'll be lucky if I don't have her down on my head as well."

"You won't," Nicolson consoled him. "She always gets Luten to do her dirty work for her. He'll handle you himself to keep her out of his own hair."

Trudie listened impatiently to this exchange. She could hardly believe that a nearly grown man like Peter should be trembling in his boots because of what his uncle would say, when the uncle himself was no better than he should be. "Tell him you bought Fandango, let him ring his peal over you, and have done with it," she advised.

"He'll cut up stiff," Peter objected.

Nicolson's chin had settled on his chest. Suddenly it lifted, and a spark of delight lit his eyes. "I say, Clappet. Your uncle has an excellent lodge—Sable. Dozens of rooms, and enormous stables. It would save us a bundle if he asked us to stay with him."

"Where is his lodge?" Trudie asked.

"Just three or four down from your own. The good one, at the end of the row there, closest to the main road," Nick said.

As if having Luten virtually on her doorstep wasn't enough for Trudie to contend with, Mrs. Harrington soon found them and demanded to know why she had given Mr. Mandeville the time of day, after the way he treated her in London.

"What do you mean?" Norman bristled.

There was a suspicious pause, and when no one else spoke, Trudie undertook to iron out this wrinkle. "It's nothing, Norman. He came looking for Peter at our apartment on Conduit Street one day, and Auntie didn't care for his manners. That's all. He didn't tell us he was Peter's uncle, you see. We understood his name was Mr. Mandeville."

"Peter's uncle!" Mrs. Harrington exclaimed. "Why on earth did he not say so? He introduced himself as a friend of Sir Charles."

"Great jokester," Nicolson said, hoping to smooth over the contretemps.

"It is not *my* idea of a joke! What was the point of it?"

"Point? Why, there was no point," Peter said vaguely. "He just did it for a lark."

"That is incredible," the dame declared. "A grown man playing off pointless jokes. I hope you did not encourage him in such pranks, Trudie."

"Of course not. I scolded him severely."

"Strange carrying on indeed," the aunt decreed.

Mr. O'Kelly joined them for dinner. As he was at pains to be polite to an aging lady, he found high favor with Mrs. Harrington. Not so high as to replace Lord Clappet, but he was invited to call on her some time he was near Northfield. He smiled agreeably and mentioned that as he was at the track most days, she would soon have an opportunity to regret her kindness.

"Mr. O'Kelly," she pointed out to Trudie later, "has a true sense of humor. Regret my kindness indeed! Unlike the pointless carrying on of Lord Luten, masquerading as a financier, and not even paying you your crown for the Latin lesson."

Mr. O'Kelly took full advantage of Mrs. Harrington's offer and appeared frequently in her saloon, usually just before luncheon.

"I hope you don't take the notion I only come for your excellent cuisine!" he laughed. "The fact is, this is about the only part of my day I have any spare time. You've no idea how eagerly I look forward to it. Why, it's almost like having a family to come home to. The days are pretty well filled up with business at the track, and in the evenings I have all my paperwork to do. My man of business usually has a pile of papers for my signature."

"This is business having to do with your estate in Ireland, is it, Mr. O'Kelly?" Mrs. Harrington asked, with what she believed to be very sly subtlety.

"Yes, Doneraile, the old homestead. A large estate entails a great deal of work."

"What sort of estate is it?"

"Dairy for the most part, though the forests have given me some good revenues the past few years as well. And of course you may take for granted that I also do a fair bit of horsebreeding."

Over the chops, she gave a meaningful nod to her niece. The combined activities listed could hardly be accomplished on less than five or six hundred acres, probably a thousand.

O'Kelly had still not entirely replaced Clappet in her esteem, but since Lord Luten's coming to his lodge, they had seen less of Peter. Of Luten himself, they had seen nothing, not so much as a glimpse of him or even his carriage. Trudie knew he was often at the track and began to regret her insistence that he not call at Northfield. She felt some hesitation to be seen standing around the tracks alone. Her first gratification at O'Kelly's calls had begun to fade. He was still handsome and amusing, but there was no denying he always showed up just before luncheon and left very soon after. Furthermore, she knew perfectly well he wasn't snowed under with paperwork at night. Norman often mentioned seeing him at the Golden Lion. To sit at Okay's feet and learn the arcane secrets of the turf was the only reason Norman went.

With Norman going into town for his entertainment, it meant the evenings at Northfield were every bit as long and tedious as those in London had been. She learned secondhand from Norman what was going forth. Peter and Sir Charles hadn't been invited to remove to Sable Lodge, and when the racers were returned after the day's working out, she usually went to the stable, just for the company.

When the head and shoulders clock on the mantel showed five o'clock, she set aside her novel and said, "I'm going down to meet Norman, Auntie. Dinner at six, as usual?"

"Yes, and don't keep Norman there past five-thirty. I want him to wash the stench of horses from him and change before he comes to the table."

March had finally passed, and April's balmier breezes were awaft in the air. They brought an unsettled, wistful mood with them. Trudie told herself it was Walbeck Park and her old friends she was missing, but some atavistic wisdom whispered a different song. It wasn't the friends and neighbors from home she secretly craved, but one special new friend. When these feelings settled around her, she often thought of Mr. O'Kelly, but despite his many free lunches, no real romance was offered. If he favored either lady, she would have to say it was her aunt who was being courted. Of course, it wasn't unusual for a gentleman to play the gallant to a young lady's chaperone; what was unusual about it was that Mr. O'Kelly took no advantage of his new intimacy with the family. There were no soft smiles exchanged behind Aunt Gertrude's back, no meaningful looks or double entendres that only she would understand.

She had an instinct that Lord Luten would not be such a dallier in the primeval art of romance, and the wish was born tha she might put her instinct to the test. All these thoughts flitted through her mind as she walked to the stable, and flew out of her mind as soon as she opened the door and got a whiff of the smell. She saw a group of blue jackets clustered at the far end and advanced. "Lord, I don't know how you can all stand the stench of this place. It smells worse than the pigsty at home."

She gasped and lifted her hand to her mouth. There was an extra blue jacket in the throng, and as it turned toward her, she saw it was occupied by Lord Luten. "What are you doing here?" she demanded sharply. Her voice sounded angry, but it was embarrassment that lent it that rough edge. Why had she blurted out that likeness to pigsties? Was she forever doomed to appear a hoyden in front of that man?

His reply was more than civil; there was something very like an apology in its humble tone. "Norman asked me along to have a look at True Lady's ankle," he said. They gazed at each other curiously, as though meeting for the first time. The Lord Luten standing before her today seemed different from before. His habitual expression of disdain was softer, and something in her regard brought a small smile to his lips. "I didn't plan to encroach so far as your saloon," he added.

She brushed past him. "What seems to be the trouble?" she asked briskly. It was a foolish pose to pretend that she knew the first thing about horse management.

"I think True Lady kicked herself," Norman said. "She does have a little tendency to toe in. There's some swelling between the fetlock and the knee,'' he said, tenderly rubbing his fingers along the cannon while True Lady whinnied in dismay.

Luten joined him, and Norman stood back to let Luten repeat the same procedure. ''There's a little fever here too,'' he said.

''I use mud and vinegar to lower the fever. The skin's not broken, so it'll be easy. There's been a little damage done to the ligament—feel the swelling,'' he said, placing Norman's hand on the appropriate spot. ''When the fever comes down, you'll want a liniment to tighten and toughen the injured area. I'll give you a can of the sort used at Danebury. Keep True Lady off the track for a few days, and bandage her the first time out. If the leg is not swollen after a few runs, you can dispense with the bandage.''

''But do you think she'll do it again?'' Norman asked. A sharp frown worried his brow. ''Is she going to keep kicking herself every time out?''

Luten didn't have the heart to admit his feelings. ''It may be a recurring problem. All horses have problems, and a badly formed leg is one of the most difficult to overcome. When you see a thoroughbred going at a bargain, Norman, there has to be a reason. It's usually the legs.''

Sir Charles had edged forward. ''While you're here, Luten, would you mind having a look at Lightning? These shin bucks have me worried.''

''You're driving her too hard.''

''But at Danebury they drive them into the ground! Everybody knows that.''

''No, they stop just short of driving them into the ground. Danebury's in the business of training horses, not burying them.''

Trudie fetched the vinegar from the cupboard and watched as Luten showed Norman the proportions, then applied it with extreme gentleness to True Lady's swollen leg. His long fingers moved carefully, and while she watched, she could almost feel those fingers stroking her own skin.

"When should I take this off and put on the liniment?" Norman asked.

"When the fever's gone. It'll take a couple of hours at least." He sent off for the liniment.

"It looks like you won't be coming into town tonight then," Sir Charles said to Norman.

"You and I might as well toddle off," Peter said.

They left, but Luten remained. It was after five-thirty, and Trudie knew she should be hurrying Norman up for dinner, but disliked to do it with Luten still there. When the mud pack was on, Norman settled the matter by saying, "I hope you will stay and take your mutton with us, Luten. It'll only be pot luck, but if that's all right with you, we'd be happy for your company."

Luten looked at Trudie. "Some other time, perhaps," he said, but there was that in his eyes that suggested he could be persuaded without too much trouble.

"There's plenty of ham" was her mild encouragement.

"If you're quite sure—I wouldn't want to inconvenience Mrs. Harrington. But no, I'm not dressed. . . ." Even this impediment didn't remove the look of interest, however.

"That's no matter. There won't be anyone but us. Do stay," Norman urged. "You can tell me when you think the fever's down enough to put on the liniment."

"I'll tell Auntie," Trudie said quickly, before Luten could change his mind or make it up really.

The excited smile that lifted her lips had to be tamed before she went frowning into the saloon. "That clunch of a Norman has asked Lord Luten for dinner," she scolded.

"What on earth for?"

"He's giving Norman a hand with True Lady's swollen leg. It'll take half the night, so we can hardly turn him from the door without feeding him."

"Is Peter with him?" Mrs. Harrington asked, hoping to find some good in the arrangement.

"No, he and Sir Charles have left. It'll just be Lord Luten. I'll tell the Bogmans."

The Bogmans were made aware that the table was to be loaded with every piece of silver in the house, the best crystal and dishes, and Trudie herself went into the garden and grabbed a handful of early flowers for a centerpiece. She wouldn't change, since Luten must wear his afternoon clothes, but Mrs. Harrington had no intention of entertaining a marquess in anything but her best burgundy silk and white wool shawl.

She sat as stiff and forbidding as an archbishop when Luten and Norman came in after washing up. Luten made a graceful bow and melted some small ice buildup by looking around the room and congratulating her on its renovation.

"You are an admirable housekeeper, ma'am. I was afraid, when Mr. Johnson showed me the damage done by his tenants last year, that Northfield would become an eyesore to the community. You have achieved remarkable results in a very short time."

She pulled in her chin and received this praise with dignity. "We never would have let Norman hire it if we'd had any idea how bad it was."

"I noticed your gardener has cleaned up the grounds as well," Luten said.

Having a gardener added to the household went down very well. "You'll soon see more improvements in that regard now that spring has finally arrived," Mrs. Harrington said. "I think I can rescue some of those roses in front, now that the weeds have been rooted out. I should like to set Bogman to work with a bucket of paint as well, but it would hardly pay, when we shan't be here long."

"Such an outlay as that is best restricted to your own

property," he agreed, and received a chilly smile for his proper thinking.

It wasn't till Luten proclaimed the ham the best he had ever tasted that the chill melted from his hostess's smile. By the time he had requested her chef's receipt for peach chantilly, he was accepted enough that she confessed she had no chef, but only a plain cook. "For in the country, you know, hiring a male chef is considered showing off. No one has one but Lord Gratton, and he is in London three-quarters of the time."

Trudie found herself strangely tongue-tied, and though she squirmed at many of her aunt's rustic utterances, she could think of nothing clever to say herself. Even when a speech occurred to her, she heard it as one in a dream, being passed to Luten through the medium of Aunt Gertrude.

"Perhaps Lord Luten would like some more chantilly, Auntie," she suggested.

"There's plenty left," Mrs. Harrington said, reaching for his plate. "These youngsters will be gobbling it up for breakfast if we don't get rid of it. You wouldn't believe what Norman ate this morning. Two pieces of apple tart and a glass of milk. If he had waited ten minutes, Bogman would have had gammon and eggs on the table, but no, he must bolt his food and run. It's all the fault of this racing mania that's struck him down. We'll be fortunate if he doesn't bankrupt us."

A little later, Trudie suggested to her aunt that "Perhaps Lord Luten would like another cup of coffee."

"If he's not afraid of being awake half the night, I'm sure he's welcome to it."

"It's been an hour, Luten. I think I'll nip down to the stable, but you stay and have more coffee by all means, if you like," Norman said.

Luten knew what was expected of him and declined the

second cup. "We'll have port when we come back," Norman said.

There was no point lingering at the table, so the ladies retired to the saloon. "Lord Luten seems a rational man. I cannot for the life of me imagine what got into him in London, to be playing off those practical jokes."

It was still odd, but not so odd as it had been before the request for the peach chantilly receipt. The ladies heard Norman and Luten return to the dining room for port. Trudie thought that on this unusual occasion port might be taken in the saloon without breaking any important laws of etiquette. Luten thought so too, and suggested it to his host.

It seemed the evening was to be a repetition of dinner, with Trudie sitting tongue-tied while Mrs. Harrington pointed out to their guest where she had mended the hole burned in the sofa, and the six gouges in the marble mantel from what she was convinced could only be bullets. Luten was suitably impressed with all these domestic details. Before he could find a moment for any private talk with Trudie, Norman hauled him off to the stable again.

In fifteen minutes they were back. The fever was rapidly coming down—another half hour should lower it enough to apply the liniment. Trudie determined that she'd make good use of that half hour and spoke up brightly to Luten before her aunt could ensnare him again.

Her intention was to be charming and gracious, but as this eliminated virtually all of their past encounters, she heard herself saying, "What do you think of Peter's having bought a colt and joined turfing society, Lord Luten?" She thought she already knew his opinion on that score, and regretted that their first private talk must be a harangue.

His mild answer amazed her. "I'm not surprised. I only wish he had consulted me before making his purchase. If you're going to race horses, then you ought to race ones that stand some chance of winning."

"You don't give Fandango much chance?"

"Not much, the way he's being trained. It will be a lesson to Peter. Horse-racing is like everything else—you may hear lectures till the cows home, but in the end, we all learn by making our own mistakes." He looked across the room, where Norman was talking with his aunt. Assured of some privacy, Luten began veering toward more personal matters. "I, of all people, am in no position to accuse anyone of making mistakes. I hope I haven't stumbled into your black books again by coming here this evening, after having been hinted away. Norman asked me to come and take a look at True Lady—I hadn't meant to hang on so long."

She was impressed at the change in his attitude and rushed in to assure him of his welcome. "I was only afraid Auntie would fly into the boughs, but you've conned her entirely, so it's no matter now."

His lips moved unsteadily at her plain speaking. "It took some doing, I can tell you! I shall be eternally grateful to the clutch of scoundrels who defiled Johnson's saloon."

"Well, I shall not! It took us hours to cover up the sofa arm, and besides it still looks hideous."

"I've done my duty in regard to the fixing up of this saloon, Miss Barten. I hoped we might speak of other things."

"Oh!" she said, on a soft breath of pleasure. "What other things did you have in mind? You must know by now that I'm no wizard in horse management."

"I've also done my duty in that respect, with Norman. There are other subjects available to us."

"Yes," she agreed, but none occurred to her.

"You're acquainted with Mr. O'Kelly, I think?" he asked.

She assumed the subject he had chosen was jealousy of a rival and was well satisfied with it. "More than acquainted. We are very good friends," she replied.

The quick scowl that drew his brows together was gratifying. "You choose your friends as badly as Norman chooses a filly."

"Why, Lord Luten, you're not suggesting that Mr. O'Kelly toes in!" she laughed. "I have always found him to be in excellent form."

"You'll discover an odd kick in his gallop before the Season's over. O'Kelly is a parasite. He lives off credulous youngsters. I wish I could discourage you from any association with him."

"He'd have slim pickings trying to live off Norman," she answered bluntly.

"Quite—it can't be Norman he's after. I'm afraid it must be Peter."

"Then it would be up to *you* to handle him, *n'est-ce-pas*? I seem to recall you handled that other parasite, whom you imagined to be gulling Peter, quite effectively. Perhaps you could arrange another of those delightful Kent Street Ejections."

"I had nothing to do with that! My dish is full enough without ladling that mess into it. And I was certainly not putting you and your aunt in the same class as O'Kelly. He is dangerous; you are merely . . ." He came to a stop as a pair of brilliant hazel eyes examined him.

"Pray continue."

"Oh, no. We've just begun to be friends. I came here tonight for that reason. You shan't goad me into folly this time."

The tea tray was brought in, and the company sat together around the table. Any privacy was over, but there was one more effort at friendship before Luten left for the stables with Norman.

"Since True Lady won't be working out tomorrow, Norman," Luten said, "it would be a good time for you to have a look at Cheveley Park. I promised to take you there one day. I have a mare who is due anytime now, and I'll be

141

going to have a look at her. Would you and Miss Barten care to come along? And Mrs. Harrington as well, of course, if she's interested.''

Mrs. Harrington declined at once. Trudie was of two minds. She wanted to see Luten again, but almost any other place than a stud farm would have been more pleasing to her. When Luten mentioned his hope that they would take tea with him after at Sable Lodge, her mind was made up.

''It sounds lovely!'' she said.

''I should like it of all things!'' Norman exclaimed, much more enthusiastically.

This was the subject of discussion till tea was finished. Mrs. Harrington took little interest in it, but she was always happy for any treat that came Norman's way, and remained friendly. It was after nine when the gentlemen returned to the stable, and Mrs. Harrington decided it would be overly civil to receive Lord Luten again that night. She and Trudie left the saloon.

It proved unnecessary. Luten did not return to the house but expressed his thanks to his hostess through Norman and left. Trudie spoke to her brother after their aunt went upstairs.

''Did Lord Luten say anything about Okay O'Kelly?'' she asked. Her real aim was to hear what he had said of her, but Norman, being a male, was unaware of her subtlety.

''Yes, he says we ought to stay away from him. To tell the truth, I had begun to suspect he ain't quite the thing. I've heard a few unsavory comments. Mind you, he knows as much about winning races as anyone on the turf, but I think I shall hint him away from taking his lunch here.''

''But what's the matter with him? He seems very nice.''

''He had some run-ins with the Jockey Club. None of the old track hands have a good word to say for him. It's only the new ones, like Nick and Peter and me, that give him the time of day. Luten is a good fellow, ain't he? The way Peter talks, I thought he'd be a mile high in the instep, but it's no such a thing. Taking us to Cheveley—imagine! And he was more than polite to you and Auntie too. Lord, I nearly died to hear her blabbing all that stuff about not being able to afford painting the house. I have half a mind to set Bogman at it.''

''Why don't you?'' Trudie urged.

''Because I can't afford it. The way Fandango is eating up the stalls, I'll have to rebuild the stables when we leave. Speaking of eating,'' he added, ''did Luten finish the peach chantilly?''

''No, there's some left.''

They went to the kitchen, and Norman ate his breakfast a few hours early. Trudie's closest questioning did not reveal a single word Luten had said about her, except that he feared she would be bored at Cheveley Park, and he was a little surprised she had accepted the invitation. She feared she had slipped into hoydendom again, but this time it was Luten's fault, so her mind was easy.

Chapter Fourteen

The sky was so heavy with clouds the next morning that Norman doubted he could have taken True Lady to the tracks, even if her leg had been better. No matter how black the sky, it wasn't dark enough to shadow his spirits that day, with the trip to Cheveley Park before him. Trudie didn't think the clouds would keep Mr. O'Kelly from his lunch either and was a little worried that Norman would be rude to him when he arrived, but luck was with her. Mr. O'Kelly, having learned that Norman was at home, stayed away.

"I wonder where Mr. O'Kelly is," Mrs. Harrington said when they had taken their places at the table.

"You don't mean he comes every day!" Norman scowled.

"No, certainly not," she assured him, though he came often enough that she had to lower her brows at Trudie to keep her silent.

"I mean to hint O'Kelly away from us. Nick was telling me this morning when he came for Lightning that Luten gave O'Kelly a warning as well."

"Against coming to us?" Mrs. Harrington demanded, fire in her eye. If this was one of Luten's jokes, it wasn't funny. And if he was serious, it was even less humorous. "I hardly think we are so close to Luten that he can decide whom we entertain under our own roof.''

"No, he warned him from trying to gull Peter," Norman explained. "Luten did a little checking up at the inn, and it seems O'Kelly hasn't paid a penny since he moved in there. He's run up an enormous bill and still owes something at the other place he was staying as well. He left his watch as security.''

"He takes a bit much on himself, to be blackening Mr. O'Kelly's good name with that sort of carrying on. Furthermore, it's ridiculous," Mrs. Harrington declared. "O'Kelly is well to grass. He owns a thousand acres of prime dairy land in Ireland. And what did he pay for Sheba, Trudie? Some enormous sum there as well. Very likely that is what's left him a little short.''

To hear Norman issue a decree was a new thing. As far as Mrs. Harrington was concerned, the matter of Mr. O'Kelly's admission to Northfield was left up in the air, and that was exactly where she wanted to keep it. She had developed a maternal interest in him, and if the poor lad was actually hungry and unable to pay for a meal, why, it would be unchristian to turn him off. She must certainly guide him away from the turf before Trudie fell in love with him, though. An estate encumbered with mortgages was not what she wanted for her niece.

Miss Barten listened in silence. She was not unusually vain, but she was intelligent enough to know that Luten liked her, and she put his condemnation of O'Kelly down to jealousy as much as anything else. She wouldn't encourage O'Kelly, but she wasn't docile enough to cut him dead only because Luten wanted it.

She went upstairs immediately after lunch and began her toilette for the trip to Sable Lodge. In her mind, that was the real treat of the day. Careless of what outfit might suit a stud farm, she knew well enough what would look well behind a tea table afterward, and put on her prettiest sarsenet gown of forest green, which turned her eyes to emerald. She brushed her coppery curls till they glowed, and made sure to take her best lace-edged handkerchief to hold to her nose at Cheveley Park.

At one minute to two, Norman's chaise drew up to Sable Lodge. "I say, this is a bit of all right, ain't it?" he said as they approached the sprawling brick house. There was no peeling paint in evidence here, no weed-strangled garden or dusty windows. They were met at the door by a butler and shown into a saloon done up in the first style of fashion. Lord Luten came to greet them even before he was called, and offered wine.

"Couldn't we do that after we come back from Cheveley Park?" Norman asked, so eagerly that no one had the heart to deny his wish.

They transferred to Luten's stylish carriage for the short trip, just half a mile up the road past the Boy's Grave. Cheveley Park was not so grand as Norman had been imagining. The setting was picturesque, with old stands of cedars, backed by limes, but the stud groom's lodge was a small brick affair built onto an insignificant cottage. The stables loomed behind, and as soon as they dismounted, that old familiar reek of horses assailed Trudie's nostrils.

Lord Luten made them acquainted with Mr. Heffernan, whom he called Heff. The man looked like an ordinary provincial groom. He wore a somewhat grimed jacket, and longish hair, but there was an alert intelligence in his eyes and an air of authority that put him on equal terms with his noble patrons.

"You've come to have a look at your Athene, have you, Luten?" he smiled. "Your groom is there. I was about to go to her myself. Her teats had lost their wax this morning, and a bit of milk was oozing out, so she'll be due today. Now, you mustn't worry yourself. She's healthy and roomy. All will go fine.''

Heffernan led them to the brood mare's paddock. As they walked down the hall, lined with stalls on either side, Norman felt that this was about as close to heaven as he was likely to come, unless by some miracle he actually won the Triple Crown. He had never seen such a collection of prime horseflesh. Knotted muscles were coated in oil-smooth shades of gold and brown and black. The mares were high-strung thoroughbreds. They snorted and pranced and stamped the ground.

From a stall at the end, there issued an almost insane whinnying. "She's coming. She's coming!" Heffernan shouted, and ran forward, with Luten a step behind him. Norman hastened his pace as well, but Trudie lagged. She took one peek into the stall and fell back. She saw a mare on her side, her head tossing, her eyes alive with fear. Her coat was covered with curdled sweat, and she thrashed about on the floor, with a horse doctor and the other men huddled around her.

Suddenly Trudie felt faint. She turned and ran from the barn, out into the fresh air. Though she had been raised on a farm, she took little interest in animals. She had witnessed a foaling before and found it frightening. She didn't want to see the foal struggling to its feet in the slippery afterbirth, looking as if it were not quite ready to be born yet, with its unopened eyes. She walked around the grounds for half an hour, and when she returned to the barn, the men were just coming out.

"What a splendid delivery!" Norman exclaimed. His eyes were bright, and in his excitement, he babbled like a boy. "She's a girl, Trudie!" he called. "That is, a filly," he amended when Heffernan let out a burst of laughter. "What will you call her, Luten?"

"Perhaps Miss Barten can tell us what Athene's daughter ought to be called," he said, turning to Trudie.

"I'm afraid you've presented me with an impossible job, milord. Pallas Athene didn't have a daughter."

"Then we'll call her Minerva, the Roman counterpart of Athene. As she had a Latin scholar present at her birth—or nearly—we must give her a classical name. Why did you leave? Don't tell me a country-bred lady is squeamish!"

"Count yourself lucky that she did leave," Norman said. "Athene whinnying her head off was bad enough. If Trudie had been there, she'd have been hollering louder than the mare. But you should have stayed, Trudie. Minerva was on her feet within five or ten minutes, a regular Trojan. I wouldn't be surprised if she's feeding already. Can we have a look around at the rest of the setup, Luten?"

"Shall we begin with last year's Derby winner? Heff, Lord Simcoe won't mind if I show my friends his stalls."

It seemed a long time to Trudie that she was walked through barns, being told by Norman, and often Luten as well, that every bit of blood she looked at was "the best in England," and in some moments of excess, "the best in the world." All had "the look of eagles" in their eyes, but it more closely resembled the look of a mischievous boy to her.

At last the tour was done, and they returned to Luten's carriage for the drive to Sable Lodge. Norman's day was over, but Trudie's was just beginning. She was shown upstairs to a chamber to freshen up and spent the greater part of her time admiring the brocade draperies and bed hangings, the gleam of polished mahogany and the soft woolen carpet. She found herself wondering what Luten's London house was like, and his country estate. He had hinted that he'd like her to attend his ball, and now that he had weaseled his way into Mrs. Harrington's and Norman's affection, the offer might be renewed. But how could they accept, when hiring

148

Northfield and training True Lady had eaten up all their money?

She went belowstairs and found Luten alone in the saloon. It was a handsome but not overpowering room. There was a masculine air about it, conferred by the heavy furnishings, the oak paneling, and the rather plain decor. Luten poured wine and brought her a glass. He sat beside her on the sofa and smiled a warm smile.

"Norman will join us shortly. He's still freshening up. I'm afraid today's outing was no treat for you, Miss Barten. To tell the truth, I was surprised—delighted!—that you accepted."

"Oh, well, I've heard the boys talking about Cheveley Park forever and was curious to have a look at it."

"Norman's had his treat. Next time, I shall devise an outing to please you. What would *you* like to do?"

Nothing about Newmarket pleased her entirely. She would have liked to attend a ball or at least a rout party but could hardly suggest such a troublesome entertainment.

"We might drive over to Cambridge one afternoon. Would you be interested to see where Norman studied?"

"That wouldn't be much fun for Norman," she parried.

There was no misinterpreting the warm look in his eyes. He spoke on to make his meaning perfectly clear. "I meant just the two of us. Would you like to see it? There are some lovely drives and walks around the university."

She felt a warm flush suffuse her cheeks and found herself slipping once more into rusticity. "Mrs. Harrington would have something to say about that. She's very strict about whom I drive out with."

"I had the distinct impression in London that it was you who were in charge. You convinced her that Mr. Mandeville was acceptable; surely you can sway her opinion of Lord Luten."

Norman came pouncing in at the door before anything

was settled about the outing, but in the bottom of her heart, Trudie felt that something much more important had been accomplished. Luten wouldn't have asked her to drive out with him alone if he weren't seriously interested. Not necessarily in love, she admitted, but at least interested enough that he wanted to know her better. She was hard put to imagine what had attracted him. He had seen her always at her worst. She wasn't wealthy enough that her dowry could be the motive, and she didn't even profess any love in racing, his avocation. What could he possibly see in her?

They went to the dining room, where she presided over the teapot, feeling ill at ease under Luten's scrutiny; but with Norman present to keep the conversation rolling, there were no embarrassing silences. It wasn't a conversation that showed her in her best light. They spoke of horse breeding. "Breed the best to the best, and hope for the best" was their motto. The aim was "a nick of the right bloodliness"—that magical chemistry that occurred only one time in ten thousand and brought forth a winner.

"And even if you're fortunate to breed that special one," Luten said, "that's just the beginning. Then there is the long and expensive process of training, and hoping that nothing happens to break the horse's spirit—or his legs. Horse-racing is called a rich man's game; I think it ought by rights to be called a rich fool's game. It requires life-long dedication."

Norman sat listening, not frowning exactly, but with a pensive look about him. "I daresay it's pretty uncommon for a chap to win a big race his only—his first season at it."

"As far as I know, it would be unique," Luten said.

"Did you ever hear of a nag that toes in winning the Triple Crown, Luten?" Norman asked.

He shook his head. "When you realize you've landed yourself with a flawed nag, the only thing is to get rid of it and start over. Sell or trade it, and . . ."

"I could never sell True Lady!" he objected. "She's like a part of me."

"You have to be hard, Norman. Racing's part business."

"But when she looks at me, Luten . . . Oh, dash it, you must know what I mean."

"Yes, I know what you mean. She might win a few smaller races for you, and at the very least, she'll make a good hack. Take her home to Walbeck and keep her for a spare mount. Who is looking after Walbeck during your absence?"

Norman was lured into a description of Walbeck Park. He felt a lump rise up in his throat as he remembered his heritage. No other brick home seemed to glow so beautifully in the sunlight. And the setting too, backed by a rising hill, with three spreading elms at the summit, was like something out of a painting. He had intended to enlarge the conservatory for his aunt this spring. The wheat would be in by now; the rolling fields of new green shoots was a particular delight to him every spring. His dairy herd too would be increasing, and the sheep yeaning. But his sister thought that it was the silent memory of Georgiana Halley that brought that suspicion of a mist to her brother's eyes.

"I hope you've left it in good hands. It sounds an excellent estate," Luten said.

"Neighbors, the Alexanders, are running it for me. I daresay old George forgot to mend the east fence. Betsy is a terror for sneaking through the fence and foraging in the road. She'll get run down by a carriage if he ain't careful. She's the best milcher there ever was, Luten. And produces the best milchers too. She's getting on now, old Betsy. I hope she don't decide to stick her fork in the wall while I'm away."

"Don't be morose, Norman!" his sister exclaimed. "Mr. Alexander would let us know if any such a thing happened."

151

"He didn't let me know the old oak tree in the meadow got knocked down by lightning. I had to hear of it from Georgiana."

"Not the old oak!" she exclaimed, but almost as disappointing was to hear that he was corresponding with Georgiana.

"I always hire a steward myself," Luten said blandly. "A farmer working his own place can't reasonably be expected to put anyone else's interest before his own. It's a big job, running two estates."

"There's no point going back home now, even if True Lady hasn't any real chance of winning. I've let the place for a year, you see. And besides me, there're Trudie and Aunt Gertrude to think of. I couldn't expect Geo— anyone to take two ladies into the house for the better part of a year."

"That's true. The ladies have certainly been subjected to more than enough inconvenience already." Luten said no more, but Norman was intelligent enough to acknowledge that he'd been foolish, and extremely selfish as well. In fact, that suspicion had already occurred to him more than once. He felt guilty when the ladies talked about their old friends, and regretted missing certain social functions at home.

The tea was excellent, and very daintily served, but after the discussion of Walbeck, a pall descended on the party. As soon as they had finished, Norman suggested he and Trudie ought to go home. They thanked him for the outing and parted on good terms. Luten went out to the carriage with them and found a moment to speak to Trudie in private while Norman had a word with his horses. He always greeted them by name and said good-bye when he left.

"I hope you don't think I've been too hard on him. Someone ought to have said what I said before now. This was a harebrained scheme, rooting you and your aunt out of your home and squandering good money on a bad horse. He has no chance of winning, you know, and the sooner he gets back to his real business, the better it will be for him.''

''I hope you haven't given him the idea he should go home and get married. That's the main reason I went along with it—to prevent him from marrying Miss Halley.''

''Is it the institution or the woman you object to?'' he asked archly.

''The woman.''

''What is amiss with Miss Halley?''

''Nothing in particular. Norman's only twenty years old, and Georgiana is barely eighteen.''

''That is a bit young, but absence makes the heart grow fonder, you know. You may have inadvertently rushed the wedding forward. He looked quite wistful. I couldn't figure out whether it was Betsy or Georgiana he was missing.''

''There's not that much difference between them,'' she snipped. ''A great, placid, cow-eyed girl.''

''A placid woman would suit Norman. He's not exactly a high liver. I can see him happily settled down with a brood around his easy chair.''

''Can you see Mrs. Harrington and me as part of the brood? It's the Halleys' easy chair he'd have to occupy if he went home before the year was up. I, for one, have no intention of billeting myself on the Halleys. I'd rather go back to Conduit Street and have the neighbors all smirking at me.''

''I happen to know a little cottage standing vacant at Tunbridge Wells,'' he said with a mischievous smile.

She had been uneasy ever since she had learned Norman was writing to Georgiana. His stumbling mention of her and Aunt Gertrude staying with the Halleys had further unnerved her, and she knew that such a thing had never occurred to Norman before Luten had put the idea into his head that he was selfish and foolish. That she agreed with Luten did nothing to alleviate her ire.

She stuck out her chin and answered before thinking.

"I'm sure you'll soon have it occupied, if you can convince any of your high flyers to leave London, that is."

Norman turned back from the carriage, waiting for his sister to join him. "Thanks again, Luten. I'll let you know how True Lady's leg is coming along."

"I'll drop around your place and have a look at her. About True Lady's gallop, Norman. It isn't desperate, you know. I'll speak to the men at Danebury and see if they have any ideas. There might be some exercise to help her or some contraption they can attach to her fetlock to straighten out that ankle. Possibly by next year . . ."

"I won't be here next year," Norman said sullenly. "I shouldn't be here now, if I had any sense."

Trudie cast one long, accusing stare at Luten. "Thank you so much for your *help*," she said, and strode angrily to the carriage.

Chapter Fifteen

Mrs. Harrington and Trudie felt bad when Mr. O'Kelly didn't show up for luncheon the next day. They feared Norman had hinted him away, and Trudie at least knew it was Luten who had put him up to it. A further strain was put on family relations by Norman's morose mood. He wasn't surly or authoritative—he was much worse. He turned solicitous on them. With True Lady incapacitated, he was around the house more than was quite comfortable, and finding a fault with everything. The house was a shambles; he must have been mad to bring them there, when they had a fine home at Walbeck Park.

"Nonsense, it is much better than our rooms in London," Mrs. Harrington assured him. "And with us all staying together, it is cheaper too."

"I am a selfish fiend," Norman mourned. "You should have told me what a jackanapes I was. I don't know the first thing about racing, and after seeing those bloods at Cheveley Park, I am convinced there's no hope of winning anything with a filly who toes in. Mind you, she's a beauty for all that. Maybe the groom from Danebury will come up with something."

"I thought you had no opinion of the Danebury method," his aunt reminded him.

"I won't let them do anything that will hurt True Lady. I believe I'll go down now and make sure that bandage we put on this morning isn't too tight."

Mrs. Harrington looked at her niece and said, "You know what this fit of the dismals is about?"

"It's waking up to reality, I suppose. We were stupid to go along with this idea."

"Reality—aye, there's the culprit, but it's not True Lady that worries him. It is that untrue chit of a Georgiana Halley. I had a letter from her mother this morning. She made two mentions of Georgiana's going out with Harold Rampling."

"Good!" Trudie exclaimed.

"Rubbish. If she had any notion of accepting him, she wouldn't have told Norman. She's only trying to frighten him back home."

"You shouldn't have showed him the letter."

"He grabbed it out of my hand before I had a chance to read it myself. It was addressed to the family. I have no objection to Georgiana—she is very eligible and docile."

"And a barnacle," Trudie added.

The mood lightened somewhat when Norman sent word upstairs that he was taking a ride over to the tracks to see Peter and Nick. It brightened further when O'Kelly came prancing to the door a quarter of an hour before lunch and was persuaded to take his mutton with them.

"We've missed you, Mr. O'Kelly," Trudie said.

"As to that, you may as well get accustomed to my absence, ma'am," he informed her. There was an air of gravity about him that was very becoming. His blue eyes, usually dancing, were clouded with sorrow. She felt he had come to tell them he was *persona non grata* at Northfield and was squirming in embarrassment.

When Mrs. Harrington declared firmly, "You are always welcome here, Mr. O'Kelly," she knew her aunt felt the same thing.

"You have always made me feel so." He smiled for-lornly. "But I shall be leaving the neighborhood entirely, and unless I can convince you to visit me at Doneraile, I fear this may be the last time we meet."

"Going home! Why, what has happened?" Mrs. Har-rington demanded as she piled the cold mutton on his plate, and he looked around the table for hot mustard.

"It is a family matter," he said reluctantly. "I shan't trouble you ladies with a litany of my problems."

His genteel reluctance was soon overborne, and the sad tale came pouring out. "It's my sister," he said. His low-ered eyes rested on his plate, a set of infamously long lashes making a curled crescent below. "I don't know whether I told you about Maureen. She's a widow—three children to clothe and feed. I've been giving her what help I can—financial help, that is. In fact, just last month I had to send her rather a large sum of money to pay her mortgage. It left me short myself, but I don't mind that. Now it seems she owes a few debts back home, and the bailiff is after her. I must abandon racing this year and go home to help her. Even Sheba, I fear, must go." He drew a long sigh and slowly picked up his fork.

"What a pity!" Trudie said. "Norman says she has the fastest time of any blood he's checked on the track. Couldn't you borrow . . ."

He shook his head. "I wouldn't want to fall into debt. And I doubt anyone would lend me money in any case. Lu-ten has been bruiting my business about town. I blush to confess it, but I have been asked to either pay my bill or leave the Golden Lion. I've been living on tick till my mon-ies arrive from Ireland, you see. They have become rather peremptory about it. I plan to sell Sheba and pay my bills with the proceeds. That will leave me plenty to get home and see what I can do about Maureen."

"I don't see what business it is of Luten's!" Trudie exclaimed.

O'Kelly just shook his head at her naivete. "He wants to win the Triple Crown himself. He knows he hasn't a chance while Sheba is running, and this is the ruse he's used to be rid of the competition."

"But won't whoever buys her win, and still defeat Luten?" Mrs. Harrington asked.

O'Kelly disliked such reasonable questions from a lady. He expected better of her and had to do some quick thinking. "He'll be after her himself, if I know anything. I've had a very good offer from a fellow who I happen to know hasn't a sou to his name. He offered cash. He's a very close friend of Lord Luten," he added significantly, and looked to see if Mrs. Harrington was clever enough to interpret this as he wished.

She didn't disappoint him. "You mean he's acting for Luten—buying Sheba for him!"

"Precisely. Of course, he didn't admit it, but I don't know who else would be in a position to offer me seven hundred guineas for her."

"That is shocking connivance. I am surprised at Luten," she said.

"Well, I am not," O'Kelly stated solemnly. "Badly as I need the money, however, I shan't sell to Luten, not even indirectly. Luten runs his horses into the ground. They seldom last longer than two seasons under his training. Someone like Norman, who feels as I do that racers have feelings . . ."

"Norman isn't in a position to buy such an expensive filly," Trudie said quickly.

Mrs. Harrington nodded her head in agreement. "Kind of you to offer, Mr. O'Kelly, but it just isn't possible."

"Naturally I wouldn't charge Norman such a sum! The half of that would see me out of my trouble. My first consideration isn't recouping the sum I paid for her but seeing she is handed over to someone who will take proper care of her.''

''Even three fifty is quite impossible,'' Trudie said.

Mr. O'Kelly accepted it without any ill-bred insisting or any further haggling. ''I just thought I might be able to do him a favor, since you have been so very kind to me.''

Mrs. Harrington smiled indulgently at his thoughtfulness and bethought herself of that hint of seeing them at Doneraile. ''Your sister, Maureen, she is entirely your responsibility, is she, Mr. O'Kelly?''

''Naturally I plan to take care of her. Family after all! But I shan't have that pleasure for long. She is extremely attractive. Some fortunate gentleman will marry her up when her half mourning is finished. It wouldn't be nice to mention names, but a certain Lord Someone has already made overtures in that direction.''

''I see.'' The ladies exchanged a look across the table. ''I hope Doneraile is doing well?'' Mrs. Harrington inquired idly.

''Excellent. Couldn't be better. I may have to cut down a few acres of hard wood that I hadn't planned to, to provide Maureen a little dot, but I shall make that up in no time. My dairy herd promises excellent increase this spring. I wish I could show you Doneraile. My place is just on the north shore of Dingle Bay. You haven't seen green till you've come to Ireland. I'd like to take you out in my yacht one day too. Is there any chance I might convince you to hop across the Channel and spend a little time with me before you return to Walbeck Park?''

''That would take a little planning,'' Mrs. Harrington said, but her tone was by no means repressive.

Over an apple tart, Mr. O'Kelly's favorite dessert, a time was discussed. Nothing definite was settled, but the ladies rather thought that after the Triple Crown, and before their year's exile from Walbeck Park was over, seemed the most appropriate. Norman too was invited *in absentia*, and promised a pleasant visit, for Mr. O'Kelly's breeding stables were always busy.

He took his leave, not promising to return, but there was a possibility that he'd drop around to say good-bye, and in any case he would write. "To you, Mrs. Harrington. I know you wouldn't approve of my writing to your niece—yet." That tantalizing "yet" implied the fiancé's privilege.

"Indeed the invitation has no point unless that is what he has in mind," she explained after he left. Trudie already knew it very well, and wasn't displeased with the prospect of an offer.

"But Luten says he is not at all the thing," she countered, a frown worrying her brow.

"Of course he does! He's jealous as a green cow of Sheba. Trying to arrange a deal to buy her, using a friend as an intermediary to trick Mr. O'Kelly. But then he was always odd. You remember his coming to us under the guise of Mr. Mandeville in London, my dear. And he never did pay for that Latin lesson either. That shows a certain lack in his scruples."

"It's odd Mr. O'Kelly only has one filly here, when he has a whole breeding farm at home. Do you think he might be bamming us, Auntie?"

"I had a little suspicion of it, to tell the truth. But a man who interrupts his own business to take care of his widowed sister—that shows his true nature. She will be no bother in future either, with her three children. I could not like to see you sharing a house with so many, but she will soon marry and clear out. All that might have been invented as well, of course, but when he invited us to Doneraile—well, there is no way he could pull a fine estate and a yacht out of his pocket, is there? It must be true, or he wouldn't have invited us."

"Yes, that's true."

A very motherly smile settled on Mrs. Harrington's face. "Thoughtful of him to give Norman first bid on Sheba, and at such a bargain too! Not that I am suggesting Norman be encouraged to accept! In fact, I don't mean to mention a word of the offer to him, but there will be no difficulty selling her. Mr. O'Kelly will have enough money to pay off the inn and get home in style. That will be an exciting trip— Ireland? I wonder how much it will cost to get there. And of course we'll come home for the wedding at Walbeck Park."

"It's a bit premature to start planning the trousseau, Auntie!" Trudie laughed. It wasn't too early for a little day-dreaming, though. She pictured herself in a creamy white satin gown, with a long veil nearly touching the floor. She also pictured Lord Luten in the congregation, looking daggers at her.

Norman returned early to keep an eye on True Lady's injured leg. At five, he went to the stables to talk to Peter and Nick when they brought their racers home, and Trudie went with him. She thought Lord Luten might be there, for he had said he'd come back, but he had seen Norman at the tracks and had fallen into bad aroma again.

"He had a fellow from Danebury with him, and you'll never guess what he suggested. A restraining brace on True Lady's fetlock, pulled so tight it changes the direction of her kick! It sounded a demmed awkward contraption. Can you imagine how it would hurt the poor girl?" he said, tenderly rubbing the bandaged fetlock.

"How's Fandango working out?" Trudie asked Peter.

"He's so full of splintered wood he couldn't keep up the pace. I wish I had a filly like Sheba."

Trudie saw a means of doing both Peter and O'Kelly a favor. She found a moment to speak to Peter in private and told him the filly was for sale.

Peter's eyes grew with shock and hope. "You don't mean

161

it! Why on earth would he sell her when she's the finest bit of blood at Newmarket? And a Newmarket nag too—bound to win the Oaks at Epsom. The Boy's Grave is covered with wildflowers."

"Ask your uncle," Trudie said tartly.

"What has Luten got to do with it?"

"He caused some trouble at the Golden Lion. They've asked O'Kelly to settle his account, and his pockets are empty. He had to send his sister money for her mortgage."

"What's he asking for Sheba?"

"The price he mentioned was seven hundred guineas."

"Oh, lord, I could never raise the half of that."

"That's a pity, then, for he offered to let Norman have her for half price, to keep her out of Luten's hands. Your uncle was trying to buy her, using some go-between so O'Kelly wouldn't find it out."

"He'd have stuck Luten for a thousand," Peter laughed. "And worth it too—but why would he sell her so cheap to Norman?"

Trudie blushed prettily. "He's a good friend of the family," she said.

"He'd never let *me* have her for that price."

"He'd give you some kind of a bargain, Peter. Why don't you speak to him?"

"I will," Peter said at once. "Wouldn't I like to see the look on Luten's face when I step up to take the prizes."

"But don't tell Norman!" Trudie cautioned.

"And don't *you* tell Luten. I shall consult with Nick, though. He's a knowing 'un."

Sir Charles strolled over to chat to the others. There was a whispered conversation about Sheba's being up for sale. Nick was shocked, and soon found it suspicious.

"She's a goer, no denying, but she always races alone. Who's to say she ain't gate-shy? Luten thinks so."

Trudie and Peter exchanged a knowing look. "If that's

what you think, why don't you insist on racing her with your own nags before you buy?" Trudie suggested.

Sir Charles saw nothing wrong with this idea. He was by no means averse to outwitting Luten.

"I want to be there," Trudie said. "Let me know when the race is to be held, and Auntie and I will go."

"I'll drop around to Okay's room tonight and set it up," Peter replied.

"And if he won't race, don't buy. She's gate-shy," Sir Charles decreed.

While Peter and Sir Charles made these arrangements with a willing O'Kelly, Norman stayed home, reading and rereading Mrs. Halley's letter and silently cursing Harold Rampling. Trudie began to think that even trying to raise the wind to buy Sheba might be preferable to Norman's darting home to marry Georgiana; but before she told him the filly was for sale, there was a knock on the door, and Lord Luten was shown in.

He couldn't account for the chill in the air. Was it his having come in pantaloons when the family hadn't changed for dinner? He couldn't think so, when Miss Barten looked so very lovely in her afternoon gown of a deep peacock blue that turned her emerald eyes to sapphires. Norman, he knew, had balked at the idea of restraining True Lady's leg with a brace. Maybe that was it. He set about showing that such harshness was not his own preference.

"I think you're prudent not to go for the brace," he said, settling in for a chat. "But what will you do with True Lady? Race her and hope she doesn't injure herself?"

"Yes, I'll try her, and if she packs up on me, I shall pull her out of duty. Just keep her for a spare mount. I couldn't part with her."

Luten assumed a sympathetic pose and said, "One becomes very attached to animals."

Trudie turned a sapient eye on him and added, "Some-

163

times people are even attached to other gentlemen's animals.''

He supposed she had seen through his pose and meant he was feigning an interest in True Lady. He smiled and agreed. ''Sometimes there is a reason for doing so.''

Her nostrils pinched in scorn. ''I must congratulate you on managing to make trouble for Mr. O'Kelly at his inn, Lord Luten'' was her next conversation. ''You will be happy to hear he is returning to Ireland very soon.''

''Yes, I *am* happy. We have enough of our own blacklegs and touts around the tracks, without adding Ireland's. I wonder if he'll take Sheba with him.'' She gave him a very speaking glance but said nothing. ''Where did you hear this?'' he asked.

Mrs. Harrington frowned at her niece and said, ''Peter and Sir Charles dropped around this afternoon.'' It wasn't a lie, she consoled herself. It just didn't answer his question. She wasn't morally obliged to answer any question Luten decided to pose.

''They didn't mention it to me,'' Norman said.

''It was Trudie who heard it,'' Mrs. Harrington prevaricated—still not lying. She didn't say Trudie had heard it from Peter or Sir Charles.

''Did he try to sell them his nag?'' Luten asked swiftly. There was a spark in his eye, easily misread to show jealousy.

''No, he didn't,'' Trudie answered, also not lying, but certainly concealing the whole truth.

''He'll palm her off on some gullible soul before he goes,'' Luten said. ''She might make a good brood mare.''

''Are you interested in purchasing her, Lord Luten?'' Trudie asked bluntly.

''I might be, but not at the price O'Kelly will be asking.''

''What would you consider a fair price?''

''I might go as high as fifty guineas. That's what he paid

for her. She was so wild they couldn't do anything with her at Cheveley Park. She don't care for stallions, so even breeding could prove a problem, you see.''

"I understood Mr. O'Kelly paid somewhat more than that," Trudie said. She didn't even try to keep the scorn from her tone.

Luten lifted a black brow. "You mustn't believe everything you hear, ma'am."

"I am perfectly aware of that, milord."

Norman had roused himself from his reveries of Walbeck Park and Georgiana and noticed some tension in the air. To alleviate it, he offered wine. Luten accepted a glass, but he could see he was making no headway with Miss Barten. Something had put her in the boughs. He decided she had still not forgiven him for having made Norman aware of his family duties. He wanted to give a hint that there was a better house waiting for her than the cottage at Tunbridge Wells, if she didn't wish to live with Norman and Miss Halley. It was difficult to do, with Mrs. Harrington in one corner of the room and Norman in the other.

His opportunity did not come till he was leaving. Her offer to accompany him to the door gave rise to hope. "We haven't arranged a day for our drive to Cambridge yet," he said, as though the outing was settled and only the date remained.

At the bottom of her heart, Trudie still harbored some resentment about Luten's treatment of her in London. It was aggravated now by his underhanded dealings in trying to get Sheba from Mr. O'Kelly. And though Lord Luten quite obviously admired her looks, his slippery character made her doubt a serious interest in her. The best she could hope for was a month's flirtation at Newmarket while he was deprived of his regular flirts. Such a man ought to be taught a lesson, and once Peter was safely in possession of Sheba, she wanted to see Luten's face.

He stood entranced while these thoughts were mirrored in her eyes. He saw the flash of scheming, the light of interest, and the final smile of satisfaction. "I've been wondering if you had forgotten," she said archly.

"No, certainly not. I couldn't forsake True Lady in her hour of need, but I think I can safely divert my attention to the first lady of *my* choice now. Shall we say, the day after tomorrow?"

She smiled again, in relief that he hadn't named tomorrow. She thought Peter and Mr. O'Kelly would arrange the race for tomorrow, since Mr. O'Kelly was so anxious to get his money and return to Ireland. "I'm flattered that only True Lady takes precedence over me!" she laughed. A set of matching dimples quivered at the corners of her lips. He stared, entranced, then peeped into the saloon, where neither Mrs. Harrington nor Norman was in his line of view.

He lifted a finger and traced the dimples, first on one cheek, then the other. "Charming. You should smile more often, Miss Barten."

"You should be at more pains to amuse me," she answered pertly.

The dark eyes that gazed into hers weren't smiling. There was a serious light in them, heavily tinged with admiration. "I shall take that as an invitation to return soon, and often, to Northfield. I can't amuse you from Sable Lodge."

"I'm sure Norman would be happy for your company," she said in confusion. "We—we are home most evenings."

"Then I shall do myself the honor of calling on Norman very soon. And if his sister happens also to be home—would *she* feel any pleasure to receive me?"

She stood mute, just looking at him. What struck her forcibly enough to turn her silent was the way he looked—just the way Norman looked at Georgiana. She would have been horrified to know she looked very much the same way herself.

Luten lifted her fingers to his lips and kissed them, without ever taking his eyes from hers. This simple gesture moved her as his violent attack in the carriage had not. He hardly seemed to be the same man. All the arrogance had gone out of him. She had to remind herself that he had caused so much trouble for Mr. O'Kelly.

"You'd better go now, Luten," she said softly.

"I had better, before I do something you will dislike. I hope the next time, you won't dislike it so much."

She didn't have to ask his meaning; she had just been thinking of it herself. She did feel obliged to conceal the fact, and looked at him questioningly. "What do you mean?"

"Just what you think, Miss Barten. *À demain.*"

He bowed, set his curled beaver on his head, and left. Trudie soon made an excuse to retire to her room. Was it possible she had attached two gentlemen in one day? It looked very much like it. Her mind told her Mr. O'Kelly was the more worthy of her affection, but her heart couldn't quite come to terms with it. When she went to bed, it was Luten's face that was in her mind—the way he had looked when he kissed her fingers. A deep look, right into her soul.

And what a nest of intrigue was there! She'd gone behind his back, involving Peter in buying Sheba. What if Sheba was really an unmanageable filly, and Peter went into hock to buy her? What if O'Kelly had only paid fifty guineas, when he'd said he paid seven hundred? But if that were so, O'Kelly wouldn't consent to the race. She hoped he wouldn't. She hoped she'd never see Okay O'Kelly again. It never even occurred to her to tell Luten the truth, and reveal herself such a bad judge of character.

Chapter Sixteen

O'Kelly moved with such celerity in arranging the race that Lord Clappet had to scramble to raise the funds to buy Sheba. His options were few. The bank wouldn't lend him another penny, and in any case there wasn't time to return to London. Luten, besides being a regular skint, would be against the plan. Neither Norman nor Sir Charles had any spare money. Clappet cast his eyes over his possessions and began selecting those to be placed on the shelf. His watch, a fine Breguet, was the first thing to go. Various fobs, tiepins, the beloved crop, and a set of chased silver brushes and comb were added to the pile on his bed.

Sir Charles eyed them askance. "You're looking at ten guineas—fifteen tops," he informed his friend.

"Demme I paid that much for my watch alone."

"Very true, but you ain't buying now; you're selling. Used merchandise. Besides, look at the gouge in that silver-backed brush," Sir Charles said, shaking his pretty curls in dismay. "We both know what has to go if you want Sheba, my friend. Your gig."

"You mean my curricle!" Clappet corrected with an icy stare. Meaner wits might insist on calling a gig a gig, but it was curricle-hung and ornamented with all manner of silver-mounted lamps, sword case, and splashing boards.

"Curricle," Sir Charles agreed, biting back a smile. "You can jog along without it. You have a phaeton."

"I don't have it here."

"You might buy yourself a proper curricle, after Sheba wins a few matches for you."

This rosy future mitigated Clappet's sorrow remarkably. "What do you figure I might get for it?" he asked.

"Selling it in a blind rush, I'd say fifty guineas. With those toys on the bed, that makes sixty-five. Put Fandango on the block, and you're looking at two sixty-five. I know, you paid more than two hundred for Fandango, but selling in a blind panic, you know, you'll be lucky to get half what you paid."

"It seems a shame to be giving away all my worldly possessions."

"Okay's in a heat to get home to his widowed sister."

"I have some money left—the training expenses and the track fees I paid in advance, but I have living money for the inn and so on," Clappet said, thinking aloud.

"How much?"

"Three hundred."

"Okay's a reasonable man. We'll work out something. Perhaps he'd take the junk as part of the payment, and hawk it himself. I know he don't have a watch, for he had to leave it as security at the inn he first stayed at."

They had only an hour in which to peddle Clappet's wares. At Sir Charles's suggestion, they got a written estimate from the pawn shops for the personal objects, and from a carriage shop for the gig-curricle. Peter withdrew his three hundred from the bank, and at one o'clock they headed out to the spot chosen for the race. It was a private track between Newmarket and Bury St. Edmunds. Their grooms had taken the racers out earlier in the morning, to allow them to rest up for the race. The gentlemen shared Clappet's gig. He wanted to have it there, to point out to Okay its many excel-

lencies, and he and Sir Charles could return with Norman
Barten, who had been informed of the race the night before
and planned to attend.

"Who all will be racing against Sheba?" Sir Charles
asked.

"My Fandango, of course. All a hum that Sheba cuts up
stiff with other nags. Okay didn't bat an eye when I suggested the race. Your Lightning, and a filly belonging to
Okay's friend Munger. A pity True Lady can't compete, but
between you and me and the bedpost, Nick, Norm's got
himself saddled with a clinker."

Sir Charles smiled knowingly. "A blessing in disguise.
Old Norm ain't cut out for the harsh realities of the turf. I
mean, can you see him with a nag like Sheba, stuffing her
full of oats and apples till she's so fat she can hardly waddle?
I swear True Lady's put on a stone since he bought her. Besides, it's a rich man's game, and Norman has only a com-
petence."

"Like you," Clappet added.

"I mean to marry an heiress. Since Luten has cut me out
with Trudie, I shall quite vulgarly marry for money."

Peter turned a scornful face on his friend. "Luten and
Trudie? What a bag of moonshine! She's full of pep and vinegar, and Luten, you know, would cut off the cat's tail if he
caught her playing with it. It's Okay she has in her eye."

"Get up all the rebellions you want against it, my friend,
but you'll have Miss Barten as an aunt before this Season's
over."

This news assailed Clappet's ear with all the reassurance
of a scream in the night. Trudie knew all about the race and
buying Sheba, and to think she might go blabbing it to Luten
was outrageous. "Where did you get that idea? I never
heard her say a good word about him."

"It ain't what she says about him; it's the way *he* talks
about *her*, and the way he looks when he talks. You know he
170

took her and Norman to Cheveley Park, and to Sable Lodge for tea after. Now you tell me, Clappet, would he go so far out of his way to grease Norman Barten? Not likely.''

"But Trudie ain't in his style—not in the least."

"She ain't in the style of his high flyers, but he don't ever plan to *marry* them. What *is* his style in a wife? He never seriously courted any lady in London."

"A trip to Cheveley Park can hardly be called serious courting!"

"And a rout in her honor?" Sir Charles asked, eyebrow lifted knowingly. "Oh, yes, he's having a rout party at Sable Lodge next week. I happened to hear him mention it to a couple of fellows the other day. 'The cards will be in the mail shortly,' he told them. I daresay we shall be invited as well. And you know as well as I do, Clappet, that he never had a party at Newmarket before in his life. He ain't seeing any other lady hereabouts. It's Trudie he has in his eye."

"He's whistling down the wind. She wouldn't give him the time of day."

"Would she not? A marquess with lord knows how much blunt, and two of the finest estates in the country? Start practicing up to say 'Aunt Trudie.' "

Such a tremendous piece of imbecility on Luten's part required deep thinking by both travelers, so they fell silent and looked out on the grassy face of Suffolk till they reached the track. The Bartens were already there. Mrs. Harrington had declined the treat. Clappet looked at Trudie with a keener interest, and before they had exchanged a dozen words, he began to suspect that Sir Charles was right. She had changed, even from last night. There was a worried look about her, and she soon got him aside to explain it.

"If Sheba acts up, Peter, you mustn't buy her. Luten says she is restive with colts or stallions."

"Well, Luten is dead wrong. Fandango's in the race, and Okay agreed to it."

"Yes, well the other thing is, Luten said O'Kelly only paid fifty guineas for Sheba, because they couldn't do a thing with her at Cheveley Park."

"Deuce take it, we both know Luten wants to buy Sheba himself. *You're* the one who told me so. Did he deny that?"

"No," she admitted reluctantly. "But he only thought she might be useful for a brood mare, if they could get the stallion near her."

"I see Luten has become quite a god with you!" Peter scoffed. "I never thought you were the kind of girl to marry for money, Trudie."

"Marry?" she gasped. "Where did you get that . . ." Words failed her. Was it possible Luten actually planned to marry her?

"We know all about it, me and Nick. And if you've gone running to tell Uncle about this race, Trudie . . ."

"No," she said weakly. Her head was in a whirl. She remembered those dark eyes that had gazed into hers the night before, the pressure of his lips on her fingers, and that other kiss in the carriage. "You must be mistaken," she said, looking hopeful.

"Mistaken, and the pair of you smelling like April and May? Well, I have nothing against you for an aunt, so far as that goes, as long as you didn't tip Luten the clue about Sheba. Of course he'll know after I buy her, but by then it will be too late for him to do anything."

A groom came pelting out from the stables, calling Lord Clappet. "Your nag's gone crazy!" he hollered.

"What?" Clappet darted off, and Trudie was left alone to conjure with the impossible new idea that had been put into her mind.

Sir Charles and Norman also went to the stables, and she stood at the track railing, thinking again of that long satin gown. Several minutes passed, but they passed so happily that she was unaware of it. It was twenty minutes before she was joined by the gentlemen and the race was about to begin.

The racers were led to the starting gate. There was a chill in the air that day, and a mist rising up from the heath. Munger's filly was a sleek Barb called Jet. She was well behaved at the gate, while Sheba frisked sideways and tossed her head. Trudie gave a warning look to Peter, then checked to see if Sheba was running next to Fandango.

"Why, Peter, where's your colt?" she asked, for as she looked, she saw only the three fillies lined up.

Peter blew a gust of air from his lungs and wiped his brow. "The curst screw has gone mad. He was bucking and rearing like a wild stallion. I think he burst a blood vessel in his lungs, and can't run. There was blood coming from his nostrils. I can't imagine what got into him. He's completely useless. I *have* to get Sheba now. Look at her, Trudie. Did you ever see such an eye?"

"No, nor such a frisky starter either."

"There, the jockey's got her under control now. Why don't they start the race?" he asked, looking over his shoulder in case Luten should come pelting down on him.

The starting fire was given, and the three fillies bolted from their gates. There was no such refinement as racing silks; all jockeys wore their normal jackets and peaked caps pulled low over their eyes. Both Lightning and Jet were beautiful goers, but Trudie found it impossible to watch any filly except Sheba. There was that imperative quality of a beautiful woman about her; when she was present, all competition fell into the shade. Even Sir Charles didn't watch his Lightning as closely as he felt he ought.

Sheba didn't so much run as fly. She was certainly a filly of unparalleled grace, perfect balance, and extremely elegant form. It was no race at all, but an exhibition. Before the three fillies reached the section of the rail where the viewers stood, Sheba was already two lengths ahead, and gaining.

173

She moved effortlessly, ignoring the field behind her. There was a flash of flexed muscles, a dull gleam of her golden coat, a thundering of hooves, and flying of mane, a wind from her passing, and then there was a view of retreating hooves and tail, while the huge haunches moved as regularly as the pistons of Mr. Watt's steam engine. When the other fillies raced past, it was an anticlimax. They were only flesh and bone and sinew. Sheba was made of rarer stuff—fire and light and air.

"By Jove, that's something like!" Peter crowed.

"And the jockey was holding her back, I swear!" Norman squealed.

"She'll distance the field," Sir Charles said, stunned. "I knew she was fast—I didn't know she could move like a bullet."

Sheba not only distanced the field; she won by over two hundred yards, without half trying.

O'Kelly turned to the gentlemen. "Well, what do you say? Convinced she isn't a savage, as some folks say?"

"I never saw a better-behaved filly," Peter praised. "What we have to do now is settle on a price."

O'Kelly gave a sad smile. "As I said last night, Clappet, money is not the first object. Just enough to get me home and pay off my sister's debts."

"I can get sixty-five guineas for hawking my curricle and some trinkets I have at the inn. I have three hundred in cash. Demme, I won't get a sou for Fandango, with that burst blood vessel. I suppose I ought to have a look at him."

"Yes, but let us settle up the payment first," O'Kelly said. "I have to leave immediately. I don't want to rob you of your curricle, Clappet, and your personal items—it would be too farouche to take them. Though I do need a watch. A Breguet, I think you mentioned . . ."

"A dandy watch!"

"Perhaps the watch and the three hundred guineas, and—

but that will leave you without any cash to go on here. I have it—I'll take the watch and Fandango and two hundred guineas. What do you say to that? I know Fandango isn't worth much, but I am a horse breeder, and I could find some use for him at Doneraile.''

"I paid four hundred for Fandango," Peter said doubtfully. "He might recover from the burst vessel.''

"I was just trying to lighten the burden for you, but if you prefer to give your gig and the three hundred and the watch . . .''

Sir Charles nudged Clappet in the ribs. "Fandango and two hundred," he whispered under his hand.

"I shan't want two racers, I daresay," Clappet said, still uncertain. He wished for one inexplicable moment that Luten were there to advise him. "Very well, two hundred and Fandango, and I shall keep my gig—curricle!''

"And I get the watch," O'Kelly added. "Er—do you have the cash on you? If I dash off immediately, I can take care of a little business I have in town and leave for London tomorrow to make my arrangements for going home to Ireland. I can take Fandango now. . . .''

"You'll want his papers," Sir Charles reminded him.

"That's right. I will. Let us all meet at the Golden Lion for dinner, shall we? I should be free by seven. Dinner is my treat—I insist.''

It was agreed, and the group began to break up. O'Kelly stood for a moment, stealing quiet glances at Miss Barten. "Would you care to drive back to Northfield with me?" he asked hesitantly.

She feared he wanted to discuss the trip to Ireland, and knew she would decline, but turning him off would best be done in person, so she accepted.

As they left, conversation wafted after them. "What a first-rate bargain!" Peter crowed.

"A real gentleman," Sir Charles added. "Imagine

O'Kelly taking that screw of a Fandango off you, when he could have got your gig and three hundred pounds.''

"And paying for dinner for us all!" Norman added happily.

O'Kelly smiled modestly at his companion. "It was foolish of me to accept Fandango, but I couldn't like to leave Clappet without a gig, and without any money. Some blackleg would have offered him a few guineas for his colt, and the animal would have ended up at a glue factory or pulling a dun cart.''

"You're just like Norman," she chided, but with much approval glowing in her handsome eyes.

"I take that as a great compliment, ma'am," he said, and handed her into his carriage. "I wanted to have a chance to talk to you privately, before leaving. We must settle the time for your visit to Ireland."

For one instant, she felt a strong instinct to go to Ireland and make her life with Mr. O'Kelly. He was a true gentleman, and really more handsome than Luten. Why was it that she preferred the harsher man?

"I—I don't think we shall be going after all, Mr. O'Kelly," she said gently.

"What!" His face was a mask of astonishment, though the jarring of the carriage might have been partly to blame, for they were rattling along at a very fast pace. "But surely it is settled!"

"No, it was never settled, only discussed. I now feel—oh, I daresay nothing will come of it, but I am—interested in another gentleman."

"But you must know I—that is, I know I never asked you, for with my finances up in the air, I hesitated, but you must have guessed . . . Oh, Miss Barten—Trudie—are you quite certain?"

His hands clasped hers in a tight grip, and his brilliant blue eyes, fringed heavily with lashes, were sad.

"Quite certain," she said, and pulled her fingers from his.

He looked at them a moment, with his long lashes fanning his cheeks. His lips moved unsteadily, and she feared he was going to sob. "I'm sorry," she said gently, and patted his fingers. "I'll always remember you, Mr. O'Kelly. I have enjoyed your acquaintance."

"Enjoyed?" he asked in a voice muffled with emotion. "Not so much as I have enjoyed yours, I think."

"We shan't argue about that," she said primly, and, to change the topic, asked why they were driving so quickly.

"I am in a bit of a hurry—I told my groom to spring them. Who is the lucky man who won you? Anyone I know?"

"Nothing is settled."

"Clappet?" he asked. When he lifted his head, a laughing blue eye regarded her. There was an expression in it that she'd never seen there before. She couldn't quite put a word to it—it seemed intimate, even conspiratorial. The speed of the transformation too made her suspect he would soon recover from his heartbreak. "An excellent match! I congratulate you."

"Not Clappet!" she exclaimed.

"Surely not Sir Charles. Clappet is much better to grass."

"Actually, it is neither one," she said, and flushed, not wanting to name Luten.

"I see. A gentleman back home, eh? Worse luck for me."

That's all. She had expected a longer period of mourning, perhaps some coaxing and cajoling. A hint that if it didn't work out, she would always be welcome at Doneraile would not have gone amiss. This new O'Kelly was difficult to gauge, but she sensed that he was hiding his hurt under a blustering good humor, and went along with it.

"Then I shall go home and set up a courting with my ex-ladylove," he said lightly. "You have inadvertently set me on the path to rectitude, Miss Barten. I meant to shab off on Lady Catherine, once my daylights got a sight of you. She's got a much better dowry, I fancy. Now that it's off between us, it won't seem encroaching if I inquire just what your settlement is. I make it between five and ten thousand. Am I right?"

She was surprised at his bluntness, but still felt sorry for him, and fell in with his mood. "Five thousand," she said. "You are wise to opt for Lady Catherine."

"Aye, and with your aunt thrown into the bargain, to be clothed and fed. I expect she'll leave you something, though, to make up for it."

"All of one thousand, to be split between Norman and me. Still no great heiress, you see. You are well rid of me, sir."

"No man is well rid of a smile like that," he said, with sufficient ardor to please her. "We might have rubbed along very well, you and I. I think we have some of the same spirit. I hope your new beau isn't a pillar of rectitude. That sort wouldn't suit you in the least."

"You need not worry," she laughed. Mr. O'Kelly was leaving for Ireland, and this little flirtation was like an unexpected gift. She could talk quite freely, without any fear of repercussions. "I have a secret I will share, if you promise not to tell a single soul."

"Mum's the word."

"My beau is so far from rectitude that he initially took me for a lightskirt. Don't laugh! He did! He even hired me a cottage for the Season at Tunbridge Wells that is now sitting vacant, already paid for. It sounded very nice too, right on the park."

"I shouldn't think he took it in your own name!"

"Oh, yes, I would be held in utter contempt if anyone ever found it out. That is why you are sworn to secrecy."

"And you would marry him after such an insult?" he asked.

"I would—if he asked me. It was all a misunderstanding, you see."

"I must know this gentleman's name. He cannot be an old beau from Walbeck Park days, as I thought."

This was coming perilously close to Luten. She had already denied both Peter and Sir Charles, and had no other friends in the neighborhood. "You would not know him," she said, suddenly stiffening up.

"You haven't left yourself much wiggle room, ma'am. But I shan't say a word about Lord Luten, except to hope you will be very happy, and to rescind all the unpleasant things I once said to you about him. You have nabbed yourself an excellent parti."

She frowned in derision. "I hope you are leaving the vicinity very soon, Mr. O'Kelly. He hasn't even asked me, and to be boasting of an attachment beforehand is not at all the thing."

"You will find this hard to believe," he joked, "but where I am going, the name of Lord Luten is quite unknown. I could bellow your catch from the rooftops, and no one would care a groat. So I shan't bother clambering up to any roofs. Truly, I am very happy for you."

They were soon at Northfield. Trudie assumed Mr. O'Kelly would come in to say good-bye to her aunt, but he had several commissions to discharge before leaving town, and couldn't spare the time. "I have to settle up all my bills and thank a few people who were particularly kind to me," he explained.

Mrs. Harrington, Trudie felt, ought to be one of those people, but she was suddenly tired of Mr. O'Kelly. He spoke of his sensitive feelings and disinterest in money out of one side of his mouth, but from the other came congratulations on her having "nabbed an excellent parti," almost before he had finished bemoaning his jilting. They parted as friends, but Trudie found herself regretting her outspokenness in the carriage. She was glad Mr. O'Kelly was leaving.

While they made the trip to Northfield, the young gentlemen went around to the stables to have a look at Peter's new acquisition.

"Fandango's gone already!" Norman exclaimed. "You didn't have a chance to say good-bye to him, Clappet."

Sir Charles and Peter exchanged a derisive look at such sentimental rubbish. Still it was odd O'Kelly had whisked the colt away so quickly, and when it had a burst blood vessel in its lung too.

"Did he have a horse doctor take a look at Fandango?" Sir Charles asked his own groom.

"No, sir, his jockey just hopped up on the nag's back and galloped out of here like greased lightning."

"He'll kill Fandango!" Norman worried. "Riding a colt in that condition—why, I'm surprised Fandango was able to walk. He should have had him looked at before riding him."

Sir Charles ran a hand over his white brow to aid concentration. "Something havey-cavey going on here," he said. "Like greased lightning, you say?"

"Forty miles an hour," the groom assured him. "And a new rider for Fandango too—you'd think the nag would have kicked up a fuss, the way he was ranting and roaring just before the race."

"He can't have burst any vessels, that's for certain!" Clappet said. "What do you suppose got into him to act so hostile, Wiggins?" he asked his own groom. "If he wasn't hurt, why did he buck and rear so?"

"He *was* hurt," Norman pointed out. "There was that blood coming out of his nostrils."

"The demmed cribber got a sliver up his snout, likely as not. If that's all it was, O'Kelly picked himself up a bargain. But not as fine a bargain as I got with Sheba," he declared, and turned back to examine his filly in more detail.

He advanced to her, hand out to pat her velvet nose. Sheba reared her head back, bared her teeth and snapped at him. Her powerful hind quarters hunched down, her front legs came up, and her hooves flailed the air. The light in her eye bore more resemblance to a Bedlamite than an eagle, and a diabolic whinnying sound rent the air. Clappet jumped back in fright. "Steady, girl," he said, trying to grab her rein.

But her flailing legs prevented it. Everyone present fell back, and Sheba came back down on all fours, glaring at them, while her tail whisked angrily.

"Get a hold of that bridle, Wiggins," Lord Clappet ordered.

"I ain't about to be trampled into the ground," Wiggins answered, but he edged forward carefully. Sheba's head turned, and she followed Wiggins's movement with glaring eyes. She almost seemed to be daring him. When his hand went out cautiously, she lunged her head forward and nipped his fingers. Wiggins jumped back, shaking his hand. "She bit me!"

"Lord, you call that a bite. You ain't even bleeding," Peter scoffed, and paced forward to try for the reins himself.

Sheba had had enough of interference. She lowered her head and butted Clappet in the stomach hard enough that he went sprawling on the floor. He had the wind knocked out of him and missed the next development. Wiggins unwisely raised his crop. Sheba lifted her front leg and delivered one sharp kick to the groom's hip. It sent him reeling back into the crowd, which at least prevented his being trampled to death.

Sheba bolted out of the stable, leapt the fence, and went

181

cavorting down the track sideways, from rail to rail, kicking up her heels and, Sir Charles greatly feared, bucking her shins beyond redemption. He had never seen such a wild, untrammeled exhibition of equine ferocity, and sincerely hoped he would never see one again. The filly had run mad. There was no doing anything with her.

Wiggins stumbled to the rail and watched her, shaking his head. "If we could get a gallon of ale into her, she'd calm down."

"Go to the closest inn and fetch one, then," Sir Charles ordered. "We can't let this hoyden run wild into town. She'll kill someone."

Wiggins ran to fetch a bucket, and when he returned to Sir Charles, Peter and Norman were with him. Wiggins was carrying a bucket, at which they all stared wide-eyed. "What is it?" Sir Charles demanded.

"Ale," Wiggins answered importantly.

"What, already? That's quick work. Put it here and let's see if she'll come for it."

"It's empty, nearly," Wiggins informed him.

"You see what he's done!" Peter exclaimed indignantly. "O'Kelly gave Sheba a bucket of ale before the race."

"Don't be such a gudgeon," Sir Charles said. "Why would he give it to her *before* the race? It would slow her down."

"And pacify her, so she wouldn't act up like a hurly-burly nag during the race," Peter explained. "It's all that kept her from running wild, I bet. Lord, you said yourself the jockey was holding her back for all he was worth. Sheba still distanced the field, but if she'd been stone cold sober, she'd have—well, I don't know what she might have done."

"Thrown her jockey for a start, with the other nags present," Sir Charles advised him. "O'Kelly always raced her alone. Now we know why. She ain't just gate-shy; she's a loner. You'll never train her to compete. Good God, look at her go, though!'' he added as Sheba bolted over the rails and streaked toward Bury St. Edmunds. ''We'll never catch her.''

''We've got to try,'' Peter said reluctantly. ''I'll be dunned for broken windows and broken bones and the lord only knows what else. Will you come with me, Nick?''

Sir Charles's groom joined them. His chest was puffed with importance, and in his hand he carried a wicker basket. He waited till the spectators had gathered around before lifting the lid. There, wrapped in a towel from the Golden Lion, a small eel, still living, squirmed sluggishly in a capped bottle. There was another smaller bottle, holding a quantity of red liquid that looked like blood.

''What the deuce is that?'' Norman Barten asked, frowning in perplexity.

''Well, I'll be stapped!'' Sir Charles said.

''What is it? What does it mean?'' Lord Clappet asked.

''It means you've been gulled good and proper,'' Sir Charles announced, not without a measure of suppressed glee. ''I see what he's done now. O'Kelly put a live eel down Fandango's gullet before the race, to make him turn wild. I've heard of that stunt before but thought it was a Banbury tale. He must have brought along this one for a spare, in case the other one died. His groom will get a good jawing for leaving the evidence behind. It *is* evidence,'' he added. ''Put it in our carriage, Norman,'' he said, handing the basket to Norman.

''I don't see why O'Kelly would have done that to Fandango,'' Peter objected. ''There's no question of Fandango being able to outrun Sheba.''

''Aye, but Fandango is a colt,'' Sir Charles said knowingly. ''Sheba was hardly under control with a gallon of ale in her, and running only with fillies. If Fandango had been allowed to run, even the ale wouldn't have been enough to hold Sheba in check.''

"What about the red stuff in the bottle?" Norman asked, lifting it up. "It looks like blood."

"It probably is blood—from a slaughterhouse," Sir Charles announced. "This is what he daubed on Fandango's nose, to make us think he'd broken a blood vessel. It gave an excuse for Fandango acting up so violently. Another Greek's trick."

"If you knew all these tricks, I wish you might have mentioned them before the race!" Peter complained.

"I never thought a gentleman like O'Kelly would resort to such low stunts."

"It explains how Fandango could gallop away within half an hour of his fit. The eel was dead by then," Peter said. A menacing frown drew his brows together. "We'll see what O'Kelly has to say about this tonight at dinner."

"Well, if you ain't a sapskull, Clappet," Sir Charles said, shaking his head in disbelief. "You saw the way he rattled down that road at top speed. We'll never see him again. O'Kelly is long gone with your money and your perfectly good colt."

"And your watch," Norman added. Then his face blanched, and he looked wild-eyed at the others. "And with Trudie!" he exclaimed. "I've got to go after them."

"I'll join you," Sir Charles offered.

"What about Sheba?" Peter asked, fearing the awesome job of catching her was to be left to him alone.

"I hope you ain't suggesting Sheba takes precedence over Norman's sister!" Sir Charles exclaimed. "Take your groom, and mine as well," he offered as a sop.

"But someone has to look after Lightning," Norman pointed out. "I see old Munger peeled off on us with his nag and his men. He was probably in on the whole rig. I must go." He darted for his carriage.

"You'll have to make do with Wiggins, Clappet. My

groom must tend to Lightning,'' Sir Charles said. He spoke to his groom and left with Norman.

''I wish I had brought my own curricle,'' Sir Charles fretted, but even Norman's laggardly team could be whipped into a good speed, and they left in a cloud of dust, while Peter went with his own groom to chase after Sheba, half hoping he wouldn't catch her.

Following her, at least, was no problem. She had left a wide trail of havoc behind her. An upset potato cart, with potatoes rolling all over the road, slowed them down considerably. The limping beggar muttering to himself about a she-devil nag was obviously a victim. An elegant black carriage just pulling out of a ditch bore further testimony that Clappet was on the right track in going into Bury St. Edmunds.

The actual damage there appeared to be slight. A host of stunned-looking pedestrians were still staring down the road, indicating that Sheba had bolted through very recently. Not half a mile from town, Clappet spotted the beautiful brute calmly grazing in a farmer's meadow, but the ordeal of retrieving her was still to be endured. And meanwhile, O'Kelly was running to Ireland with his misgotten gains.

''Oh, dash it, I wish Luten were here!'' he moaned.

It was several hours before he had accomplished the unenviable job. It involved a trip to the inn to buy a bucket of ale, gingerly putting it over the fence and waiting for Sheba to come and swill it down, and it involved a deal of convincing his groom that the beast was now safe to be taken by the reins, for nothing would convince Wiggins to mount the she-devil's back.

The sun was sinking into the west when a very tired, bedraggled Lord Clappet limped into his room at the Golden Lion and flopped down on his bed, half wishing he were dead. Sheba was temporarily at the inn stable, too drunk to

185

cause much ruckus, and with always a bucket of ale standing by to keep her relatively placid.

Clappet had one further thing to do, and that was accomplished by ringing for a servant, who informed him that yes, Mr. O'Kelly had left hours ago, early that morning, by the window. He hadn't checked out, and he hadn't paid his bill, but his room had been empty when the manager had gone to eject him at ten that same morning.

"Then I guess he won't be back for dinner," Lord Peter said, his heart falling to his toes.

The servant looked at him as though he were a lunatic. "I think we can safely say we shall not have the pleasure of Mr. O'Kelly's company at this establishment again. And while we are on the subject of paying bills, milord, might I suggest you speak to the manager before going out this evening. There is a matter of a few weeks' room and board, and the stable . . ."

Clappet fell back against his pillows. "I ain't getting off this bed tonight. Call me the day after tomorrow," he said, and closed his eyes to review the chaos of his future.

After a troubled half-hour, he saw one little glimmering of light. At least O'Kelly didn't have Fandango's papers from Cheveley Park. He couldn't race the colt or sell or breed him as a thoroughbred without the papers. It gave him courage to get up off the bed and go to his dresser to look at the papers. They were gone. O'Kelly had stolen them—presumably that morning before he had sneaked out by the bedroom window without paying his bill. He must have done it while Nick and he were touring the pawn shops. His plan all along had been to get Fandango, then. Okay O'Kelly had set him up like a proper dupe, and he wasn't going to get away with it—only he already had, and Clappet hadn't a single idea where to find him, nor what to do about it if he did, by some miracle, manage to run the scoundrel to earth.

A low, animal moan escaped his throat. He felt worse than he had felt after his first beating at Harrow. At least that hadn't been his own fault, and he hadn't had to face Luten after it with a guilty conscience.

Chapter Seventeen

Norman Barten was delighted to find his sister safely at home. The news fell tamely on Sir Charles's ear that O'Kelly had not kidnapped her, or at least ravished her in his carriage, but he was obliged to do the pretty and say he was "never so relieved in his life" to find her safe and sound. He had the pleasure of outlining to Trudie and her aunt what a rotter O'Kelly was and how thoroughly Clappet had been duped, and when this subject had been exhausted, he said, "Sorry to fly off on you, but I must see what I can do to give Clappet a hand with Sheba. I daresay she has got all of Bury St. Edmunds and half of Newmarket in a shambles by this time. Will you come along, Norman?"

Norman was nearly as eager as Sir Charles to view the debacle. "I must, since you haven't got your carriage," he pointed out, and the two of them flew to the rescue.

Their first stop was the inn, "For there's no saying O'Kelly didn't have to make a stop there, you know," Sir Charles explained. "We might manage to nab him and get Clappet's blunt back."

O'Kelly was, of course, gone; Lord Clappet had not yet returned, but the gentlemen were extremely thirsty, and stopped "Just to wet our whistles. This is thirsty work,"

Norman said by way of excuse, and Sir Charles agreed entirely.

Their next idea was "to round up a bunch of fellows to give us a hand. There's bound to be a riot in progress when we find Sheba."

The fellows naturally had to hear what necessitated this gathering of a rescue team, and did it over a couple of ales. They did finally go off in search of Sheba and Lord Clappet, but missed them, and after an hour's looking, they all returned to the Golden Lion to find Sheba sound asleep in her stall. A suspicious odor of ale hung in the air, and beside her was another full bucket, awaiting her pleasure.

Trudie's first instinct was to go with Norman and Nicolson to help Clappet, till she remembered her rather prominent part in Peter's bad bargain, at which time she elected to remain at home. In vain did she tell herself it wasn't her fault; she hadn't made Peter buy Sheba. But she had suggested it to him and encouraged him every step of the way. She had also introduced O'Kelly to Peter and Nick, and she and her aunt had made a special pet of him. Worst of all, she had done it all behind Luten's back, knowing how much he would dislike it.

She hardly remembered, or cared, that all O'Kelly's fine talk of loving her and having her and Mrs. Harrington to Doneraile had been an act. She was on nettles worrying what the outcome would be, and let her aunt do the repining over O'Kelly's crooked character. Her concern was how she could undo the harm she had caused, and what she would say to Luten when he showed up at the door to give her a blast, as he surely would. Amid her other fears was that O'Kelly would, in some evil way, let Luten know she had boasted of having attached him. Really that bothered her as much as the rest.

Several hours passed. An indifferent dinner was prepared and served and returned largely uneaten to the kitchen, and

189

all the while the fever burned. Trudie's first wish that Luten wouldn't come till tomorrow changed. She wished he would come at once and have it done with, for she couldn't endure any more waiting.

Luten didn't hear of the escapade till nine o'clock that evening, when a friend who was putting up at the Golden Lion called at Sable Lodge. "I was sorry to hear about your nephew's being fleeced by that bounder, O'Kelly," his friend said.

Luten felt a cold shadow pass over his heart. He had been afraid of some such thing but hoped his warnings had been heeded. "I haven't heard the story—enlighten me," he said.

"It's all anyone is talking of in town. I made sure your nephew would have come to you for help." Luten felt a twinge of guilt at that speech. By the time he got to the Golden Lion and had sorted the facts from the highly embroidered tales contrived to confuse him, it was ten o'clock, and too late to go to Northfield. What he had heard at the inn led him to believe Miss Barten was deeply enmeshed in the affair.

He turned a wrathful eye on Norman and said, "Pray tell the ladies I will call on them early tomorrow morning. I am eager to hear why your sister urged this bargain on my nephew. As she is such an intimate friend of O'Kelly, she might shed some light on his whereabouts."

Norman leapt to Trudie's defense. "Come with me now, this instant. You'll learn she had nothing to do with it, I promise you." He glared at Peter as he spoke. Sir Charles's mind fled joyfully to duels, of which at least two seemed to be brewing, if Norman survived Peter's onslaught and lived to tackle Luten after he had finished insulting Trudie.

"I have already learned she urged Sheba on Clappet," Luten said. Then he turned a fierce look on his nephew and added, "Not that you are innocent. I warned you away from that blackleg."

"Let's go!" Sir Charles exclaimed, and picked up his hat and crop, for he had no intention of missing such a bang-up fight as he foresaw.

Luten gave him a foul glare. "This is not a public performance. You and Clappet will wait here. I'll come back directly after speaking to Miss Barten."

"I'll tell you all about it tomorrow, Nick," Norman added, for they none of them counted on Luten to give a decent recital of events.

Sir Charles took Norman aside and said in a low voice, "You know who you can count on if it comes to a duel. I shouldn't think you'd stand still for letting Luten call your sister an accomplice in this imbroglio. As to Peter—you can either apologize or call him out. Up to you. Be very happy to oblige you. Fortunately, I brought my dueling pistols with me. I shall have a gander at the Code Duelo tonight—quite sure I can second you for two duels. Nothing wrong in that."

Norman stared. "Oh, it won't come to that—will it?"

"I hope not," Nicolson lied, "but if it does, you can count on me."

The lights were still burning at Northfield, though Mrs. Harrington had retired half an hour before. Only Trudie was in the saloon, awaiting her brother's return. She bounced from the sofa when the front door opened, and ran into the hallway. "What happened? Did you . . ." She saw Luten behind Norman, and fell silent. She backed away fearfully, for she had never seen him in such a rage. His face was white, and angry lines pulled his lips down.

"I came here in the hope that *you* would tell *me* what happened," he said in a thin, imperious voice, and stepped past her into the saloon.

"He knows what happened," Norman told her. "Luten has the cork-brained notion that you put Peter up to buying Sheba. I brought him here so you can tell him it is no such a thing. It was all his own idea. Imagine that jackal of a Clappet saying you had anything to do with it! He was just afraid of Luten's revenge.''

Luten pretended to ignore this remark, though he was shaken to hear himself spoken of in such harsh terms. His friend too had seemed surprised that Peter hadn't gone to him for help in his trouble. He turned to Trudie and said, ''Well?'' in such a cold voice that something inside her froze. She thought it was her heart, except a frozen heart could not pound so mercilessly as hers was doing.

When no words came from her, Norman spoke again. ''As I recall, it was Peter and Nick who told us O'Kelly was leaving, after he had been dunned for payment at the inn. Isn't that what Auntie said? Peter knew more about his doings than we did.''

Mrs. Harrington had indeed tampered a little with the truth there, but only to hide from Norman that Mr. O'Kelly had taken luncheon with them.

''It is not what my nephew told me,'' Luten said. His dark eyes demanded an explanation. ''Miss Barten, just tell me one thing: Did you, or did you not, act as go-between for O'Kelly in this scheme to fleece my nephew? Peter tells me you put the deal to him that Sheba was for sale at a bargain price. If he is hiding behind a lady's skirts, he will be called to account for it.''

''Of course she didn't!'' Norman exclaimed impatiently. ''Tell him, Trudie.''

Now two angry pairs of eyes glared at her. She licked her lips nervously and faced up to the truth. ''I did tell Peter, but I wasn't a go-between.''

''I'd like to know what else you would call it!'' Luten shouted, while Norman gasped, ''Trudie! You didn't!''

''You all thought Sheba was a marvelous racer!'' she reminded Norman. ''I thought it was too good an opportunity to miss, and O'Kelly needed money for his sister. At least he told us so."

"*Widowed* sister, no doubt?" Luten sneered.

"Yes, and with three children. He is supporting them—at least—well, he *said* he was. I—I suppose it is all a hum?"

Luten looked positively disgusted. "I am happy to say I am not on such intimate terms with O'Kelly as you, ma'am. I have always been a little careful whom I associate with, though you might not think so," he added.

This was interpreted by her to mean that he despised her, and regretted the association. Her fear subsided, and a lick of anger grew in its place. She felt her blood quicken under his bold gaze. Her chin went up, and her tone firmed amazingly. "No doubt that is why you used an intermediary when you were trying to buy Sheba yourself. Mr. O'Kelly took the idea it was because you knew he wouldn't let you have her. A clever move, Lord Luten, but not clever enough to fool Mr. O'Kelly."

"I made no offer. I wouldn't have the nag as a gift."

Trudie allowed a cool smile to lift her lips. "I seem to recall you were interested in her as a brood mare."

"For fifty guineas—possibly!"

"That's not precisely a gift!"

"You knew what I thought the filly was worth! I warned you she was impossible to race, and still you urged her on Clappet. That was unconscionable behavior, gulling a youngster."

"But that is exactly why I told Peter he must insist on a race before buying her," she explained blandly. "O'Kelly told us you had offered for Sheba yourself, and Peter just wanted to cut you out."

"You were trying to knife *me* in the back along with all the rest!" Luten raged. "You would take the word of that mongrel, O'Kelly, against mine. What magnificent price was I alleged to have offered?"

193

"Seven hundred pounds."

"Did it not strike you as even a little bit suspicious that this offer was turned down?"

"No, for Mr. O'Kelly feared you would mistreat the filly. Word of your Turkish practices has got abroad, milord."

Norman looked quite simply appalled. "I had no idea all this was going on. It's those lunches O'Kelly cadged from us—*that's* why he came here, and I thought he was only after the free meals. Luten, I'm afraid we owe you an apology!"

Luten was not appeased; it wasn't Norman's apology he was interested in. "It is you who deserve an apology from your sister," he said curtly. "You have obviously been kept in the dark about her dealings with O'Kelly. I would keep a tighter rein on the ladies, if I were you. From selling Latin lessons to crooked horse-trading! What next, Miss Barten? I'm surprised O'Kelly left you behind, for I am convinced the pair of you would deal famously."

Norman was on edge, feeling he ought to defend his sister, yet having to agree that she had gotten badly out of hand. Worst of all, Sir Charles's offer to act as his second loomed at the back of his mind, and he truly abhorred violence.

Trudie was made of sterner stuff. Her anger flared, and it was made worse by Norman's groveling demeanor. "I considered his offer!" she said boldly. "It is not the worst one I have received this Season, as *you* are very well aware, milord! I am sorry I suggested such a bad bargain to Peter, and to *him* I shall apologize. Not to you. If you were a proper guardian, your nephew would take his problems to you, instead of having to hide them from you. A guardian has more duties than laying down laws and distributing retribution. As a sportsman yourself, you must be familiar with the code: own up, pay up, and shut up. The bargain is done. Let us hear no more about it.''

Again Luten was assailed by a wave of guilt for his own laxity and his lack of closeness with Peter. He took a deep breath and proceeded to turn the tables on her. ''I should have known a lady who hangs about the tracks like a common tout would be familiar with the code. Apparently it never occurred to you that the code applies to women as well. You have owned up to your part in this fracas; I hear no mention of paying up.''

She looked to Norman for guidance and saw only a troubled frown. Did the comparison of his sister to a racetrack tout require an apology? He knew Sir Charles would think so and did not wish to be behind-hand in chivalry. ''Now see here, Luten,'' he blustered. ''I'm afraid I must demand an apology!''

Trudie knew there was no hope of an apology from their intransigent caller, and rushed in to divert disaster. ''I am perfectly willing to bear the expense, if everyone agrees the fault is mine.''

Luten made a batting motion with his hand, dismissing her offer out of hand. This too angered her. ''I have my dowry. I insist on paying!''

Norman looked at her aghast. ''Trudie!'' he squeaked, sounding very much like a frightened mouse.

She arose majestically. ''Please tell Lord Clappet to send me the bill.''

Luten arose and ran a withering eye from Miss Barten's titian head to her daintily shod foot. ''I can assure you you will not be hearing from Lord Clappet again. The matter is settled, so far as we are concerned. He will be removing to Sable Lodge with me, till I arrange to send him back to London. I only came here to see if you can tell me O'Kelly's whereabouts, but I see it was foolish. You wouldn't tell me

195

the truth if you acted in concert with him, and if he is the only scoundrel, then you don't know where he is."

Norman said, "I really must object . . ."

"No, you need not," Luten said brusquely. "I believe your sister is only headstrong and foolish, not O'Kelly's assistant. Good night."

On this unconciliating speech, he turned and strode from the room. Norman, the gudgeon, said "Good night," but at least she was able to restrain him from accompanying Luten to the door.

"He's got a lot of nerve!" Trudie said when they were alone. "To be laying the whole sorry mess in *my* dish! As if *I* knew anything about getting horses drunk and putting live eels down their gullets."

"You shouldn't have offered to pay. It ain't your fault. Not *all* your fault," Norman answered.

"I'd rather pay than have him saying I fleeced his blasted nephew. I was only trying to do him a favor."

Norman did not cut up at her, since he knew he had been backward in calling Luten to account. "What we ought to do is go after O'Kelly and make him pay up. Since he was all but living under my roof, perhaps you can tell me where in Ireland he lives?"

"He said on Dingle Bay, but I doubt he owns a shanty, much less an estate of a thousand acres. Was Luten saying he didn't want us to see Peter again? Is that what he meant by saying he was moving him to Sable Lodge?"

"What do *you* think? I hardly expect he'll invite us back for tea," Norman said very ironically.

"You must find out from Peter just how much I owe him."

"You ain't paying a sou. O'Kelly gulled us, the same as he gulled Peter. I have no money to spare, and I won't let you squander your dowry on Clappet's bad judgment," Norman said firmly. "I will call on Nick, though, and hear

196

what Luten had to say when he went back to the inn. I must apologize to Peter. I swore up and down you had nothing to do with advising him to buy Sheba. I all but called him a liar. Still, I think he might have protected your name and taken the blame himself. I'm sure Nick agrees with me, for he was rolling his eyes the whole time."

"It was that wretch of a Peter who begged me not to tell Luten; then he spills the whole story himself."

"He didn't spill it. Luten knew the worst, and just asked how Peter got bamboozled; that's all."

"I want to hear every word that's said tomorrow."

"I doubt they'll be suitable for a lady's ears. Let us not trouble Auntie with all this brouhaha, Trudie. There is no need to have her ringing a peal over us. I'm demmed sorry I ever took to the turf, if you want the truth. There is that old slice of a Rampling oiling around Georgiana all the time I am away. I think I shall cut my losses and go home."

"Home to where?" she asked. "We can't go back to Walbeck Park till the tenant's lease is up."

"I daresay we could sublet Northfield—probably at a profit, with the Season drawing closer—and rent up some little cottage near home. I am going to look into it."

"Oh, Norman," she sighed. "You mean to marry her, don't you? I hoped this year would provide a cure."

"It has. It's cured me of the racing bug. It's not what I thought it would be at all. It's all business and worse—trickery! The owners don't care for the horses at all. It's just winning the money and plate. Can you imagine how poor Fandango must have felt, with that live eel in his gullet?"

"Yes, I have a very good idea how he felt, for I feel the same myself," she answered sadly. Her sadness spread to encompass Norman. He would go home and become leg-shackled before he was twenty-one; but if that was what he wanted, she wouldn't fight him any longer. Perhaps it was what he was cut out for. Now that he was cured of turf fever,

197

he would settle into a good country squire, but she could not with equanimity face sharing a roof with Georgiana Halley, even if her name did become Georgiana Barten.

Perhaps it wouldn't be for too long. She would marry someone, but the local gentlemen would seem even more tame and unsatisfactory after Luten.

"We might as well go to bed," she said.

"You run along. I have a letter to write."

"To Georgiana, or the real estate agent back home?"

"Georgiana."

A soft smile took possession of his face. Trudie's wore a totally different look. She would pay for Peter's folly out of her own dowry and wipe that condescending glower from Luten's proud brow. But first she would see what could be done about finding O'Kelly. He couldn't just vanish. Someone must know where he was to be found.

Chapter Eighteen

It was late the next afternoon before Trudie heard the clatter of hooves advancing toward Northfield. She turned quite white and darted to the window. "It's Peter and Nick!" she exclaimed, peering down the road to ascertain that they were unaccompanied by Luten. She didn't know whether the slowing of her heartbeat was due to relief or disappointment.

"Excellent," Norman said. "It will save me the trip into town to apologize. I would have gone sooner, if I hadn't been busy with the real estate agent, putting Northfield up for hire."

Mrs. Harrington was so happy with this plan that she·was already in the kitchen with the Bogmans, explaining what meals were necessary to use up all the perishable food in the house before they left.

Norman steeled himself to do the proper thing, and Trudie remained in the saloon, intending to offer to pay the whole cost. She knew as soon as she saw the embarrassed face of Clappet that he regretted having drawn her fair name into the fracas.

"Clappet, I owe you an apology," Norman said even before the guests had taken a seat. "I was unaware of my sister's part in all this wretched business."

"No, please! I am here to apologize myself. It was scaly

of me to hide behind a lady," he said, turning to Trudie. "I
don't know what got into me, but when Luten goes into one
of his freezes, I turn into a babbling idiot. I thought he
would be less angry if he knew *you* were involved," he explained.

"I *am* involved, and I shall certainly repay every penny to
you," she assured him. "Does Luten know you're here? I
think he would dislike it very much."

"Of course he knows."

"Sent him," Sir Charles added, which earned him a
scowl from Clappet.

"I had every intention of coming anyway," Peter said.
"Luten told me you had offered to pay, and I want you to
know that I wouldn't hear of it. For him to be telling me you
are more a gentleman than I am—well, you can imagine how
small I felt. And it's true too. Did Uncle cut up very stiff last
night?"

"Yes," Norman admitted, "but not so stiff as Trudie.
She combed his hair with a rake. Have you heard anything
about O'Kelly?"

"We've been scouring the town talking to anyone who
knew him," Sir Charles said. "Luten says we ought to go
after him, but we've come a cropper. No one knows where
he has gone. It turns out he's earned himself such a reputation in Ireland that it's very unlikely he went there, as we
first thought."

"London, then . . ." Norman suggested.

Sir Charles shook his head doubtfully. "I think not.
There's a band of desperadoes on the lookout for him there
as well. Shaved cards, bad debts, and quite possibly a young
female whose family would split his head open if he showed
up. He's a cur. He didn't pay any of his debts at Newmarket
either. Luten says the only good in it is that he won't dare
show his phiz back here for a few Seasons."

"He headed south out of Newmarket. His carriage was

seen flying along at a great pace, with my poor Fandango bringing up the rear,'' Clappet explained.

''He has to be somewhere,'' Trudie said impatiently.

''Luten feels he's hiding out in some little center that wouldn't have heard of him,'' Sir Charles told them. ''He says September at Doncaster is the earliest we can hope to find him. He won't dare to race Fandango himself, but will sell him, since he stole his breeding papers. He'll summer at some cheap resort area, pull off a few more rigs, and go back into business. He goes to the tracks early in the season, as he did here, and fleeces some Johnnie Raw, then nips away before the Jockey Club catches hold of him.'' Peter grimaced to hear himself so disparagingly described, but remained silent.

''Then we should make a tour of the cheap resort areas,'' Trudie said. ''Which would you think likely, Nick?''

''Not Brighton. It'd be Margate, Weymouth, or Tunbridge Wells—somewhere like that. I, for one, don't intend to waste my time looking for the blackleg, but if I ever see him . . .'' His ever-present crop was lifted, pistol-fashion, and his trigger finger quivered.

A light of interest flashed in her eyes. ''Tunbridge Wells, did you say?''

''That's one possibility,'' Peter said. They exchanged a meaningful glance. Norman, who still had no idea of Luten's infamous proposition to his sister, failed to read any significance in it, but Sir Charles perked up.

''Of course, O'Kelly would have no way of knowing there was a cottage—er—standing idle there. Would he?'' he asked.

Trudie had a hunch so strong it amounted almost to knowledge that that was where O'Kelly had gone to hide. It would suit him right down to the ground—free, and holding the irony of another offense to this group he had diddled. She had told him the exact location, and he had even asked whose name it was hired in. He had been seen heading south too.

She shook herself back to attention. "No, he wouldn't know that."

"There would be cottages standing idle in all those summer places at this time of year," Norman said. Trudie gave a nonchalant shrug and agreed.

"Did we tell you Luten is giving us rack and manger at Sable Lodge, and stabling our nags too?" Sir Charles asked.

"He mentioned it last night," Norman said. "It is just as well, for I am leaving Northfield, and going back home."

This was discussed at some length. Norman heard with apparent equanimity that he was too soft by half to be a proper man of the turf. He already knew it, and though he resented the description, he was glad of the fact. "I wasn't raised to think winning was everything," he said simply. "I leave the field to Luten and his sort."

"Speaking of Luten," Sir Charles reminded Clappet, "he is having his groom time Lightning this afternoon. We should be going, Peter."

"Was he very hard on you, Peter?" Trudie asked.

"Well, you know, the oddest thing is, he wasn't half so hard as I expected. He said it was as much his fault as my own that I hadn't come to him in my trouble, and in future, he wanted me to feel quite free to consult with him on anything. It was demmed close to an apology. He must have been bosky."

"He was, a little," Sir Charles agreed. "It was brandy he was drinking, not wine. He don't usually drink brandy. Something had him upset. I daresay it was being bested by O'Kelly that accounted for it."

"But he won't forward me any more money," Peter said. "I shan't be able to buy another colt till next spring."

The guests soon left, promising they would all meet again before the Bartens left Newmarket.

"I'm happy that is patched up," Norman said. "It was generous of them, apologizing when it was all your fault. And we needn't worry about having to pay anything."

"Norman," Trudie said, choosing her words carefully, "it *is* my fault, and I insist on paying, whatever they say. No, not out of my dowry!" she added hastily when his face took on its mulish look. "The thing is, I know where Mr. O'Kelly is hiding."

"How could you possibly know?"

"I just know. He—he happened to let slip that he knows of a cottage paid for and unused at Tunbridge Wells."

"I thought Nick said he *couldn't* know about that cottage. What cottage is it anyway?"

"He *does* know. I told him. It's—it's a cottage one of Nick's friends hired for a ladybird, but at the last moment, she flew off on him."

"Trudie, I'm shocked that you talked so broad to O'Kelly. Why, he must think you're no better than a hurly-burly girl." His first spasm of anger subsided, and he saw the possibilities of bringing O'Kelly to justice. "We must tell Peter and Nick about this."

"No! No, it's all my fault. I want us to go. I have it all worked out, Norman. We'll tell Auntie we're going back home to hunt out a cottage and will come back for her when we've found one. She hates traveling and won't insist on coming with us."

"But she'll want you to stay with her while I go. Actually, that makes more sense. I can't take you along to Tunbridge Wells, but Nick would love to go."

"Not now, when Luten has taken him under his wing. It wouldn't be fair to drag him away when he's training Lightning. Why, it might cost him the Oaks, or even the Triple Crown." And it would rob her of the pleasure of showing Lord Luten she not only knew the sportsman's code but followed it.

It took a deal of talking, but eventually Trudie had convinced her young brother that the best solution was for the two of them to go after O'Kelly alone. Once convinced, he began to appropriate the idea for his own.

"And they said I was soft! This'll show them. Even if I ain't the sort who believes in pounding a perfectly innocent filly into the ground till her poor shins are busted, I'm not so soft as to let a blackguard like Okay O'Kelly off scot-free. We shall leave first thing tomorrow morning. Would you like to tell Auntie, or shall I?" As she wanted to make sure their aunt didn't talk him out of it or convince him to go alone, Trudie told Mrs. Harrington herself.

They packed and left . . . early the next morning. In their rush, they didn't think of such details as procuring a pistol, but it occurred to Norman that evening, after they had stopped for the night at an inn.

"You don't suppose he would do anything foolish like resist?" he asked.

"We'll take along a constable."

"Yes, that makes sense. And he'll be trespassing, along with all the rest. What was the name of the fellow who hired the cottage? A friend of Nick's, you said. I must know him."

"Mr. Mandeville," she said, hoping her brother had forgotten Luten's name.

It was no such a thing. "Luten?" he asked, staring. "What a wretched fellow he is. Imagine Peter having such a libertine for a guardian."

"It's shocking," she agreed, and quickly changed the subject.

It was a long trip from Newmarket to Tunbridge Wells, and though they got an early start on the second lap the next morning, the afternoon was well advanced when they drove through the picturesque hilly moorlands where Kent and Sussex join, into the town of Tunbridge Wells.

They had spent a few weeks there when their mother was ill some years before, and were familiar with the layout of the place. They decided to hire a room at one of the inns on the Common. This was a large area of gorse and bracken behind the Pantiles. They drove along this promenade, which was the town's chief gathering place and boasted a colonnade on one side, the other bordered by a row of lime trees.

"It's fourpences to a groat we'll see O'Kelly on the strut at this hour of the day, and we'll confront him right in public if we do," Trudie said. As the moment of confrontation drew near, she was strangely loath to meet it.

"That would be best. And we shall have a constable along with us as well," Norman reminded her. He was no more eager than his sister to tackle the large Irishman, virtually alone. Trudie could do the arguing better than he could, but she'd be little help if it came to a brawl, as it very well might.

Trudie had already foreseen a host of difficulties, the first of which was presenting herself as Miss Barten, the lady in whose name the cottage had been hired, without letting Norman know it. "First, of course, we must make sure that he's here. Why don't you hire us the room, Norman, while I run around to the real estate agencies and find out if O'Kelly got the key for the cottage?"

"You can't go alone."

"Of course I can. No one knows us here. Meet me outside the Pump Room in half an hour." She pulled the check string and hopped out.

Most of the shops and offices were on the Pantiles Parade, and at the third real estate office, she discovered what she wished to know. Her cheeks were bright pink when she presented herself as Miss Barten and inquired if this was the place where a cottage had been hired in her name by Mr. Mandeville.

"Ah, Miss Barten," the clerk said, running his eyes over

her in an assessing way. "Your patron is impatient for your arrival. He is already in residence. He took the key with him when he hired the place. I noticed yesterday as I drove by that he has moved in. The windows were open, and there was a groom out back at the stable."

"Oh, good." She blushed. "He managed to get away earlier than he thought possible. Could you just tell me exactly which cottage it is? My friend only told me it is on the park. A Queen Anne cottage, I believe he said?"

She was told the precise location. There was a bad moment when the clerk explained about her patron having taken the key when he rented the place, but it was impossible Luten had come back. It had to be O'Kelly. He had broken in, since he wouldn't know what name Luten had used when he leased the cottage.

She thanked the clerk and walked briskly to the southwest end of the parade, to wait for Norman at the Pump Room. He had the carriage and told her that he had hired two rooms at a famous bargain at Bishop's Down.

"O'Kelly is at the cottage. We might as well go and speak to him now, before dinner," she suggested.

"I am very hungry," Norman said. "It's nearly six o'clock, Trudie. O'Kelly would be out for his dinner at this time. I'd prefer to confront him on a full stomach."

She knew very well her brother would prefer not to have to confront him at all, but as she was far from eager herself, she agreed to dinner first. They went back to Bishop's Down and made a fresh toilette before ordering dinner, in Trudie's room, to save the price of a private parlor. They both drank a little more wine than usual, to give them courage. When they were finished, Norman stood up briskly and said, "We'll stop at the constable's office, and bring him along with us."

"Yes," she agreed, but her knees were already beginning to tremble.

The clerk at the inn gave them directions to the constable's office, where another barrier was encountered.

A sly-looking constable peered at them over a counter while Norman outlined the situation. At the end of the story, he gave a shake of his head and his decision. "That's all fine and dandy, sir, but I'll need some evidence before I go arresting a citizen. This ain't France, where they throw folks into jail for no reason. What evidence have you got?"

"He stole our friend's colt, and two hundred guineas!" Trudie exclaimed.

"And his watch—a Breguet," Norman added.

"The way your story sounds to me, he didn't steal nothing. He may have diddled the lad somewhat. A sharp operator, he sounds like, but as to stealing—no." He shook his head slowly, and smiled his sly smile. "It was a bargain between gentlemen, with no coercion. What you'll have to do if your friend wants his blunt back is get out a warrant against this O'Kelly person. Bring me a warrant, and I'll be happy to tag along and arrest him for you. Sorry, but there's nothing I can do."

"He's trespassing!" Trudie remembered. "He's occupying Mr. Mandeville's premises without his permission."

"Then let Mr. Mandeville come forward and lodge a complaint. I don't see that it's up to you to do it, miss."

She could not say, in front of Norman, that the cottage was in her name, so she gave vent to her frustration by insulting the officer of the law. "I should like to know what we pay your wages for, if you refuse to help innocent people!"

"Injured parties is who we help," he riposted, and turned back to his paperwork.

Norman took her arm and they went out into the street. "All this trip for nothing," Norman said, shaking his head. "We shall get a good night's sleep, and go on to Walbeck

Park first thing tomorrow morning. At least Auntie will be none the wiser.''

"Norman!" she gasped. "You don't mean you are afraid to confront O'Kelly without a constable to protect you!"

"Of course not, but what would you have me do? We have no evidence against him. We can't have him arrested. He has got Fandango's papers, and in the end it is we who would end up in the roundhouse. It was stupid, our coming here without Nick and Peter. It's not up to us to lay charges against O'Kelly. At least I shall write Peter and let him know where he can find O'Kelly.''

"But it's all my fault! We are the ones who must settle the affair ourselves. You heard what Luten said. He goaded me for not paying up like a sportsman.''

"I would like to see his face when we walked home with Fandango, and Peter's blunt.'' He smiled.

"We'll sneak up on O'Kelly,'' she said. "We don't need a pistol. A cane or a piece of wood will do as well. And your groom will come with us.'' She hurried him toward the carriage as she spoke, before the encouraging effect of the wine wore off.

"We'll do it, by Jove. We'll see who is soft.''

They drove at a hot pace to the little Queen Anne cottage by the park and decided to have their groom take the carriage into the park and tether it to a tree, to allow them to sneak up quietly. John Groom had orders to join them at the house as soon as possible. There were lights blazing in several rooms downstairs, and they crept forward quietly.

"Let's peek in the windows and see if he's there,'' Trudie whispered. They edged forward, and there was O'Kelly, lounging at his ease before a warm fire, reading, with a bottle of wine beside him. He seemed to be alone, which was excellent. So far as they knew, O'Kelly had no servant except his groom. He had removed his jacket and sat revealed in a pair of shoulders much diminished from formerly, though the jacket hanging on the back of another chair was quite as large as ever, with shoulders that set out all by themselves.

"His figure was all padding!" Norman scoffed. "I think I could take him without any help!"

"Go and look in the stable—see if Fandango is there, and the groom too," Trudie whispered back.

She waited while Norman darted to the stable and came back. "Fandango's there, right enough, and he's alone. We could lead him off right this minute."

"No, we want the two hundred guineas as well, and we need Fandango's papers too. We'll just wait for the groom before tackling O'Kelly."

When their groom—a large, burly fellow called Bullas—arrived, Norman told him to arm himself with a stout branch. When this was done, Norman got a good grip on his own crop, stepped up to the door and banged the knocker. They heard the sound of footsteps advancing, and suppressed the urge to run into the shadows. The door opened, and O'Kelly stared at them in astonishment.

"What are you doing here?" he demanded rudely.

It was Trudie who gave him an answer. "We might ask the same of you, sir. Lord Luten didn't give you permission to move into his house!"

O'Kelly counted the heads, measured the size of the groom's shoulders, and reached for the door to slam it in their faces. Trudie pushed him back and rushed in, her cohorts behind her. There was no entrance hallway. They stood in the little saloon, modestly furnished.

"Well, what of it?" O'Kelly asked. He crossed his arms over his chest and smiled, but it wasn't his old conning smile of yore. It was the disparaging smile of one who felt himself infinitely superior to the company in which he found himself. He hadn't shaved since leaving Newmarket, for he had every intention of lying very low. His soiled and rumpled shirt was open at the neck. He looked like what he was—a blackleg.

"I shouldn't think Luten sent you," O'Kelly said, and laughed. "Hardly the way a gentleman would treat his fiancée, Miss Barten—or have you managed to bring him up to scratch yet?"

"That has nothing to do with it!" she said boldly. "We are here to get Fandango and Lord Clappet's money, and you'll hand them over without an argument if you know what's good for you."

"A bargain's a bargain. I don't hear young Clappet bawling."

"Now see here, O'Kelly," Norman exclaimed, and put a hand on his opponent's chest to push him back, "you know perfectly well you conned Lord Clappet, and you ain't going to get away with it."

O'Kelly glanced through his saloon doorway to the dining room behind, then adopted a conciliating mood. "Perhaps you're right." He smiled, and while the Bartens were silently congratulating themselves on his easy capitulation, he swiftly raised his fist and drove it with all his force into the pit of Norman's stomach. Norman grunted and fell to the ground. Trudie made a rush at O'Kelly to claw his eyes out. She looked to the groom for help and screamed. Advancing silently behind Bullas was O'Kelly's groom, with a poker in his hand. She watched in mortal terror while the metal rod was raised and came crashing down on the groom's head. He too fell to the floor in a heap.

O'Kelly smiled an oily smile at his man. "Good work, lad. Haul that pair off to the stables and tie them up. Miss Barten and I have a little unfinished business. Now, you were saying, my dear," he said, reaching out to grab her hands.

Norman groaned to consciousness and tried to get up. O'Kelly's man lifted his poker and brought it down again. It made a terribly hard sound as it hit Norman's head. Trudie tried to go to her brother, but O'Kelly held her hands fast.

"I'm flattered that you came running after me, my little love," he laughed. "If I'd known you were that fond of me, I'd have brought you along. It occurred to me, but the dot was a bit on the slim side. Five thousand wouldn't last me long. But that doesn't mean we can't enjoy ourselves, now you're here."

He watched as his man dragged first Norman, then the Bartens' groom, out of the room. Trudie tried to free herself from his grasp, but his fingers were like stone, immovable. And to make her position worse, she actually felt sick to her stomach. She didn't know whether it was fear or hatred of that viciously smiling face above her that caused it.

As though she were about to die, the past weeks ran vividly around in her mind. The trip to London, when any wonderful thing seemed possible; the advent into their lives of Lord Luten; the awful catastrophe of O'Kelly and Sheba; and, most regrettable of all, how close she had come to attaching Luten. How had she ended up here, with this dyed-in-the-wool villain who would do anything he wanted with her? What would such a wicked creature as this want? And Norman—if he ever survived that blow on the head, he'd be lucky not to end up a moonling. She had brought herself to this pass by her own rashness, and if she were to escape, that must be done by herself as well. There was no hope of rescue. She hadn't told anyone where she was going—more folly, sneaking behind Aunt Gertrude's back.

At last the groom was gone, and O'Kelly pulled her toward the sofa. "You'd better not molest me, or you'll have to deal with the law," she warned, but her voice was weak.

"We're old opponents, the law and I," he said softly. Such a menacing softness. "If they ever catch me, I'm done for, so I might as well take what I can get. I'll just tame you down a peg for Lord Luten."

She swallowed convulsively, trying to hide her terror. He pushed her past the sofa table, laughing at her efforts to free herself. From the corner of her eye, she saw that the paper he had been reading was Fandango's breeding certificate. Even that detail he had arranged. What hope had she against such a clever enemy? She dug in her heels and tried to resist, to stall for time in hope that Norman or the groom might revive and come to help her. She looked around for a weapon as well, but the room was empty of small objects. Just the tables and chairs and sofa that came with the hired house were there—and the poker that had been used on Norman and his groom!

Her eyes widened when she spotted it. O'Kelly noticed where she was looking. Still holding her by one hand, he picked it up and stuck it into the middle of the blazing fire. "Now don't make me put my brand on you, my little love," he said, and threw her onto the sofa. The air caught in her lungs as she looked into his awful, smiling eyes. She didn't doubt for an instant that he'd use the hot poker on her, and with pleasure.

Chapter Nineteen

Lord Luten's temper had caused him difficulties before without jeopardizing the fulfillment of his wishes. He disliked apologizing but knew he must make the first overture if he were ever to see Miss Barten again. Allowing Peter and Sir Charles to go to Northfield was a step designed to appease the lady. He had some hope that Peter's account of the merciful treatment he had received might further soften her. But still, when he remembered those flashing eyes, whose shade changed with every gown, he thought it wise not to approach her till another day had passed. By the time he called at Northfield, he was told by a very disapproving Mrs. Harrington that she was very happy to tell him the Bartens had left on a little trip that morning and would soon be gone for good. She did not inform him of their destination, but he already knew from his nephew that they intended to leave Northfield soon.

"They are coming back?" he asked, aware of the alarm in his tone and unhappy with it.

"As to that, I really couldn't say," she said, and closed the door in his face. She knew very well they were returning but was accustomed to misleading Luten, and even took some pleasure from it.

Luten darted back to Sable Lodge to quiz his nephew.

"No, I didn't expect them to leave for a few days, Uncle," Peter said. "They wouldn't have flown off home in such a pelter—we were all supposed to meet again before they left."

"Where else could they have gone—to London, do you think?"

"With Norman's pockets to let? I shouldn't think so."

"Dammit, they must have said *something*, given some clue. *Think*—what did you talk about yesterday?"

"About you," Peter admitted, "and O'Kelly, and how it was a shame he got clean away. Trudie thought we ought to go after him."

"She would, of course," Luten said, but in no condemnatory way. There was something suspiciously like a smile about his lips. "I suppose you told her my opinion that he would be at one of the cheaper watering holes?"

"I did, I believe. She perked up when Tunbridge Wells was mentioned, but as Nick pointed out, there's no way O'Kelly could know your lovenest is standing empty."

"Unless she told him," Luten added doubtfully.

"Said she hadn't. They must have gone home. Norman is involved with a girl there—Miss Halley, a fubsy-faced lady."

But Miss Barten was opposed to that match, and Luten didn't think she had catapulted her brother off home, no matter how fevered she was to show him a lesson. No, out combing the countryside for O'Kelly was more like it. He wrote Trudie a letter and addressed it to Walbeck Park, feeling that if she were visiting neighbors in the vicinity, the new tenant would know it and forward it to her. But really that was just insurance; in his heart, he felt sure she was finally paying a visit to the cottage he had hired on the park. Of course the hoyden would have told O'Kelly. The two of them had probably had a good laugh over it.

He regretted the headstart the Bartens had on him. It was

fortunate Norman's team couldn't match his own. He learned before he left Newmarket that the Bartens' carriage had gone south, not west to Walbeck Park. He knew then that he was on the right track, and whipped his bays to a faster trot. They would not attempt to make the trip in one day, and his hope was to catch up with them before nightfall; but as they had left so early, and he so late, he was obliged to pull in for the night before overtaking them.

Inquiries along his route the next morning told him he was gaining ground. At Hornchurch he was three hours behind; at Tilbury the gap had narrowed to just over two. Unfortunately, he had to hire a fresh team at Tilbury, and from there on, the time between their passings held steady at two-and-a-half hours. He was on thorns by nightfall, when he reached Tunbridge Wells and drove straight to the little cottage on the park.

He saw the lights burning downstairs and didn't bother to hide his carriage. He hopped down and ran to the house. Like the Bartens, he decided to take a peek in the window first, to see just what he had to deal with. When he saw the outline of O'Kelly on the sofa with his arms around Trudie, a nauseating revulsion came over him. She was alone! She hadn't come with Norman at all but had arranged somehow to fly to her lover. Common sense fled, leaving a blind, surging fury in its wake. Hardly aware what he was doing, he lifted his fist and smashed it through the window. The shattering of glass was accompanied by a lusty and accomplished oath.

O'Kelly jumped up first and looked at the window, then Trudie flew up from the sofa. She ran to the grate, lifted a poker, and dropped it when it burned her fingers. Undeterred, she raised her skirt and used it for a pad. Luten still couldn't figure out exactly what was going on. Had she taken up that weapon to use against the intruder—him? He watched, his heart pounding painfully while O'Kelly darted

215

to the window, calling, "Who is it? Is that you, Rooney?" Trudie wasn't a step behind him, and their relationship was no longer in doubt. Through the broken window Luten heard her say, "Be thankful it's not your face, you brute!" just before she slashed the red hot poker against O'Kelly's arm. The next sound was an agonized howl from her tormentor.

By that time, Luten was already on his way to the front door. Trudie was still brandishing the poker when he pelted in, for she had an awful premonition that it was O'Kelly's groom she would have to deal with next. Luten took one look to see she was not noticeably damaged, then lunged at O'Kelly. His only regret was that he couldn't give him the thrashing he deserved. His sportsman's instinct forbade him from beating up an injured man, so he merely bloodied his nose and sent him to the floor with a fist in the gut.

He turned to Trudie. At the sight of him, she dropped the poker, which burned a deep black gash in the carpet, and burst into tears. Luten rushed forward and pulled her into his arms.

"You foolish, darling girl," he scolded fiercely in her ear, but even while he spoke, his lips were beginning to skim across her wet cheeks, to find hers. He felt her small, soft body tremble in his arms and drew her more tightly against him, to protect this cherished hothead from the world.

The trembling from fear subsided, and a new shaking began deep within her as Luten's lips firmed on hers. It was really very much like his first rough embrace in the carriage, but frequent memories of that moment had accustomed her to it now, and it no longer felt repulsive. It still felt a little frightening, but at the same time reassuring and exciting and a host of other delicious things. When he stopped kissing her, a jumble of angrily loving words poured from his

216

mouth, while his handkerchief brushed her tears away with infinite tenderness.

"Are you sure you're all right, darling? Why the devil did you . . . Dammit, Trudie, have you no sense at all? You're quite sure he didn't hurt you?" And before she could reassure him, he kissed her again, as though he would never stop.

It was sometime later that she withdrew and looked shyly at him. Her eyes looked nearly black tonight, in the dim shadows of the saloon. "Luten," she breathed, "I am so glad you came. How did you know?"

He ignored the question and asked again. "Did he hurt you?"

O'Kelly moaned on the floor. "Not as much as I hurt him."

"He didn't . . ."

Her eyes flashed dangerously to the moaning body. "No, but he intended to. He said he was going to *tame* me," she scoffed. "Whoever heard of a jackass taming anyone? We had better call the constable. I daresay *now* he will come, when we no longer need him. You'll have to lay a charge of trespassing to hold that mawworm till Peter can get here and swear out a warrant against him for the other things."

"Why did you and Norman run off without telling me?" Luten asked.

"Norman!" she exclaimed.

"Where is Norman?"

"In the stable, I think. Rooney cracked him and our groom over the head and hauled them away. Oh, Luten, it has been such a horrid night. Such a horrid spring," she added on a sigh.

"And it's all my fault," he said humbly.

"Oh, no! Not all!" she assured him, for she was magnanimous in victory.

"It is. If I had taken proper care of Peter, all this never

217

would have happened. I want you to know, I have mended my ways.''

"In any case, it's over now. We shall be going to Warwick immediately from here. We shan't even return to Northfield,'' she added, to hasten along anything he might want to say in that regard. She cast an inviting peep at him from the corner of her eye.

"Surely *you* don't have to leave Northfield. *You* aren't marrying Miss Halley.''

"I can hardly stay alone!'' she pointed out. When he just stood frowning, she tossed her curls and said, "We'd better go to Norman.''

"Yes,'' he said, and turned to leave. She followed him through the dining room. "You could stay with me at Sable Lodge,'' he pointed out.

"Luten! Good God, you're as bad as O'Kelly! How could I batten myself on a bachelor?'' He opened the back door, and they went out into the chilly night.

"I mean after we are married, naturally,'' he said angrily. It wasn't the proposal he had intended making, nor the one she had dreamed of receiving, but it was what popped out, and she made do with it. "Well?'' he asked sharply, to hide his concern.

"You'll have to speak to Norman,'' she said modestly, while hurrying to keep up with his long strides.

"Since when have you put yourself under that gudgeon's protection? You may rule the roost at Walbeck Park, milady, but there'll be no Latin lessons, and no hanging around the tracks with the likes of O'Kelly when you are married to *me*!''

"That sounds very dull; just when I was becoming interested in racing too,'' she said, and tossed him an arch smile that didn't deceive him for a minute.

His scowl gave way to an anticipatory smile; he stopped walking and pulled her to him by the hand, just in front of the stable door. His fingers stroked her cheek, which glowered in the moonlight. "Any hanging around the track must be in my company. I'll even teach you the difference between an unmanageable jade, like Sheba, and a winner," he said, but in a voice that had nothing to do with horses.

She drew a glorious breath of night air. "I have the most ravishing wedding gown in mind," she said softly.

Luten pulled open the door, and as the sharp stench of the stable assailed their nostrils, he said, "Good, but first let's see if Norman will be attending our wedding."

Rooney lunged from the shadows, a raised stick in his hand. Norman Barten achieved one bit of glory to clear his reputation of softness. He flew up from the straw and pulled the stick from Rooney's hand, allowing Luten to flatten him.

The law was much more biddable when dealing with Lord Luten than with the Bartens. Mr. O'Kelly was held on a charge of trespassing, while Clappet and Sir Charles came bounding down to Tunbridge Wells to lay charges, miffed that they had missed out on all the fun. They never would have thought Norman had such pluck. They all gathered in the cottage on the park, where Luten had decided to stay, since he had hired the place.

"I say, Uncle," Peter said, "now that I have got Fandango back, I will be able to enter some races this season after all."

His uncle shook his head. "No, cawker, you will sell that cribber and pay for the damages Sheba has caused at the Golden Lion. A carriage and several stalls smashed, a groom with a broken thumb, to say nothing of the bill for all that ale!"

"Yes, but I am rid of Sheba now. Rooney has gone to bring her back to O'Kelly, thank God, and Fandango really is a sweet goer. Nick is sure I can sublet my flat on Poland

Street in London in two minutes—there's fifty guineas right there—and I shan't have any expense living with you at Sable Lodge.''

"I'm not at all sure Lady Luten will want such rowdy guests when we are on our honeymoon," Luten said with a caressing smile at his fiancée, whom he caught nodding and winking at Peter.

"But Trudie is going to coach me in my Latin, remember?" Clappet tempted.

"On the contrary, she has given up coaching," he said firmly. "You will remember it is those Latin lessons that have caused all our problems. I will have enough problems convincing Lady Clappet my wife isn't a lightskirt, without you and Sir Charles forever dragging at Trudie's heels to remind her. At least it is Mrs. Harrington she has fingered as the wicked woman in the affair. Which reminds me, Trudie, we must write to your aunt and inform her of our plans."

"I already have," she said, and smiled luxuriously.

Not half an hour later, Mrs. Harrington ripped open that same missive and went flying down to discuss it with the Bogmans, who were busily packing up to remove to Warwickshire. "The shatter-brained chit! Can't she see it is another of Luten's freakish practical jokes, like taking Latin lessons? And he never paid her the crown either."